THE LAST CHANCE

THE LAST CHANCE

RON WELLING

First published in Great Britain in 2022 by
The Book Guild Ltd
Unit E2 Airfield Business Park,
Harrison Road, Market Harborough,
Leicestershire. LE16 7UL
Tel: 0116 2792299
www.bookguild.co.uk
Email: info@bookguild.co.uk
Twitter: @bookguild

Copyright © 2022 Ron Welling

The right of Ron Welling to be identified as the author of this
work has been asserted by them in accordance with the
Copyright, Design and Patents Act 1988.

All rights reserved. No part of this publication may be
reproduced, transmitted, or stored in a retrieval system, in any form or by any means,
without permission in writing from the publisher, nor be otherwise circulated in
any form of binding or cover other than that in which it is published and without
a similar condition being imposed on the subsequent purchaser.

This work is entirely fictitious and bears no resemblance to any persons living or dead.

Typeset in 11pt Adobe Garamond Pro

Printed and bound by CPI Group (UK) Ltd, Croydon, CR0 4YY

ISBN 978 1915352 330

British Library Cataloguing in Publication Data.
A catalogue record for this book is available from the British Library.

To Simon, Paul and Philippa

Happy Reading

1

The day was hot; the train from Brighton was crowded; London was too busy with tourists blocking the traffic. Being kept waiting for a meeting in a formal, uncluttered room was never going to be Stone's favourite place to pursue a deal. And Stone did not yet know how he was going to find £2.5 million.

He paid off the taxi in Grosvenor Street in London's Mayfair. This road smelled of an outwards show of wealth; the area was tidy with trees; and no waste bins spilled onto the road, spoiling the façades of the pristine buildings. For a minute Stone stood and looked up at the white-fronted town house before he went in.

An officious young woman led Stone up a spiral staircase to the third floor and into what he was told was a boardroom. She did not look at him and said nothing further except telling him to take a seat as she then left. This was not a place hanging with cobwebs, with dusty corners that had no veneer to hide anything, where Stone preferred to confront difficult business. And now, left on his own, with no noise of anyone moving around in the corridor, it began to add to Stone's irritation. Stone was a man of impatience; he would rarely wait for anyone beyond fifteen minutes, and that time was now running out.

But today was different. This meeting was important; he had come here to buy Marine House, and that somehow stretched his short fuse without snapping. He was going to see this out.

There were seats all round a long table, and Stone walked to the far end and stared blankly at a full-length portrait hanging on the wall. It was of a lady in bright-red robes. Her eyes looked straight to the end of the table – this was her place. There was silence as he stood on his own for another three minutes. He ran his hand through his hair. The door suddenly opened. Almost as one movement, a middle-aged woman, followed by a younger man – who had a red face as if he had been hurrying too much since lunchtime – came into the room. There was hardly a pause before the woman spoke.

'I'm Lady Ruth Jackson, and you must be Mr Harry Stone,' she said and noisily took a chair without a handshake. 'Please take a seat, but my son and I haven't got much time; we have other more important business to attend to, so what have you come to say, Mr Stone?'

Stone sat at the end of the table. He looked back at the woman and the muscles on his face tightened. This was the same person whose face was in the portrait looking down the room at him.

'You know why I'm here. I've sent you my offer for Marine House, £2.5 million. It's right on top market value, so I'm surprised you're not snatching my hand off for it. Remember, too, I am the sitting tenant – that should put me top of your list, so I want to know today that the sale is on,' Stone said.

'I thought you were coming here to tell me you can afford to pay the rent for the next twelve weeks. We shall need to know that you've cleared what you owe when you leave at the end of your lease,' Lady Ruth said and glared at Stone.

'If you're trying to sell Marine House over my head, I would remind you I don't have to leave that building until the very last day at the end of those twelve weeks. And that's a bank holiday Monday.'

'Your offer is too low; we've told you that three times. And our advice is that there are plenty of people out there who are about to put in bids. It's a valuable property, seven bedrooms, and because of its prominent address central to Brighton seafront, I will also make sure it goes to the right person. And, as I understand you intend to redevelop the place if you ever get your hands on it, I'll remind you that Marine

House is a listed Regency building. As a lot of people knew it as our family home, it still carries our name, and we want to make sure it's not turned into something ghastly. Something out of keeping with the other elegant houses nearby, a monstrosity,' Lady Ruth said.

'Mr Stone, let me introduce myself. I'm Josh – Lady Ruth is my mother.'

The son leant across the long, bare oak table; he left a card a few inches from Stone's hand.

Lady Ruth put her hand up to stop him talking; he sat back again quickly and idled with his fingers on the table. And she had not finished.

'Before we go any further, we need to get some matters straight,' she said. 'So, you'd better listen to what I'm now going to tell you, Mr Stone. What has come to light, in case you've already forgotten, is that you have attracted a lot of dubious publicity in the past year. We've seen reports of early morning police raids looking for expected money laundering and drug dealing going on from Marine House. This publicity doesn't get around unless it's true, and you obviously don't understand how it damages an important address like Marine House. And I expect we'll find some physical damage you've caused inside the building with your criminal friends visiting. But we'll do an inspection soon and send you a bill for anything we find.'

'That's all nonsense. It's now history,' Stone said quickly and fidgeted in his chair.

'That may be so, but it was still in print for the whole world to see.'

'It was just the gutter press poking around for easy idle gossip to fill their pages. And it doesn't help you to sell Marine House if you spend your time raking up that rubbish you're trying to throw at me.'

'Mr Stone, please. Arguing with Mother won't help, and of course we want you to enjoy Marine House right up until the end of your lease,' Josh said.

'I'm not here to argue with anybody. I'm asking you to remember my offer's top value and firm. And I want to know when you're going to accept it.'

'I think I need to remind you that you have not always been regular in paying the rent when it falls due,' Lady Ruth said. 'And whatever figure you might put at the bottom of a piece of paper when we do bank searches, my son and I are beginning to wonder if you have the necessary money to buy Marine House. So, are you just here today as a speculator trying your luck with us?'

'Don't question my money – it's real; it's in the bank ready to be paid the day we sign contracts. And I'm the only prospect if you want an easy, quick sale.'

'Not so. It is most unlikely we are going to sell to you, Mr Stone. Because when we put it all together you need to know we don't think you are the right sort of person to buy such a prominent building. We shall put it out to tender and that will really sort out who the highest bidder is. So please don't come here to bother my son and myself about it again.'

For now, Stone hid his clenched fist that he had wanted to bang heavily on the board table. He picked up the card that Josh had placed in front of him.

'The valuers I've consulted tell me you won't get a higher offer than mine. That's £2.5 million, and I've got the money ready and waiting. So, keep me top of the pile on your table – you have my number; I'll look forward to your call. Soon.'

Without looking at Lady Ruth, Stone left the room, pulling the door hard so that it closed with a thud. He hesitated as he walked down the three floors of the spiral staircase. Had he just left the room too quickly? Would Lady Ruth and her son ever call him again? At that moment Stone felt probably not. And it was then, as he moved, that Stone suddenly felt a sharp pain in his back. For a moment he held the stair rail. It was hot in this stifling place – he was becoming very uncomfortable.

Once on the Mayfair street, Stone took in big breaths of the fresh air. But it did not temper his instant dislike of Lady Ruth Jackson. Stone thought he knew how to handle people, but with this titled lady and her condescending attitude, even tone of voice, he could see she was going to be very difficult. And he was unsure of Josh, who sat there twisting his fingers, his gaze mostly turned to the window, as if he wished he was outside. But drag Josh away from his mother, then maybe he was someone he could do business with.

Walking along the busy street, all Stone could feel was growing tension. It was being reminded by the pretentious titled lady of what happened just a year ago that hit him. She had not only derided his ability to buy Marine House but also his past. It left him numbed. And how could he not remember the early morning police raid on Marine House? The fraud squad had been tipped off – Stone never knew who had grassed on him.

There was a knock on the door at six in the morning, and all eight of them thundered around the place. They had expected to find a dump of laundered money with dubious bundles of £20 notes tied together with red elastic bands. They had expected to find the proceeds of racketeering and drug dealing stashed around the place. They had searched the seven bedrooms, even box rooms in the attic, for three hours, but they found nothing. Not even Charlie the police dog could sense a whiff of cannabis or anything stronger. The police raid, in all its force, noise and disruption, had missed what had really been going on in Stone's erratic world.

The speculation of something big happening at Marine House just a year ago had buzzed around. It was still sticking. And as Stone waited for a taxi to cruise by, in his paranoia he believed he could see a menacing shadow from his past moving towards him. He could see a dark shadow of a gangland thug, Xavier, leader of a ring of racketeers and dealers in narcotics. The man had a big face, bald head with rippling neck, and with his gang of heavies, not short of inflicting GBH, he had squeezed Stone into the squalor of illicit money laundering. He had even brought a slobbering dog into Marine House just to frighten him.

But Stone had stayed on in the large building, alone, living comfortably in just a few rooms. And driving him today were grand plans for turning Marine House inside out, into apartments. There would be three of them – selling them on, he would then double his money.

He climbed into a taxi to take him to his train to Brighton. His backache was developing into a constant, nagging pain. Rising in his right hip, every time he stretched, the ache was getting stronger, almost biting at him. Before leaving Brighton that morning, he had taken two painkillers with a glass of whisky, but that had all worn off, and on that warm afternoon, his belligerence had turned up a few notches. He now wanted another drink.

The growing discomfort in his back was beginning to trouble him. And he was wary of the sharks from his past circling him again as he scratched around for £2.5 million to get the prize, Marine House.

2

A fire razed Arrow Hall to the ground two years ago. It was arson. Working for Harry Stone, Claire had once known that medieval building as home and today, meeting with architects on the site of the burned-out wreck, made Claire excited. Drawing up plans, searching old, coloured photographs of the historic house, Claire dared to think that Arrow Hall could be rebuilt.

There was a small cabin on the site that was the office. The architects had left and, alone, Claire stared at the plans and drawings with colour wash that showed how this Elizabethan house in the middle of the Essex countryside could be rebuilt to just as it had been four hundred years ago. Claire walked from the cabin; the site was empty, with only the rustle from tall trees at the entrance, and for a moment, she breathed in the serenity of the surrounding landscape. The grass was even growing in the old, dried-out moat but with thistles now encroaching. She stood for almost a minute before she sat in her car ready for the tedious drive back to London.

The sudden voice right up close frightened Claire.

'I'm looking for Harry Stone. Last time I saw him was right here. And my boss, Mr Xavier, has got a message for him.'

Claire put her hand to her mouth as she tried to close her car door. But it was kept open by the strong arm of a man standing very close to her. A large face with grey, wispy stubble and wide, bloodshot eyes stared back, and he was not going to let her go.

'Listen to me, lady.'

'Leave me alone,' Claire shouted as she again tried to close her car door.

'This is his place, so where is he? Is he hiding somewhere in this pile of rubble?'

Without thinking, Claire punched the car hooter with her fist. It blared out with a penetrating noise, and it killed the stillness that Claire had felt only a few moments ago in this deserted place. But the blast lasted only a few seconds before Claire's arm was pulled away with a tight grip and a force that made her scream. She tumbled from her car seat onto the long, wet grass. The man stood over her for a few seconds but made no attempt to help her to get up from the ground.

'Don't do that,' he shouted as he moved away from her. 'And now you tell me where Harry is and then we both get on with the rest of our day. Eh, lady?'

'This site's nothing to do with Harry Stone; he's finished here, so leave me alone,' Claire shouted at the top of her voice.

But her shout went into the air as if it was nothing, and the unwelcome visitor watched as Claire scrambled back into her car.

'Don't play with me; you know where he is, so give it.'

'Brighton seafront. Marine House,' Claire shouted again.

As suddenly as he had come, the man with the unkempt stubble ran from Claire down the track that led to the entrance of Arrow Hall. But she expected him back someday. The address she had shouted was only what she had read in the papers. There had been a police raid at Marine House searching for traces of money laundering and drug trafficking.

Claire was shaking; she sat back in her car and closed and locked the doors. Phlegmatic, level-headed, not much fazed her. But suddenly there was an uncomfortable aura wafting around the empty site, and Claire's excitement was jolted. The ghost of Harry Stone she had exorcised was surely still hovering.

It left her grasp of rebuilding Arrow Hall hanging by a slender thread, just like a spider's gossamer web.

3

It was not until the day after meeting the haughty lady in her Mayfair house that Stone's antagonism towards Lady Ruth Jackson and her son softened. He walked across to the beachside, just to stand and stare at Marine House. It was big, imposing, and he had less than twelve weeks of his lease left. Nobody was going to tell him how to buy and sell property, however big. It is what he did. He knew the human nature of bargaining, greed even, but he had always found the money. Dealing with the Jackson family, he would have to wait and watch, play a long game. But he was not going to let this slip away – whatever happened, he was going to buy Marine House. That was all there was to it.

He crossed the road to the front door, and, standing on the top step, he practised a growing ritual. Before he let himself into the large, empty house, Stone looked along the street, and he hesitated. He was on his own – he thought he could see a hazy figure staring back at him, but it was getting dark; his paranoia was growing.

Stone went to his study, a dark room with windows looking over the back garden of the house. The growing ache in his back suddenly stretched to his right hip and he caught his breath. Just like a stab, it jerked at his nerve ends. He poured a large whisky; he took painkillers, but they would take time to subdue this insidious pain.

Loud banging on the rear door of Marine House, at just before 6.00 that evening, was unusual. He had closed his eyes for half an hour in a deep armchair; there was a bell which was always used by tradesmen, but this insistent noise roused Stone. At first, with eyes still firmly closed, he tried to ignore it. But a minute later it started again. Stone swore as he pulled himself from the chair and walked quickly along the hallway to the kitchen. He unbolted and opened the door. His mood was belligerent as he confronted a big, wide face with very white teeth and watery eyes. There was a bristly white beard on his face which stared hard at Stone. After a few seconds, he spoke with a snappy voice.

'It's Harry Stone, ain't it, mate?'

Stone started to close the door; his heart rate quickened; he thought he knew that voice. But the visitor held the door open and easily pushed Stone inside. A hand was placed on his sleeve which he tried to brush off, but this thickset man standing next to him was not going away.

'What do you want?' Stone shouted.

'A quarter of a million. That's what my boss Mr Xavier says you owe him. Money he lent to you to launder clean for him.'

'That thug Xavier's in prison. Sent down for five years. He's behind thick iron bars where he belongs. So, don't bring me idle threats demanding money. And get out of my way.'

'Mr Xavier might be sleeping in a room that's not as big as he's used to, but he still knows what's going on. He's all ready for the day he comes out. And anyway, being inside is just a little holiday for him. You should try it one day, Harry.'

'Go back to that extortioner and tell him for the last time I'm not joining in his games anymore.'

'They're harsh words, Harry, from someone who's in debt big time. That money's been outstanding too long, and he sent me to tell you that you've got just two weeks now before the big man gets really angry. And I can tell you, if you ignore him you won't like what'll happen to you.'

'I'm going to call the cops,' Stone barked again.

'I wouldn't advise that, mate. Me and Mr Xavier don't like the cops.'

This man with malodorous breath laughed and again placed his hand on Stone's arm. He barged Stone further into the kitchen with a wide, mocking grin. Stone tried to push him away, but it had little effect on the bulky, muscular body in front of him. He was on his own in this large house, and he felt vulnerable to whatever this intruder wanted to do.

'Okay, Harry. Here's a deal. I'm coming to see you each week so you can tell me how you're getting the cash together to repay Mr Xavier's big quarter of a million. And what say I leave the physical stuff off if you slip me a hundred quid each time I pop in to see you? Like today, we don't want to make a fuss in this nice kitchen, do we?'

'I told you, get out of here, you scum,' Stone bawled.

Stone moved to pick up his mobile from the kitchen table, but his arm was grabbed and squeezed tightly as the black man's face came close to his.

'Leave that. Give me a hundred quid now or I smash your face in. What do you want, man?'

Stone pulled a draw open from the kitchen table and fumbled with some spare notes. Without counting them, he pulled out £20 notes and threw them on the floor.

'Now clear out. Rats like you should be locked up inside the same place as Xavier is. Got it?'

The intruder picked the notes from the floor and there was a strange odour as he lent into Stone. In one movement, which Stone did not see coming, he landed a fist hard on Stone's right temple. It sent him sprawling across the empty kitchen and the wide thug loomed over him as Stone righted himself. He put his hand to his cheek and rubbed it as if he needed to feel where the punch had landed. He pulled himself up, dazed, and adjusted his shirt over his shoulders.

The thug wagged his finger in Stone's face.

'Don't play with me like that. This ain't going away until you pay up.'

'Last time. You're getting nothing from me.'

'No, it don't work like that. There was the whole quarter million slipped through your greasy hands. Mr Xavier trusted you to wash it white, clean, for him, money he could then splash around again. And he just don't believe the fairy tale you made up. Who would?'

There was the unnerving, sour smell of cannabis, and Stone stood back, but the thug caught his left arm.

'Instead of washing it through his shops, your mate lost it all gambling. And on the blackjack table at Monte Carlo and then the Cheltenham races. Now come on, Harry, there's a whole quarter million left dangling, so don't make me laugh.'

In the dark of the early evening, Stone watched the intruder leave and he closed and bolted the back door. In the elegant sitting room, Stone poured another large whisky. With a growing mood of defiance, he opened the balcony doors. He breathed in fresh air, and he stood, as he had often done in the past few months, and stared across to the sea. But today he was soon feeling cold; he closed the doors and slumped onto the chaise longue.

The darkening clouds of violence, lingering from an unpaid debt, left Stone feeling edgy. Not for the first time in the past two years, he was wary of these ruthless gangsters who were well practised in slashing knives, disfiguring faces. How could he forget the quarter of a million pounds that had been right inside this elegant room? He stood for a moment and looked at the cushioned seat he had been sitting on. It was there, just for a short while, that the illicit money had been in a briefcase hidden under the elegant red rosewood Regency settee. The bundled notes were to be washed white from the indelible stain of drugs and racketeering they carried.

Stone had always kept his distance from squalid puddles of dirty water. But this criminal shark had squeezed and taunted him, and too often threatened random violence, until he washed white dirty, tainted paper money. All flowing from drugs, extortion rackets. And maybe worse.

What stung him today, as sharp as a barbed bee stinger in his skin, was, just a few hours ago, the taunt from Lady Ruth about a heavy-booted police raid on Marine House. He would never forget how close that had been – the police had missed the case of money by just a few days.

Stone paced the sitting room and suddenly he felt the pain in his back. He tried to ease the discomfort by straightening his shoulders. He was unsure, nervous even. What was going on to cause this insidious pain? His febrile temper was bubbling. He went to the bathroom and saw the large, black bruise on his right temple. Dabbing at it tentatively, it felt sore, a reminder that there was a bunch of crooks out there who would call again. He ran his hand through his hair.

Later that evening, after more glasses of whisky, Stone eased himself into bed. But as ever at this time of day, Marine House was very quiet, with not even the noise of a mouse scampering or a seagull circling outside. And it was not even broken by a call from Lady Ruth Jackson.

It was an ominous silence.

4

More often in the past few weeks, Stone spent a restless night. Today he left his bed after a few hours' fitful sleep, and it was still dark as he took his shower. Drying his legs, he stretched and felt his ankle. He recoiled – the heavy scar, deep into his flesh, was where he had been bitten by a slobbering dog. Right here in his bedroom. Just a year ago, the snarling animal had been held, hovering over him, by Xavier, a gang leader of thugs dealing in heroin and crack cocaine, from south of the river. Selling to crackheads in his patch was his speciality.

But it was the line in money laundering, racketeering, to wash white the proceeds from his street dealing, that he had dragged Stone into. The threat of nastiness – today it came as a demand for repayment of a quarter of a million pounds – was hanging over Stone like a noose which at any time could be tightened. Stone shuddered; the memory still felt very close.

He finished drying himself, dressed, and he then sat at the kitchen table with a mug of tea. Stone remained alert, nervous of the amorphous, invisible, drug dealing ring out there. He looked again at the bolts securing the back door and he peered through the window to the gloomy back garden. Right inside Marine House, he was satisfied that he was safe, but he still felt the lingering menace that Xavier and his cronies threatened.

Stone walked into the elegant sitting room and stretched on a large sofa to ease his pain. His second mug of tea he drank quickly, but the pain in Stone's back was becoming insistent, more than just an ache. Taking painkillers, sometimes above the right dosage, had not helped; they just left him feeling tired. He tried to read a newspaper but could not concentrate and soon threw it onto the floor in frustration. Feeling restless, unable to sit still, he could put up with it no more. He rang for a private appointment with his doctor. The doctor would see him later today.

In his growing discomfort, he was fidgeting, and he walked into his study to fill his whisky glass. He picked up a black-and-white photo of a row of eight Victorian terrace houses in London's East End. Stone liked to think of himself as self-made; he had pulled himself up over his sixty-five years by his own bootstraps and he handled the picture as if he could touch those houses. He had bought them out of nostalgia. The narrow road would always be sharply engrained on his memory. It was where he had been brought up by his mother and a mostly absent father who was an alcoholic. But he had sold the houses just six months ago after too many tenants defaulted on their rent payment.

Piled untidily on his desk were bank statements for the last year, and he flicked through them. They told him what he already knew. Just under £2 million, money from selling those properties stood out in a nice row just like the terraced houses. The seven figures stared back at him.

After shuffling the papers back into a tidy pile, he ran his hand through his hair. He was growing restless again as, even with selling his row of houses in London's East End, he was still £500,000 short of the price the Jackson family were demanding for Marine House. And Lady Ruth Jackson had hit him on a soft spot about his money. Was he just a speculator trying it on?

He clumsily searched through a thin plastic file to find the papers with details of a secret account in Panama. Out of sight, he had squirrelled away a large bundle of US dollars, and they were what was needed to narrow the gap of half a million pounds to buy Marine House. Getting that money back to London was becoming urgent.

It was early in the day, but Stone called Roger Garon in his smart office on the tenth floor of a block in the City of London. Never a mate of Stone, Roger was just someone he had known for a long time and one of the few people he trusted.

'Roger, I need to talk to you.'

'Make it quick. I'm off to a meeting and I've got a taxi waiting,' Roger said.

'It's my bank accounts in Panama. Dollars piling up. I need to get the money moved. Back to London. You know how I work, so how do I do it?'

'What're you up to this time?' Roger asked.

'I've got a big property deal bubbling. Getting hold of that pot of gold will help to fill the gap to pay for it,' Stone said.

'That's not going to be easy if you need it quickly. How much have you got there?'

'There's $400,000 there. It's serious money.'

'Be very careful because any money coming from countries like Panama will attract immediate attention. Snoopers in high places do nothing else but look out for that sort of cash sloshing around into London banks. And they'll ask some awkward questions if they find you at it. Like how you got it and whether you paid tax on it.'

'You're being negative. I'm not in the mood to listen to bad news,' Stone said firmly. 'I did a property deal in Sicily. I put some cash up with a mate to build apartments in the small town of Corleone. It was all looking good until I had a knock on the door of my rented villa late one night. The Mafia got interested. Have you ever worked with the Mafia, Roger?'

'No, I haven't. And you were naïve to get into building work in any Italian town. That's always going to attract the stinging wasps to the light bulb.'

'Yes, it was a large car with blacked-out windows and large bodies with dark glasses. But that's history.'

'Are you sure you want to tell me all this?'

'Only that I got out of the deal. They paid me off in bundles of dollar bills. The money went straight through a London currency exchange bureau and was deposited anonymously into Panama. Easily done. It's still there. Not forgotten.'

'You walk into some crazy situations, don't you? Laundering cash is explosive stuff if it ever got out. So, I'm going to keep my distance and pretend I haven't heard what you've just told me about your misfiring business.'

'My money's hard earned, not laundered, maybe bypassed tax people somewhere but that's different. So, you stay white, Roger. You always do,' Stone taunted.

'Yeah, so what? Somebody has to. But I've got to rush now. Give me time and I'll check it all through for you. And I'll call. I just remind you that you pay me a fee for counsel so listen carefully this time and don't ignore my advice,' Roger chided. He closed his phone.

It left Stone unsure. Maybe Roger was right, the dollars were stuck there forever. He ambled back to the empty, quiet kitchen. His body was shouting at him loudly. He could feel the pain reaching across his back; it was now too intense. The whisky bottle on the table offered strong temptation, but he resisted. More urgent than playing with money was going to see his doctor, and it was never going to be a good consultation if his breath was smelling of drink.

What would his doctor find?

5

Stone called a taxi to keep the appointment at his doctor's surgery. Before he left, in the hallway cloakroom, he looked at his face in a mirror. He tried to wash the tiredness from his eyes, tiredness from the sleepless nights in the past week. But it did not work. He saw the tiredness and he felt the tiredness.

His doctor, an Irishman called Sean, saw him promptly. He listened to Stone's symptoms closely.

'On the couch please, Harry. I need to do a physical examination. It's internal, I'm afraid.'

There was silence for several minutes as Stone removed his lower clothing and slipped onto the couch. It was a quick examination and, in silence again, Stone redressed slowly and sat next to the small table that was Dr Sean's desk. That part of the consultation was just five minutes.

'Anything to tell me?' Stone asked.

'Not yet. We need some blood. Roll up your sleeve, Harry.'

Again there was silence as a routine sample of Stone's blood was taken from his left arm. For a moment Stone looked the other way before he rolled his sleeve back down.

'Right, before you go, I'll check blood pressure and give you a prescription for stronger painkillers. They should help with your back pain.'

There was again silence for another minute and Stone closed his eyes.

'Blood pressure's running high. I've known you a few years, Harry, but today you look tired. So, what are you up to that's pushing your blood pressure up? Some more tight deals?' Sean laughed as he said it; he knew he would not get a straight answer.

'A big property deal, and a bit here and a bit there. And some people are just impossible to deal with.'

'Okay but, Harry, slow it down is my advice. The blood results will be available in three days. But in the meantime, I'm going to make an appointment for you at a London clinic in Harley Street. I think you should see a urologist. It'll be at least a week, but I'll give you a call.'

Stone was uncertain that he wanted to see another doctor in Harley Street. He wanted to know more but he never asked a question when he would not like the answer. He was sure that his doctor already knew what the result would be. It left Stone with a dry mouth, certain that his blood pressure was rising even higher.

Stone stood to leave, and Sean looked with interest at the grey bruising on Stone's temple. He noted too the ashen colour on his patient's face.

'Where did you get that from?'

'I had a small accident in the kitchen. Tripped over a chair.'

His doctor laughed at Stone. It was obvious that even his patient did not believe a simple explanation like that was likely. They parted with a handshake and Stone collected the prescription at a nearby pharmacy. With the sun on his face, he walked the mile and a half along the seafront to Marine House. As he climbed the three steps to the front door, the pain in his back was stronger and he could feel it round to his right hip. He sat in the kitchen and took two painkillers and within half an hour he was feeling drowsy. He slumped into a deep sofa in the sitting room with a glass of whisky and, gradually, the pain subsided.

As his day in pain finished, he was still uncertain if he would want to hear what the result would be if he followed his doctor's advice and went to Harley Street. He tried to push the uncertainty away, he did not want it to interrupt closing the gap in the money he needed to get Marine House. But his world was soon to change. In ways that he could never have planned.

6

'Claire, while I'm away I know you can look after everything. It's a long way to New Zealand; I won't be visiting down under too often. But buying a wine estate is not a quick and easy fix and I've got to make sure I get it right. So don't expect me back for at least six weeks, maybe more. But I'll call; I'll text; and we'll talk.'

'That's a long time,' Claire said as Rick packed some notes and brochures in his briefcase, at the same time drinking from a cup of coffee. 'This apartment, as comfortable as it is, can be very quiet when you're away,' Claire said.

'You'll be too busy to be lonely. From what I've seen in the plans, rebuilding Arrow Hall is a very big job. When you get stuck into it you won't wonder what to do with yourself for a few weeks.'

'This might sound odd, but I'm a bit nervous of Arrow Hall's long history. It'll be like resurrecting something from the dead, and when the building's up, the historic house is to have no trace of any of its ghosts,' Claire said.

'You've never told me of ghosts before. Have you seen them?' Rick looked at Claire with a mocking grin.

'It's just the previous owner of Arrow Hall, Harry Stone. The man you bought it all from. He let the place get burnt down and I'm not sure how I'll clear him out from my memories of the old house,' Claire said.

'No, you shouldn't be worrying about Harry Stone. He's finished; he's right out of it now. You must clear your memories. Stand back.'

'I've never counted Harry Stone out. And knowing that man as I do, I doubt the day will ever come when he doesn't still think he owns it.'

Claire suddenly felt uncomfortable talking about Harry Stone. And this morning, just saying goodbye to Rick, she felt a growing tension. It was 5.00 in the morning; a limousine would shortly be calling to take him to Heathrow for his flight and right now Claire could see he had other thoughts demanding his time.

'The house is yours to rebuild, not his. There's a lot to do and soon you must find time to go to the site to meet James, a surveyor I've used for a few years. He didn't know it before the fire, and he'll just see it as a load of bricks, timber and tiles like any other building. Let him get on with managing the building work and deal with all the technical stuff. He's young, knows what he's talking about, but just to warn you, the downside is he can be too aggressive with builders. You deal with all the money and be firm, control James's spending. He'll always run over if it makes life easier.'

'Yes, I'll keep a grip of the money, but if James is as good as you say he is, then it won't be too difficult.'

'You're going to be working closely with him, so try to get to know James – have a drink round the local sometime and you'll find him quite different to his brash site style.'

'I remember the local well from when I lived in Arrow Hall. I'll look forward to that.'

'James does know there's an absolute top spend of £300,000. It can't go beyond that; and I will no longer get my money back if I have to sell it.'

Claire looked at Rick. She felt growing doubt about Rick's intention for rebuilding Arrow Hall. It was not the first time he had spoken like that.

'But it's not just to sell on; it's to be our country house, isn't it?' Claire said.

'Yeah, but everything has a value, so let's see how it all goes.'

'We've not talked about Arrow Hall much, and I can't get very excited with the project unless it's somewhere I will live again.'

'Let your emotion go; you'll feel different as the building takes shape. But first, there's some money to give to James. £25,000 in hard cash, it's in the small safe on the floor in my dressing room. It's £15,000 now, and he can have the rest if he needs it,' Rick said.

'What's that for?'

'Casual labour. Greasy palms and all that, and we do need the site to run smoothly. But £20 notes are easy to give away so watch how James spends it.'

That was just how Harry Stone used to manipulate deals, and it is what Claire had come to distrust. She had seen notes dropped around like confetti. It was bribery – you didn't pay up, you didn't get. And that is just what had happened to Arrow Hall first time around.

'Before I go, I've got a little present for you. Something to look forward to away from the mud and dirt of a building site. When I'm back we'll go to Wimbledon. Ladies' final. Something to dress up for. How about that?'

Five minutes later there was a light hug and kiss. Claire stood on the landing as she saw Rick into the lift from his penthouse to the waiting car. It left her very uncertain of Rick's feelings. He was going to a beautiful place on the other side of the world to buy a wine estate. He was going to have a holiday without her. And the money was all that concerned him in rebuilding Arrow Hall.

In the clear freshness of early morning, Claire was now on her own. She stood and gazed at the wide, sweeping view across the Thames from the living room, which, even at this time of day, had boats moving on it. And she watched for many minutes as the sun was gradually rising from the east. There was a fresh, very clear view of the cloudless blue sky.

Claire turned away, her unease growing. The ghost of Harry Stone clinging to the five-hundred-year-old building would still be there. And talking to Rick was leaving her cold. Whatever he said, Arrow Hall was never really just hers to rebuild.

7

Feeling angry and anxious from her first visit to the Arrow Hall site, Claire called her friend Jennie. Meeting for lunch was quickly arranged. Jennie preferred the classy Michelin-starred restaurants around London's West End where she always had ease in making a reservation. And Claire enjoyed an embrace from Jennie as they were shown to their table.

With a glass of wine, Claire slowly relaxed.

'Your visit to Arrow Hall has shaken you, especially being on your own. And Harry Stone, somebody searching for him at the site doesn't sound good. Have you heard anything from him?' Jennie asked.

As she sipped from her glass, Claire was almost breathless. The words "Harry Stone" hit her again.

'No, not a word. But just visiting the derelict site earlier, the memories flood back.'

'I can see from the tense lines on your face, he's right in your thoughts again.'

'Yes, it was that awful day two years ago, when I saw Harry standing at the door to the old building. The image is indelible, his face red with rage, the flames flicking to the sky. I can still see the inferno that took hold of the historic Elizabethan manor house. In less than a few minutes it had gone.'

'Are you sure you're ready to rebuild Arrow Hall? You're carrying too much of the past with you,' Jennie asked.

'I'm trying not to let that awful day stop me. But the frightening thing is the arson was all about money. Protection money he wouldn't pay to a drug cartel after a broken property deal in the Caribbean.'

Jennie looked at Claire, who was not eating much of a large Dover sole on her plate.

'But, Claire, you walked out of the mess that man left in his trail after the fire. It's not your problem.'

'I worked for him for many years; I knew the inside of all his business; and I can't just blot that away.'

'But you've moved on; living with Rick surely must make it all different for you,' Jennie said.

'Yes, and I'm still hanging on to the shiver of excitement when Rick told me that he had bought the cinders of Arrow Hall from Harry. And when it was rebuilt, it was to become our country home.'

'Rick must have seen something in it – buying a burnt-out wreck of a building is hardly something to be eager about.'

'Back then I was so excited, the adrenalin flowing like a river. But now…' There was a pause as Claire watched the waiter refill her wine glass. 'I'm not sure anymore.'

'Just let the good times roll, Claire. You've had plenty of them.'

Claire put her knife and fork on her plate and pushed it away. She was not hungry. The waiter cleared the table; Claire sipped her wine and leant back in her chair.

'Rick's left for New Zealand; he'll be away for some weeks. Looking to buy a winery business.'

'Why aren't you going with him?'

'Rick's never asked me to go. He wants me to stay here, to sort out Arrow Hall, and that'll mean being in the mud and dirt of a building site for some time.'

Claire put her wine glass down on the white tablecloth and sighed. It was a gesture that Jennie noticed, and she touched Claire's hand.

'I sense all is not well between you and Rick. I'm here to listen.'

'Rick is just too busy. I live in his large penthouse with him, but I don't see much of him. He just seems to be becoming very distant, there's even a coldness between us. We now rarely eat together because he leaves early and sometimes can be away for several days. Eating at the kitchen table was always a good time to talk to him, if only just to hear what he was thinking. It's all changing, and that's not how it was even just a few months ago,' Claire said.

'Try to get motivated again about rebuilding Arrow Hall, see it taking on new life.'

'Of course, I want to see the old place rebuilt, the gardens landscaped around the dried-out moat. I loved the old house when I had a flat there, with the freedom of the countryside all around. But today I'm feeling very nervous about the whole thing.'

'That's a dark picture you're painting,' Jennie said.

'It's Rick's property, not mine, and I get the feeling he's changed his mind on Arrow Hall becoming our country house. Only once has he found time to visit the place – I'm going to tie him down and ask what his intentions are for the place. I'm beginning to think he'll sell it on after it's all finished.'

'Why are you putting your future at risk like this? You need to have a down-to-earth talk with him.'

'I'll pick my moment. But for now, I'll have to keep it all tight and close until he returns.'

'Are you telling me all?' Jennie asked, looking at the frown on Claire's face.

'Since I've lived with Rick in his penthouse apartment and enjoyed the high life, other than his pay from odd jobs, I've earned nothing. I need to find work, and that'll clash with the rebuild of Arrow Hall. So, something will have to give, Jennie.'

Claire sat back in her chair – it had been a relaxing time out with Jennie; the wine had tasted fresh and good, and they made another date to meet again. But as Claire saw Jennie into a taxi, she could not let go of the strain of the morning on the derelict site of Arrow Hall.

Rick's apartment was only a short distance and Claire decided to walk there. She took the lift to the seventeenth floor – the place was empty, cold and quiet. And that is how it would be for the next few weeks. The large rooms, balconies with wide views across London, Claire found intimidating and unsettling.

In the spacious kitchen, Claire poured herself another glass of wine. But sitting alone, Claire felt insecure. Rick was distant; these airy and elegant surroundings were no longer the place she thought she could call home. But it was also the sense she had that Harry Stone would someday soon dominate her life again.

8

Stone's phone rang, interrupting his thought. He picked it up from a low table in the sitting room. It was Roger Garon.

'Listen to this. It's about Panama,' Roger said.

'I'm listening just as long as you're going to tell me how I'm going to get my money back to London.'

'Have you ever heard of Nevis? It's a little island in the Caribbean.'

'No that one's new to me. There are a lot of them over there,' Stone said and ran his hand through his hair. He disliked the Caribbean; he had been there before. On the island of St Lucia, he had been threatened with a knife point to his throat. It was protection money he wouldn't pay, and he left the island with a collapsed property deal amongst its banana trees. The memory was still raw.

'Nevis is a very private place, anonymous, no questions asked. And Panama's not so secret anymore. Some disgruntled snitch who worked in a back office of a big Panama bank got his hands on a load of computer files. They hold the names of people with accounts there and how much they've got deposited. And this stool pigeon is selling the details to newspapers to print away so that all the world knows who's hiding money. Some big names tumbling out of the hat. So just be aware, Harry, that if the revenue find your name on the list, you'll be roasted alive. Your money'll go, and with your history with the revenue, you'll most likely go somewhere too. I'll send you some good contacts in Nevis. People who know how these things work.'

'Are you trying to scare me?'

'That's how it is. Go there and send me a postcard with your greetings from that sunny island.'

'I might need help to do the detail on Panama. So, Roger, there's something else I want you to do for me,' Stone said.

'If it's legal I'm here to help but otherwise forget it.'

'Don't get boring, Roger, because you're the only one who can help with this.'

'Tell me.'

'I'm left on my own. I've got a lot of things happening and I'm not always feeling too well just now. So, I need someone to deal with my papers just as I've always had, keeping my deals tidy so I know where everything is.'

'I know what you're going to say.'

'Yeah, why not? I need Claire back. Urgently.'

'You do remember Claire's moved on, don't you?'

'Yeah, but there's nobody else I want around at this time. Claire knows all the secret corners of my business. She set up the Panama accounts for me; she can now sort them out and help me to get the money back and close them down.'

'After the way you treated her, I doubt very much she'll want to do anything like that for you. And anyway, Claire's busy resurrecting the skeleton of Arrow Hall.'

'I know what she's doing, and I know that you sold Arrow Hall for me too cheaply.'

'You've said that before today. So don't go there again, Harry. It's too late for that. You know how these things work. You signed the deal off, and you've had the money. That deal is now dead.'

'What about you call Claire for me, tell her I need to talk?'

'No. Leave me out of it, and leave Claire alone is my advice.'

'I know she lives in a fancy apartment in Mayfair, so give me her number and I'll call her.'

'I haven't got it and I wouldn't give it to you if I had. And don't expect Claire to run around for you again – it's not going to happen,' Roger goaded.

'I don't like that talk, Roger.'

There was a pause as Stone sipped his whisky and stared from a window to the street below. The answer was just as he expected.

'Forget Claire and deal with Panama yourself. Don't leave it. I know it'll be a change for you, but you do need to take my advice, and seriously, this time.'

Stone closed the call without replying. Pacing the room, his tension increased. His thinking was racing away. He was still £500,000 short of the total price Lady Ruth Jackson was asking, but when he had grabbed his money from Panama, it would take a big bite into closing that gap.

He could feel himself being dragged to the small Caribbean island of Nevis – it was a mystery place, and he did not know what he would really find there. Online he bought a first-class ticket to Nevis for the end of the week.

He sat at the kitchen table and tugged his phone from his pocket. He called Vlad, his sometime driver and odd-job man.

'Two hundred quid for you for a little job when you're finished. How soon can you drive up past the building site in Essex?' Stone asked and he heard a grunt from Vlad.

'Tomorrow soon enough? Early morning, boss?'

'Yeah, tomorrow. But just watch the place. I want to know if there's a lady around the site, short hair, early thirties. Watch to see what time she comes and goes and what day she's there. And get me the landline number that calls right into the site office. It'll be on a site noticeboard. Don't talk to anyone, just watch, keep it tight. You'll know what I mean by that.'

There was another grunt from Vlad.

Stone had a sense of easy excitement – he was making plans, giving directions and he was going to talk to Claire. But would Claire ever want to talk to him again?

9

Early morning Stone called Claridge's, a hotel with discreet security, close enough to the London hospital in Harley Street where he had an appointment to keep. He made a reservation for a suite for the next five days. With just an overnight bag, later that day he caught the train to London. But he was alert and satisfied he had not been followed by the druggie circling Marine House. That thug would now disappear back into the malodorous air from which he had come. Or so Stone hoped.

Seeing the urologist tomorrow left Stone agitated, annoyed at this disruption to his life, and it increased the tension in his neck and back. Inevitably, his impatience with this thing was bubbling, and for the next few hours not even Marine House mattered. The visit to the urologist was all-pervading in his thoughts; he needed his pain to be cured so he could get on with his life.

The next morning, with the hospital looming just an hour away, he paced his hotel suite. Of course, Stone drank too much whisky, he knew that, but he had always been fit and well, and he often dared to think at his age he had at least a couple of decades left. Stone was very edgy, unsure how he would face up to any ominous truth to confront him. But he was also holding onto a faint hope that his doctor Sean was making a fuss just to be sure there was nothing sinister to be uncovered.

The hospital was just a few roads away from Claridge's and Stone set out to walk there. But it left him feeling cold even on a summer morning. As he checked into the hospital, he was not sure what to make of the place. The reception had carpets on the floor, more like a hotel – it was polite, clean, brightly lit and impersonal. It was also empty of anyone else around; it felt like a place just for him, where he could come and go unnoticed by the outside world. It slowly made Stone feel more comfortable.

Exactly on time, the urologist saw Stone in his consulting room on the first floor. Across a clear desk with not even a laptop between them, the consultant, dressed in a smart suit and bright-red tie, looked Stone in the eye. This man was in charge, and Stone already felt the morning would run beyond his control.

'Mr Stone, thank you for coming to see me – I have had a letter and report from your doctor. He's outlined your symptoms for me, but perhaps you could tell me when they started and how they have progressed to how you feel now.'

Stone hesitated. He could not remember when all this started. He just knew how he felt now. He fidgeted in his seat.

'I visit the small room too often, and it's always been like that. Getting up a few times in the night, I soon knew I wasn't sleeping too well. I can put up with all that, even though it's getting worse, but my main symptom now is pain. Stretching right across my lower back. And getting stronger.'

The questions continued for the next half an hour about his habits, how much he drank of all liquids, what he ate, what exercise he took, his lifestyle; the consultant made a lot of notes. It was done with a seriousness that made Stone feel even more tense. Sitting in this large office was not a place he wanted to be.

'I shall need to do an investigation, and that will include a biopsy of your prostate.'

The consultant showed Stone a diagram of the prostate and the next stage of this investigation was discussed with him. It was all very matter of fact, almost detached from the pain and unease that his patient was feeling.

He was taken down a wide corridor to a separate clinical room, where he took off his clothes and put on a surgical gown. At this time Stone felt isolated, on his own and not able to stop the onwards progress. With the help of two nurses, the consultant carried out a biopsy of Stone's prostate. It only took fifteen minutes, but the procedure was particularly unpleasant and painful. Followed by blood tests, Stone was in the hospital for two and a half hours and the time there left him feeling tired and frustrated. He was offered a cup of coffee in a small side room and refused the sandwiches as he had no appetite at all. Sitting on his own for a few minutes, he was anxious, unsatisfied at the end of all the procedures.

'As soon as I have the biopsy results, I should like to see you again, Mr Stone. They should be ready within the week. Your doctor has given you pain relief medication, I presume, to carry you over for now.'

'Nothing more you can say?' Stone asked.

The doctor gave him a look which made Stone think he did know more but was not going to say. To Stone it was almost like a game of poker. It might be good; it might be bad.

The clinic would call him for another appointment to follow it up. Feeling very uncomfortable and in a deep mood of frustration, he took a taxi back to the discreet luxury of Claridge's. Once in his suite, he felt the overpowering quietness. It was sealed even against the outside traffic of the street below. Nobody would know he was here or where he had been, and perhaps nobody would care anyway. He started to consider who he should tell if his health treatment all went wrong.

He poured a whisky from a decanter on a sideboard and spread out on a low sofa with a newspaper. With his eyes closed for a few moments, he felt the discomfort of this morning's hospital investigations. He sipped from his glass as if that would take the pain away, but it left him very unsettled. Where was this all going to end?

Sitting alone in the quietness of his suite, Stone gathered his thoughts. This illness that was impinging on his life was not going to drag him down. He was not going to let it. More than that, he still had work to do. There was money in Nevis to be grabbed and pulled back to London; it was a necessary part of closing the gap to buy Marine House.

The luxury of his hotel gave him a comfortable space, and as he sipped his whisky, he would never have believed that he would soon take a call offering a tantalising money-making deal. Or was it just a neat scam by someone he was trying to clear from his life?

10

Stone nibbled at the croissants and drank two cups of black coffee that had been brought to his suite. He was interrupted from his meagre breakfast as his phone rang.

'Who's calling?' Stone asked quickly.

'Sounds like my mate Harry. How are you today, my friend?'

Stone held the phone away and looked at it. He was not sure what he had heard.

'Are you there, Harry?' the caller persisted.

'They've just put you away, banged you up for three years with no parole.'

'Don't get nasty, Harry, just because one of my boys called on you and gave a little fist towards your face. It was a gentle nudge to remind you I trusted you, matey, with a lot of money to look after. And look where we are now. My man said you didn't want to cooperate with him, but please take it as a gentle nod between friends. You still owe a quarter of a million. That's a lot of money we won't let you forget.'

'You're not out from behind bars, are you? You were in cell block C, shut away for money laundering, GBH, fraud, racketeering is what I heard,' Stone said again in a torrent.

'Between friends that's all a bit strong, Harry. And it don't mean I don't do jobs. I lead a busy life with my mates in here. And that's why I'm calling you.'

'What're you after?'

'You listen to me for a couple of minutes, matey. I've got something for you. You do what I ask and maybe we make some money together. And maybe then you can pay off what you owe me and a few of my boys out there. Then maybe we leave you alone. No more physical stuff. How does that sound?'

By now Stone would quickly have put the phone down on any crass caller making idle threats. But today it was different. He knew this man. Xavier was his name. Was it a Christian name or something more? The name was indelibly sticking. Stone could not forget him, and he suddenly felt the closeness of this ruthless narcotics dealer as if he was in the next room.

'One more hit and I'll call the cops. I'll spill to 'em all I know about you next time. You keep your crooks right away from me,' Stone said.

'The cops and me are friends now, Harry. They even come to see me in my new home. So, I'm talking to 'em all the time. You know what I mean?' Xavier sneered.

'Your festering lump of dirty cash is gone – forget it. You've now got ten seconds before I close the call. What do you want?'

'I was talking to one of my mates over dinner last night – yeah it was good, a plateful of beef stew and I didn't have to do the washing up afterwards – and with my other pals I've made in here we could all sit round as if we were buddies, and we had a good game of poker. Do you ever play poker, Harry?'

'Shut it – I don't want to listen to all that crap. You're in jail – it's where you belong, and it's where you're staying.'

'I don't like that talk, matey, 'cos I was telling you something you might like to hear. You got a pencil handy? You can write, can't you?'

Stone found a pencil with a small pad of paper on a sideboard; he grunted and listened. There was a quarter of a million outstanding to this thug, cash which had been lost in more games than poker. The pencil hovered in Stone's hand.

'You there still?' Xavier asked.

'I said get on with it.'

'My friend I dined with last night is a man of the world. And he's had a nod from one of his partners on the outside who keeps his money interests running for him. You see, there's a corporation out there on the stock market that's going to be bought, taken over, in a few days' time. And a man of business like you will know what that means, Harry, won't you? The price of its shares will jump up as soon as that bit of very private hidden information is shared with the world. Cos that's what always happens on takeovers like this.'

'Do you think I would believe anything coming from another con like you, banged up with a hundred other thugs?'

'Electric Motors Inc. It's going to be bought out at a high price, double what it's trading at now. And we've got a couple of weeks before the party happens. So listen, Harry, a stockbroker friend is going to buy some shares for me. I've got some real cash standing around, you know, saved from hard work over the last year. Fifty grand when I last looked. And do you know what? My stockbroker friends think I'm still living at my nice pad in the East End.' There was a loud croaky laugh and Stone held the phone away from his ear.

'You're in fairyland. You'd do better to put that money on a horse; at least you can watch the thing as you lose the lot.'

'Harry, hold on. You're not the sort of man who walks away from a deal that's a dead cert for making easy money. And listen to this. I don't have to spend my own money to live in here and have dinner with my business contacts. It's all free, so today I'm putting up fifty grand to get some shares in Electric Motors Inc.'

'What do you know about Electric Motors Inc that's not out there? And why're you telling me all this?'

'Harry, they're a big business – they build engines for motors like big cars. The noise is they've got something new for electric cars and an American business is scooping up the whole lot. Beyond that, I know nothing about 'em, don't need to. But Harry, trust me cos I want you to come in on this little deal. Big chance for you to make some notes to pay off the quarter of a million debt that you're trying to wriggle out of.'

'I'm never paying you a quarter of a million, so forget it. And how does this jailbird, serving time along with all you other crooks in cell block C, know what is going on at Electric Motors Inc?'

Stone asked. 'How shady is he to be stuck behind bars?'

'Please don't call my friends crooks – that's a nasty word, and it's not one we use when we're having dinner together.'

'Get on with it – I don't have any more time to waste with you.'

'Harry, my friend's in here with me because the last time he was invited to go to The Old Bailey for a couple of days they told him he'd done a bit of fraud. Nothing serious and it's only because some rat squealed on him that he got caught. Upright gentleman otherwise with some mates in high places. And they sent him this bit of insider information – it's worth gold.'

'I'm not interested, and I will never trust what a thug like you is telling me. So, get back to your cell, and remember I'm on the outside, and you're on the inside.'

'Okay, just watch the papers then, this time in two weeks. Not in *The Sun* what you read but in the pink ones like we get delivered to us in here with stock prices,' Xavier said.

Stone groaned – he knew all about insider information, and he knew where to find prices of stocks and shares.

'I trust you, matey to keep this bit of info quiet. Don't spill it around or you'll spoil it for the next time. But think about this special stuff that only people like you and me know of. And remember, matey, until you repay a quarter of a million… well, let's leave that for another day.'

'You call your gangster thugs right off, got it?'

'Harry, calm down. You know how these things work. Get somebody onto it; get your money lined up because there's going to be a few more tips from my mate – I hear there are tips of some very private things going on. They'll be worth gold. You'll make the fastest few quid ever in your life. And with it you get a final chance to clear your debts. Okay?'

Ten seconds later, Stone put his phone down, feeling hot. That man Xavier with the shiny bald head was going nowhere today; he had a lot of time to waste on poker and stock market tips that were probably no more than prison gossip.

But Xavier would walk out of the front gates of that jail in three years' time. Stone had deep distrust of this underworld gangster and the memory was still raw of Xavier chasing his money. Stone felt his ankle – he could still see the mad dog right inside Marine House, which had bitten a lump from his flesh.

Stone sat upright. His body felt tense and the hit to his right temple was still throbbing. For some time Stone had pushed Xavier out of his sight, out of his mind. But with his heavies, he was now inching, in a permeable way, closer again. Listening to the throaty voice of Xavier from behind bars repulsed Stone.

For a few minutes he lay on the sofa and stared at the name Electric Motors Inc he had scribbled on a pad. He would maybe follow that up. Sometime. Someday. Or maybe he would forget it quickly. He was very uncertain.

11

It was late morning as Claire weaved slowly down the narrow lane that led to the Arrow Hall site. The trees that formed an arch over the road had grown bigger and darker with their summer leaves, and the intricate iron gates with green mould on the top were still there. They were stuck wide open as they always had been for as long as she could remember.

The memory should have given her tingling excitement but not today. Her dream of Arrow Hall, walking in its newly landscaped gardens, was fading. It had been raining on the site and her car squelched in the mud. Claire stopped and shuddered. Since she had called just a couple of weeks ago, ugly grey hoardings now surrounded the perimeter, with large, industrial gates at the entrance to the building work. She was tense.

As she drew up near to the container that was to be the office, the site looked empty. She parked her car next to an open-top, vintage sports car with gleaming red metal. It stood out in the eerie quietness of the place.

But loud shouting suddenly boomed into the air.

'Which planet do you think you're on, Jimmy? You don't know how to run this site, you arrogant idiot.'

The shout came from a man with heavy, wide shoulders, with a baseball cap drawn over his eyes, who appeared from behind a stack of timber.

Jimmy – a younger man with rolled up shirt sleeves, a mug in one hand and a sandwich in the other – walked quickly towards Claire as she left her car.

'Get off this site if you don't like it. I run this place, not you,' Jimmy said, and he turned towards the irate block layer as if to face him off.

'You'd better listen up this time, else work stops.'

The shouting was followed by a string of expletives, bellowed out so quickly by the builder, he struggled to pour them from his mouth. He picked up a brick, then had second thoughts what to do with it. It dropped to the ground, and he stalked away in the opposite direction. It started to rain in a sharp shower, and Claire walked into the small cabin to shelter. Inside it was hot and damp, and she peered through the window, expecting Jimmy to join her. But she saw him running towards the vintage sports car. He fumbled to pull the hood into place to keep the seats free from the rain. As he finished, three men were standing in an arc close by, and Claire could hear their jeering shouts.

'Which lady are you trying to impress today with your fancy motor, eh, Jimmy?'

Jimmy waved his arm at them.

'Get back to your tools, you layabouts,' he yelled back.

He walked into the cabin and saw Claire, and his face was taught with tension.

'You must be Claire.'

'You must be James. Or Jimmy?'

'Ignore that lot of serfs out there. I'm James and that's final.' It was said with force, as if it was an insult which he resented.

'I see you've already started on the site.'

'Yeah, I've had a contractor clear some of the debris, remains of the fire. A challenging site, this one, but I'm sure it will go well,' James said.

'I always get nostalgic when I come here,' Claire said. 'This was such a beautiful, historic building, going back to the fifteen hundreds. I hope between us we can resurrect Arrow Hall. But I guess, when it's finished, it won't look quite the same as I remember it. Have you ever seen photos of what the old house looked like? Did you know I've researched its history?'

'No, thank you. I don't want to be sidetracked by something that might look quite different to what we're going to build here,' James said.

'James, this place is going to haunt you whether you like it or not. There was a Sir William Wholinge. He built the old house. And rebuilding Arrow Hall to look and feel just like it did all those years ago – with its tall, brick-built chimneys twisted in shape, almost like a corkscrew – is what I hope we will see. Then, the taller chimneys showed off your wealth. But not today. He was the squire of the place who farmed all of this land and land for many miles around. Sir William was a man who had two wives and six children, and he was a Protestant friend of Elizabeth I. And the Queen, on one of her tours of her country, stayed in Arrow Hall in 1601. So, James, when you see the building grow, tell me which room you think she slept in.'

'We can follow the footprint of the original house. But beyond that, it'll be time to move on and forget the past.'

'My dream is that Arrow Hall will be rebuilt to show off its history from inside and outside. It's a building with its own life and we owe it that.'

James turned away, disinterested in what Claire was saying.

'Seeing it all as bleak as this, is Rick's budget of £300,000 going to be enough?' Claire asked.

'It's tight. Prices are going up all the time. Some builders are cowboys; you've just seen one, but I'll sort 'em out. Anyway, I pass you the bills, you pay up promptly, otherwise we don't talk about money. That's a deal I hope, Claire.'

James was crisp and curt in his reply, and it left Claire unsure how much James would listen to her. James looked at his watch.

'What about a drink? There's a nice country pub around the corner. Have you got half an hour to spare? And it is time for a break now.'

'No. Some other day. I've got other things I must do today.'

Standing in the cramped, dusty space that was the office, James quickly finished his sandwich and took a noisy slurp from a mug.

'I've already got a few accounts for you to pay. A contractor has cleared the debris from the fire, and diggers have started to claw at the earth for the new foundations. And there'll be a lot more to come.' James hesitated and looked at Claire.

Claire felt his stare and started to open her laptop.

'I'd like to get to know you,' James said.

'We're going to work together. You'll soon find out my foibles.' Claire laughed.

James laughed back and passed a folder to her of bills to pay.

'Have you brought me some notes I can splash around? There are a few black economy guys out there I need to keep this place tidy.'

Claire handed James a leather briefcase she had brought from the safe in Rick's apartment.

'There's fifteen thousand pounds in bundled notes in there. I shall need to know exactly how you spend it. So, keep a record for me, please.'

'Yeah. Maybe. But that's just to start with. Bring me some more money to spread around every couple of weeks. Please remember, Claire, my first job is to fix this place so it gets the building growing. But keeping records? I'm not too good at that so don't expect much,' James replied. He started to walk from the cabin without looking back at Claire.

Claire, always meticulous about money, had promised Rick she would take control over how James was spending it, and she would do precisely that. But there was a distinct edge from James; his arrogance was on show, and shouting at contractors reminded her of Harry Stone's ego bellowing down the phone. This was not a place where she would tolerate hearing that again. His dismissive response to money left Claire uncertain.

Next time she would go to the pub, have a drink with James. Today he was brash with his flashy red sports car —would there be another side away from the mud and coarseness of a building site? From what she had seen of James, Claire was already wary.

It was a slow drive back to the emptiness of Rick's apartment, and Claire was alone. Isolated from anyone to talk to, Claire had growing doubt that she would ever see life in Arrow Hall again. How much would Rick spend on the site? And would she find a black hole sucking in as much money as James wanted to splash around on rebuilding Arrow Hall?

12

From the call he had just taken from the hospital, Stone knew that this was never going to be a good day. The appointment was for early that afternoon. Looking in the mirror as he shaved, the lines on his face were deepening; his eyes looked hollow; and his hands had fingers as thin as matchsticks. With a body that was lean and lithe, he never had a big appetite, but without standing on the bathroom scales, just from the fit of his trousers round his waist, he knew that he was losing weight.

Stone felt the urgency to get today's appointment with the smart-suited consultant over. He took a taxi, and in the carpeted hospital consulting room, all Stone now wanted to know was how this man facing him was going to clear him of incessant pain. Comfortable chairs faced the doctor sitting across the desk, and Stone sat upright, rigid, his hands clutching each arm. The doctor, as last time, looked straight at Stone with a blank expression that gave nothing away.

'Harry, I've had the biopsy results, and I'm afraid it shows that your expected cancer may be developing at a fast rate. It could be aggressive, and where we go from here will all depend on how quickly we've caught it.' The consultant looked down at his notes as if he was not sure of something. 'So, tell me again, how long did you say you've been having this pain in your back and your urinary symptoms?'

'Three, four months,' Stone replied, though he knew it was closer to nine months or even a year. This thing had been around a long while.

The doctor looked away and Stone moved in his chair. He was now very uncomfortable even as he sat there.

'We should talk about treatment options. And I think a scan at this time is important to see how far it has spread. They are not a cure but hopefully can alleviate symptoms and keep you going for a while.'

'How long is a while?' Stone blurted back.

'It can vary. Maybe eighteen months but maybe a lot fewer. Until we've seen how advanced it is, we shall not know. I shall make an appointment for you to have a full MRI scan. Have you had one before?'

'No and I'm not sure I want one now,' Stone said, feeling techy.

'I understand how you feel, but it would be in your best interests.'

Stone hardly moved for the next ten minutes. He sat upright in his chair, staring to the blank white wall ahead. The consultant, in the same dark suit and bright-red tie, described the time-consuming and painful medical interventions that he could have. Possibly remove the prostate and undergo radiotherapy treatment. But Stone tried not to listen. It was becoming clear that his life expectancy, as long as he sat there, was probably getting very much shorter. In the end he agreed to have a scan, though nothing more. And even a scan, for Harry Stone, was only in the hope that he could see that this cancer had not spread and that this hospital had got it all wrong.

At just after midday, Harry Stone was ready to leave the London hospital. In a move that was just as clinical as the urologist's investigations and this morning's consultation, he was told that his credit card, presented on the first visit to the hospital, had now been charged with £3,250. He was handed the account in an envelope, but paying for professional services this morning, unusually, meant nothing for Stone. The high cost passed over him; he just felt numb from the bleak message, and he stood outside on the pavement for two minutes waiting for a taxi.

It was beginning to rain heavily and, as he climbed into the back seat of a taxi, he felt his heartbeat in his neck, and his hand was shaking. This pain in his back had been with him for many more months than he had told the doctor, but the diagnosis presented to him was as if nothing had happened until this morning. It had all just started today and again, he thought they had got it all wrong; they didn't know what they were doing.

Today left Stone tense, frightened. What would come next was beyond his control.

13

Stone's mood was low as he walked into the busy foyer of Claridge's twenty minutes after leaving the hospital. In the sitting room of his suite, he poured a large whisky. For a moment he felt an urge to throw it across the room, but he paced the heavily carpeted space and took a long sip. This thing he was faced with was real and threatening. He felt cold, and he shivered.

His phone buzzed; he was in no mood to answer, and it rang for almost a minute before he picked it up.

'I want to meet with you.'

Stone sat more upright; he knew that voice immediately.

'Josh, good to hear from you. You got something to tell me? You're ready to close the deal on Marine House I hope,' Stone said almost with a snigger.

'Can you be at the Reform Club in Pall Mall, next Friday, 10.00 in the morning? Can you be there?'

'Of course I can. Will you be on your own, or will your mother come with you?' Stone asked.

'Just me, but can you be there?'

'Yes, I'll look forward to it.'

It was enough to end the call. Stone heard it click off as if Josh needed to keep it short and quiet. Stone stared at his whisky glass and then wrote down the details from Josh.

What had the son of the Jackson family, Josh, got to say to him that he would really want to listen to? Stone had dismissed him as a top-level layabout, a playboy and probably with not much to do. And meeting in the Reform Club – a toffs' place in an expensive part of the West End of London – was not Stone's scene. Just like the meeting room in Mayfair, to Stone they were sterile places, never changing, where he could never feel comfortable.

Stone rested on the sofa for a few more minutes and stared at the ceiling. He then paced the room, and the growing nagging pain on his hip subsided for a while. His mood slowly lightened. Next Thursday there was a deal to be done on Marine House; he would put his prejudice of the meeting place aside.

Half an hour later, he poured his second glass of whisky; he was still shivering – he put on a bathrobe and started to pace the room. He pulled the bathrobe more tightly around himself. And his dark mood deepened as he again added up what money he could find. He was still £500,000 short, and he was never going to tell the Jackson family there was a deep hole in his purse.

Feeling an urgency, Stone opened his laptop and keyed into his Panama dollars. The money had been buried away for six years, forgotten, nobody touching them, and would the bank in Panama soon snatch the dollars as their own? He wanted to grab them in his hand, to feel them, to know they were real. They would close half the gap in the money for Marine House, and if he had to, he would carry them in his pocket back to London himself.

Today his body was aching; he was still dazed as the news of the doctor's words were sinking in. Whisky glass in his hand, he wandered around the sitting room of the suite. Any time he had left would not be kind to him and a journey to a small island in the Caribbean Sea would test his diminishing stamina to the end.

Suddenly feeling alone, helpless, he began to believe that the pain in his back would not let him work much longer. And maybe his time was short even to go outside just to walk a few steps. His energy was being sucked out by the certainty of this prognosis, but there was fight stirring in Harry Stone. Whatever was attacking him, he was going to get hold of his deposit of dollars in Panama. There was urgent work to do before meeting with Josh. He poured another whisky and took more painkillers as prescribed by the consultant.

14

Stone was beginning to feel hungry. He called room service. He had not eaten much; the clinic in London with the painful biopsy of his prostate and then the awful prognosis had left him with little appetite. But the tray of smoked salmon with a green salad that was quickly brought to his suite was tempting – he sat at a small table, and he ate it in only a short time.

He pulled out a sheet of crumpled paper from his pocket and he read the words Electric Motors Inc that he had scribbled down. Xavier, the inmate of HMP Belmarsh, became real again, and he could see the shiny bald head with a rippling neck. Making fast money would always drive Stone, and today, with his time left getting shorter, maybe the prize to buy Marine House was getting closer.

But Stone was cautious, his intuition pulling him back. This ruthless crook, who kept as pets snarling slobbering dogs, was trying to lure him into another blind corner that only paying up a quarter of a million pounds would get him out of. Sitting back on the sofa, he opened his laptop and he keyed in Electric Motors Inc. He flicked past the technical pages until he found what Electric Motors Inc had to say about its own money. Stone did not need to study it for long to see that this supposed money-making tip was losing cash in bucketloads. The screen showed a red arrow pointing downwards, the price of the shares had fallen today. And yesterday and the day before. He found nothing about what this business did with its electric motors that was special, unique and what somebody would want to pay a lot of money to get their hands on.

Stone smiled to himself. Aimlessly staring at the screen for several seconds, he felt the raw memory of five years ago buying some shares after an insider tip. He should have known better, but talking with somebody in a bar room, somebody he did not even know, alongside his usual glass of whisky, he had swallowed a nod about a gold mine in Africa. The price of anything gold was massive, still going up, and tomorrow the gold mine was going to hit the big time, hit it rich from rock deep underground. And wasn't everybody cashing in by selling their gold jewellery to someone who would smelt it down for its high value?

Stone had hustled himself into buying into an African gold mine just as the tip had suggested. But he waited and waited and watched as the price tumbled over the next few weeks. The tip-off had been a dud, somebody's guess at what might happen in a faraway deep gold mine. In just one afternoon Stone saw nearly £10,000 drain away.

The memory for a short while increased the sneering ridicule Stone now had for Xavier, a money launderer serving a sentence in prison. Electric Motors Inc smelled like a hoax; it was likely that this insider secret was dead – it was worthless. After closing his laptop, he nibbled at what was left of the salad and, for ten minutes, sat almost motionless on the sofa. He called Roger in his high rise city office. Stone spoke with an eager edge.

'Roger, listen to this. It's sensitive information on what I hear is going to happen in a few days' time. My informant tells me the price of some shares is going to run up. There's going to be a takeover of a business and I want to know what you think. You've got to keep this close, Roger.'

'I'm listening, but if this is another of your reckless deals with the underworld, leave me out.'

'Electric Motors Inc. My information is that the price is going to double sometime soon on the stock market. A deal's going to be announced to the world that somebody's making a bid for them. What do you think of that?'

'Harry, it sounds again as if you're talking about something right on the edge. Are you sure you want to share this with me? I mean, using insider information is a criminal offence. They lock you up for it.'

'I might spend some money buying into it. So, what's Electric Motors all about?'

'Where did you get this drivel from? And why do they want to tell you about it?'

'I have my sources; I can't disclose them – just tell me what you know about Electric Motors Inc.'

'Not much, and I don't have a clue why somebody would want to buy them at twice the price they are today. It sounds to me like some speculative deal that one of your mates has tipped you about in the pub when he was half drunk.'

'I want you to set up a stockbroker dealing account for me. You know the channels to do this so get it done and I'll transfer some cash into it when I'm ready to deal. Then in a few days' time we'll watch Electric Motors together to see what happens.'

'Yeah, sure, I'll set it up for you – it might take a few days. But you leave insider dealing alone if you want to stay in one piece.'

Stone ignored Roger's lecturing which he had heard many times before.

'There's something else. My place in Brighton I've got on a lease that's running out. I'm trying to buy it, but the owner's being awkward, a Lady Ruth Jackson. And in the picture, there's a son, Josh, maybe a daughter too. Maybe a Sir or Lord Jackson, maybe other hangers-on. Who knows? But the son, Josh, has called for a meeting. I've got to get this right, so I need to find out who they really are. Roger, dig up everything on Lady Ruth and her family. Where she lives, what she has, property, money, cars, debts, lovers, the lot,' Stone said.

'I've never heard of them, but give me some time and I'll see what I can find.'

'The meeting with the son, Josh Jackson, is next Friday morning, 10.00, St James's Square, Pall Mall. Reform Club. I want you to be there.' Stone's voice snapped the instruction.

'Yeah, I'll be there, but it'll have to be quick. I've got other important things on that day.'

'I've had some unpleasant news from my doctor,' Stone said quietly as if he did not want anyone to hear it.

There was silence for a moment as Roger was uncertain what he should say.

'Do you want to tell me more?' Roger coaxed.

'I've got eighteen months, probably much fewer, probably only weeks,' Stone said.

'Harry, what's going on?'

'Cancer in the prostate, may be spreading. Giving me serious backache even when I'm sitting still.'

'That's awful. Are you having treatment?' Roger asked.

'Not until I've bought Marine House. I've got to feel well enough to get that deal right without people fiddling about with me. It might be my last chance.'

'Why Marine House?'

'Good investment. It'll make three smart apartments when I've split it up. And that'll bring in three times the money I pay for Marine House. But there's something else. It's where I've been living for the past three years. I don't want to leave it.' Stone paused. 'But it's £2.5 million,' he added quickly as if his reckoning was not as shrewd as he had said.

'That sounds like a very big house. And £2.5 million sounds like a very big price.'

'You must come to see it sometime. Soon,' Stone said.

'Maybe one day,' Roger replied half-heartedly.

'Don't forget Electric Motors – there's money there,' Stone said, but he knew that all around that deal was the fog of where it had come from. He pressed his phone off.

The whisky decanter on the sideboard was looking low and Stone drained it to fill his glass. He sat back and took a long sip. Impatiently, he then walked round the room trying to ease his back, trying to find a comfortable position. His numbered days draining away, he now had little to lose. He was never going to know if Xavier was really onto something unless he dipped his toes in the murky water. Innate greed, he needed money to close the gap for Marine House, and curiosity pushed Stone into leaving that thought still resonating. And it would be too easy to pour £50,000 into Xavier's blind share deal just from the press of a button a few screens away on his laptop.

It left Stone undecided. Lying on a large sofa, his eyes closed, after a few minutes, he fell into a deep sleep.

15

As he woke in his suite in Claridge's, Stone felt an overpowering tiredness. That was something new, something he did not like, and he did not know how to deal with it. He tried to calm his growing anxiety, but he paced his suite uneasily. He had been told not to eat for four hours before the scan, so he skipped lunch and even a glass of malt whisky.

It took him half an hour walking slowly through the London streets to reach the hospital. He felt better for the walk and was determined not to be intimidated by what he had been told about today's procedure. It did not help as he was asked at the MRI reception to fill in a detailed questionnaire about his health and medical history as any form-filling was anathema to him.

He undressed in a side room and felt naked as he put on a hospital gown. The radiographer who was to conduct the scan met Stone as he came from the cubicle.

'Mr Stone, I'm looking after you today. We are going to scan most of your body, bone structures and internal organs. The procedure in the scanner will take probably just over half an hour.'

'You're looking to see where the prostate cancer has spread. I'm getting a lot of pain, so I suspect you've got a lot to find.'

'Well, let's see how it goes. I just ask you to lie as still as you can; you will hear rattling noises from time to time, but please wear the headphones if you prefer to.'

'No, let's get on with it,' Stone said with impatience at the whole procedure. He wanted to get this over.

'It will take a short while after today for the results to be studied, and I will talk to your urologist about them too. I will send my report to him and your doctor in Brighton in three or four days. Please now make yourself comfortable.'

A nurse took Stone to the adjoining room and for the first time Stone saw the narrow tunnel with the scanner that he would be lying in head first. Claustrophobia was his dread. This would not be easy as he lay on the motorised bed that moved him inside the scanner. He closed his eyes and listened to the rattling sound that was all around him. For the next forty minutes he resisted using the panic button to get him out of this narrow, noisy space. But why was he doing this, why was he wasting his time here?

Stone dressed slowly, a difficult part of his diagnosis now completed, and he already knew what the results would show. This was not a place to linger – he left the cubicle, quickly walked past the nurse and radiographer without looking back.

His racing heart slowed as he walked back to Claridge's, and he now just wanted to get out of this place. A short while later, his head was nodding as he was sitting in the back of a limousine to take him to Marine House.

16

Early morning Stone stood on the balcony of the sitting room and looked across to the sea and wide horizon. He breathed in deeply the fresh air of the morning. Even this time of day, his energy was sapped, and eating away at him was the knowledge that he had had this pernicious disease for much longer than he had admitted. His illness was forcing him into a black corner, but Stone had fight in him. He felt the challenge, just like a game to beat the consultant, and he was determined he would outlive the short-term prognosis that had been given to him.

His determination was reinforced by pouring a small glass of whisky. He dared to remember he was over sixty four years. Retirement was never something Stone had planned, and he was not sure what he would be retiring from. Sitting on the sofa, he took out a dog-eared photo from his wallet. It was of his younger sister who had died three years ago. Yes, of course there was an end.

And at that moment, for the first time since she had gone, he wondered if his ex-wife Sofie would want to know of his disease. For fifteen years he had been married to Sofie, but that had ended ten years ago, and he had not seen her or heard of her since.

They had no children; Stone's life had been sterile of friendships; he kept a distance from any emotional attraction. It left only one person he could really care about, even maybe care for as a parent. And that was Claire. Claire had been part of his work for a long time. But Claire had walked away, finally disliking his crude attempts to make money. And now, in his growing isolation, he felt the absurdity that the only outside contact who called him was a con in HMP Belmarsh, demanding a quarter of a million pounds and feeding him insider tips on share prices which were probably duff.

He put the photo of his sister back in his wallet and in the elegant Regency sitting room of Marine House, he lounged on the sofa just as he usually did. But he was alone, and Stone brooded. From today, Marine House was to become a place to rest in, to find time to look across to the sea with a full glass of whisky in his hand.

Buying Marine House was still a deal Stone was not going to let slip away. And there was unfinished business at Arrow Hall. The rambling Elizabethan manor house, surrounded by three acres of gardens with a dried-out moat, was a place he had owned and a place where he had lived for many years. But Arrow Hall was no longer his, the burnt-out site sold too cheaply.

Arrow Hall and Claire were two names that, for Harry Stone, remained closely entwined, like ivy flourishing as it climbed an ancient oak tree. But he had not spoken to Claire for two years and he did not know how to deal with sensitive talk like that. And how would he tell her he only had a very limited time left to sort everything out? He pushed those thoughts aside; he needed Claire, and he needed her soon.

For a short while Stone closed his eyes, but he did not sleep. His brain whirled; there was much he still had to do. His secret Panama deposit, was it valuable in a distant place? Bringing it all back to London, he would soon find out if it would help him to buy Marine House, but he was now about to play a dangerous game, keeping that money away from the eyes of nosey authorities.

With less than nine weeks left of his lease, Stone fretted. Meeting Josh at the Reform Club in Pall Mall would be no more than a vanity call, a chat with Josh just to boost his ego. But Stone would work on Josh; a door had been opened, and he was being pulled to rest in this seafront mansion.

But impulsively, Stone ran his hand to his right temple. It was still sore from the fist that had hit his face just a few days ago right inside the kitchen of this big house. The threat of a thug loitering around the place had not gone.

17

As soon as it was delivered, Stone gathered the post from the letter box. In his study, he slit open a deep brown official envelope with a long silver paperknife. He knew what it was; it did not help his mood and, with impatience and annoyance in equal measure, he scanned the letter quickly before throwing it onto his desk. It was a demand from the revenue for £25,000. A levy on his profits from selling his row of houses in the East End. His accountant had warned him the demand was coming, but worse, this demand was just the start. There was something bigger that would quickly follow.

His mood of belligerence immediately increased – this piece of paper was a hit against his scrabble for money, and in his present state of uncertain health, that was not good. But with appointments to see specialist doctors and the frightening pain in his back, Stone stood back. He looked from the window to the dark back garden to Marine House and decided he did not care about that sort of letter anymore. They could sing for the money.

From a crisp white envelope, he pulled a second letter – it was dated two weeks ago. He sat at his desk, took his time to read it and a grin spread over his face. He scanned the short note for a second time.

Dear Mr Stone,

Your donation to the Plaistow Hospice for Children of £100,000 is very gratefully received. We rely on the generosity of our patrons to carry out the very necessary work and your gift will go towards an area we are planning to landscape into gardens.

Should you wish to view what we are doing, I would be more than pleased to show you round the green spaces we are creating.

Yours truly,
David Tompkins
Chair Trustees

His sister had worked in that hospice as a nurse; it was in memory of her. Just sending the money made him feel powerful – he managed a smile of satisfaction and there was a warm glow from reading it again. Even though he was running half a million short for buying Marine House, one day he would send another gift. Soon. Harry Stone was a complex man; there was more to him than just money, a number shown on a piece of paper from a London bank.

18

Claire heard loud shouting as she drove onto the site and parked next to James's bright-red, ostentatious sports car. James and the wide-shouldered bricky were standing face to face. This was more than a loud argument; it was going to be a punch-up.

James turned to leave; he was given a hard push between his shoulders. He fell forwards and his body hit the ground with a hard thump. The bricky moved away quickly, trying to hide himself, and James, stunned, sat on his knees for some seconds before standing up.

'What's that all about?' Claire asked.

James was breathless as he walked towards the cabin.

'Not much. He doesn't like the way I inspect his work. It's not always up to my standards.'

'I suggest you don't bring that sporty car onto the site. It's asking for ridicule when you get into a shouting match.'

'Not now, Claire, please. I've had enough this morning.'

'I heard you last time I was here. Calling tradesmen you've brought onto the site layabouts, that surely isn't going to work. You go on like that and the friction you cause will soon empty this place. It'll just grind to a halt and what then?'

'Don't you question too. I've been running building sites for ten years now and I know how to deal with the kind of people you find here. So, leave it won't you?'

'You look flustered, James. You're on your phone; you're running around; and you rarely have time to stop and talk.'

'I've had Heritage England, electricians, plumbers, that fool from the architects' office, all calling for me just in the space of this morning. So how do you think I feel?'

James started to walk away but Claire called him.

'Davies, the plumber. Bill duplicated, signed off by you twice. Same work, same date. Expensive mistake, James, if we're not careful.'

'Give it to me – I'll get the money back.'

'It's £7,500, so put it top of your priority list.'

James snatched the paper from Claire and again started to walk from the cabin.

'Not so fast, James. What about the £15,000 in hard cash I gave to you last time? Have you got a list for me yet where it's gone?'

'Leave it off, can't you? That's just petty cash, and I don't keep a record of every penny.'

James left quickly without turning to face Claire. She had a prickly feeling just visiting this place. What was biting James? Why was he so hostile on this clear, sunny morning?

Claire sat alone in the cabin and totalled what had so far been spent on the rebuild. It was already quickly running close to Rick's top figure that he would spend. And the building was not yet halfway there. What would happen when the money had gone?

An uncomfortable sense of discord was growing on Claire. And it was not only the arrogance of James. Rick and Arrow Hall did not fit together. Perhaps they never had. Rick, after all, was more used to living in Mayfair in his penthouse apartment, where there was space and high ceilings with wide views from each window. A country estate with a mock Elizabethan manor house? It was not his style. It left Claire with only lingering feelings for Arrow Hall, and she felt a growing numbness at visiting this site.

Claire looked up quickly from her laptop. She saw at the entrance to the site a man in a black Mini with blacked-out rear windows. The car drove slowly towards the site. It stopped; the driver stared intensely for a few minutes and then moved on. Arrow

Hall was at the end of a small lane, and you did not drive down it unless you had a reason. And with unrest around the place, for Claire, a man staring from a car window left her again feeling very uneasy.

19

Harry Stone was restless on the flight to the Caribbean island of Nevis. He fidgeted; he walked around the cabin; he felt nervous and aggressive in equal waves. This cancer was eating away at him. For a short while, he questioned if he should take the palliative and other treatments that were being offered by his doctor. But his impatience did not let him think that far. In the privacy of his first-class seat, in a depressive moment, a single tear crept down Stone's thin face.

He had barely slept; he was tired after the long twelve-hour journey, and he did not know what he was going to find in this strange place.

At the small, dusty terminal that was Nevis's airport, the humid heat hit him. His growing depressive mood was not lifted in the sunshine, and as he climbed into a taxi, it started to rain heavily. The forecast was for a hurricane to roll in that would ground all aircraft for several days. He could not get this visit over quickly enough.

Charlestown, the centre of Nevis, is not a big place, and Stone wandered down the main street half an hour later. The town had no buzz to it; there was little noise; it was not busy, and he started to doubt the advice from Roger. This looked an unlikely location for his money to be anonymous and safe. Panama City had high-rise, solid buildings; they gave a signal that his money was at least shielded behind the concrete structures there. And Nevis was small, rustic, with tin roofs, unsophisticated and without the noise of fast-moving traffic, hooting in a cacophony of sound.

In a side street he found the address he had been given by Roger. It was a small, wooden building with a red roof and a balcony that opened onto the road below. Inside it was barely cooler than the humid heat of the road; a Caribbean lady looked at her computer and finally announced that they were expecting him. Roger had cleared his way, and he was soon introduced to an American woman with long, blonde hair hanging over her shoulders who was just half his age. She was sitting at a large, almost bare, desk but with three landline phones on the edge. A fan whirled overhead, but it was still very humid and warm.

'My contact tells me you might be able to do some business for me. I've got dollars in Panama, but I've now got to get them to London. Without any busybody knowing about it.'

'Yeah, we know all about Panama. Nasty bit of business. So, you first transfer them here, then with one or two twists we'll help you get them quietly to London. And unlike Panama, we keep all details here secure. We shoot anyone who tries to steal them.' The American laughed but her voice had serious depth to it.'

'Keep it simple; don't try to fiddle me and maybe… well, just maybe we do some business together. But there's at least $400,000. That's big money – how safe would it all be in this wooden building?'

The American woman's face turned to a wide smile. She was sitting stiffly upright, and Stone saw her searching his face across the desk as if she was looking for something.

'We deal with a lot of money being transferred around the world. First, I'll set up a company for you here in this beautiful little island of Nevis, and what say we make it owned by your business in Panama. Then you transfer your dollars across into it. Any account here will have passwords that only you know. No questions from anyone but me, nothing in writing that will let anybody know what you're doing here. All with a cast-iron guarantee we will never give your name away.'

Stone was testy – how could he trust the set up here? For some reason he felt nervous sitting in front of, and listening to, this blonde American woman. He fidgeted in his chair and his back was again beginning to ache badly.

'Yeah, okay, but words are the easy bit. How do you get my money to London? And fast.'

'We don't do bag loads of dollar bills stuffed in suitcases. Too dangerous from sniffer dogs when walking through airports. But there are other safer ways to transfer your money. You've got two options. Number one you go round London and set up ten different bank accounts with just a few thousand in each one. That'll look like normal banking and not seen as seed beds for money laundering. So, I split your money up over ten accounts, send it over the wire spaced out over the next few months. It'll be small enough in each account not to alert anyone.'

'I've already got accounts in London. But can't do ten. Too much paper to fill in, and I don't do forms. So, tell me something else.' Stone turned away and stared towards the window.

'Okay, number two. Ever dealt in diamonds, Mr Stone?'

Stone looked up. Now was the time to sound naïve.

'Diamonds? No that'll be new to me.'

'If your dollars are as big as what you say, we'll give you three very high-value, cut and polished, five-carat, lab-certified diamonds. Cut to size and shape, they shine with brilliant colour. And to make up any balance, we'll throw in a few rough, uncut diamonds. We'll make them all add up to the same value as your Panama money.'

The American woman's face relaxed into a tight grin.

'Come on then, what's the catch?'

'It's sound business. We have traded this way before, and graded diamonds are the easiest way for you to get a good swap for dollars. They can be sold for sterling. You then no longer have to worry about unusable dollars stuffed in Panama.'

'How do I know your diamonds are worth my four hundred grand dollars?' Stone asked.

'We only deal with people who have been recommended and you come from my contacts in London. And I remind you, Mr

Stone, we trade worldwide, and I'm not going to blow it all on some fake stones. That enough?'

'You sure I can carry them just like that?' Stone asked.

'They're small enough to slip into your pocket and there's no way anyone's going to find you've got them. No customs checks are likely to find diamonds. They don't leave a marker; they're invisible money and not even sniffer dogs get close. So, unless you're stopped with a full body search, you pass easily through the airport. But why would they want to search a smart gent like you?'

'What do you get out of all this? What's your pay-off?'

'Ten per cent. Flat. You get ninety per cent; I get ten per cent.'

'Show the gems to me. Do you keep them here?'

'Sure, why not? Give me two minutes, Mr Stone, and I'll show you what we have to offer you.'

Stone stared at the young American woman as she left the airless room. He walked to the balcony. The rain was hitting the roof of this two-storey building noisily; the wind was gusting just outside in the wide road and Stone was beginning to feel sealed into this place for a few days if he did not get away soon. And he was very uncomfortable; he had not taken painkillers for twenty-four hours – he walked around the room and then sat again heavily into a chair to rest his back.

This wooden building with its verandah, plain and simple, looking down to a quiet road, did not feel real. Had Roger ever been within a hundred miles of this place to see a gem dealer hiding away in the middle of the Caribbean? Even a smart American, sounding as if she knew what she was talking about, adding sophistication, was only a veneer.

He suddenly felt that diamonds for dollars was too easy to be real. It was just like dealing with share tips from a con in jail. But his reckonings on buying Marine House were hanging right on the edge, and that was when he felt the strong tug to get his dollars cleared. He looked at his watch; he wanted to get away.

With loud talking, the American returned, followed by a big, imposing Caribbean man well over six feet tall and with shoulders as wide as a New York Yankees quarter back. He had a freshly laundered white shirt. He grinned and placed a tray of seven glinting diamond gems onto the desk. Three large ones stood out, glistening in blues and yellows as he turned the desk light onto them.

'I'm sure you understand that we must have strong security with such valuable items as these. But handle them, study them, hold them to the light,' the American said as she stood back to let Stone get closer.

Stone picked up the small, uncut diamonds, all of a similar size but with different shapes and colour. He held one to the light and even tried to bite it to see if it crumbled, as that is what he had been told was a true test of a diamond. But he felt its jagged edge on his gum, and he took it from his lips quickly. Then there were three big, round diamonds, the facets cleanly cut and again glinting in the light with blue colour brilliance. He handled them for a couple of minutes, held them in his hand as if he was weighing them, held them to the light, but Stone was not sure. How could he know what they were really worth?

The American saw Stone hesitating and the big Caribbean man moved away towards the window.

'The ten per cent you're after is a big take from $400,000. What about seven and half per cent?' Stone said.

'No, that's the deal we offer whatever the transaction. You want to move your money and I assure you our discretion and service is rock solid. And we have to be paid for it.'

Stone did not see the pun in the American woman's words. She watched him closely and there was silence for a minute as Stone studied again each of the big-cut diamonds in his hand.

'How much is each of these worth?' Stone asked.

'I will guarantee when you want to cash them in you will get your money in full. You take two uncut and this five-carat, round-cut, very valuable stone with you today. This one is worth up to $110,000. Its clarity and colour you can see, and let me show you this tiny number lasered into the girdle. Take that one with you to London – if it's ever lost or stolen, it can be identified by that number. So, I'll know where it is if you don't bring it back.' She laughed again, sensing Stone's tenseness.

'I'll take 'em, but give me time to have them valued by my contact in Hatton Garden.'

'There are lots of diamond dealers in London – get an unbiased assessment from someone who'll give you money for them. And then, when you're ready, you get the rest. Come to Nevis and stay longer another time. But you won't be able to sell the big ones without the certificates from an independent certification laboratory, and I give you those when our dealing together is finished. For my security, today you give me access to half your Panama money and I get the rest when you collect the other diamonds and the certificates. And remember, my ten per cent I take only when all your money is cleared from Panama. And that's when the deal is finished and we're both satisfied.'

For a moment, Stone just stared at the diamonds. This is not what he had expected, and he had no idea if this woman was telling him the true value of this gem. He handled again the large diamond and thought of over £80,000 just resting in his hand. It felt unreal.

'Maybe we'll talk again,' Stone said.

'Yeah, we'll talk again, I'm sure.' The American nodded.

Sitting in this humid place was making Stone sweat. The deal was clear. The American put two rough and the finely cut large diamonds in a string pouch which slipped easily into Stone's pocket. They sat together for another hour as she called in a young American man in a colourful shirt who had the forms all ready for signature to set up a company in Nevis. Without showing either of them, Stone put in his codes to transfer up to half of his dollars from Panama into this anonymous shell company.

This visit to this torrid place was already too long for Stone; he was unsure what he had done, and his pain was increasing as he sat there. Within an hour, he left with three diamonds in his pocket. A small, private plane was quickly arranged by the American to take Stone to a neighbouring island for his flight back to London.

The parting was businesslike, and he left Nevis sure that he would never come back again. His time was too short. But his dollars were moving; if he was careful, he could get them back to London and start to close the gap for the money to buy Marine House.

He kept the diamonds in their string pouch at the bottom of his travelling bag, which he never let out of his sight, as he flew back on an overnight flight to London. Inevitably, he did not sleep; he did not drink or eat; and when he arrived at Gatwick airport, he was in a hurry. But he slowed as he walked to the green customs channel, milling with holidaymakers returning from the Caribbean. A young customs officer looked at Stone, almost singling him out as a sniffer dog ran around his bag.

'Just one moment, sir,' the officer said.

Stone said nothing, but he felt his scalp tingle with nervousness. He turned to face the officer as he saw the sniffer dog again walk around his bag.

'Are you travelling alone today?'

'Yes.'

'Where have you come from?'

'Antigua.'

'Have you been on business, or a holiday break?'

Stone wanted to get on and he felt his back stiffen.

'Bit of each,' Stone replied.

The officer's attention was drawn away as his dog was sniffing closely and pawing at another traveller's bag.

'Continue your journey, sir, and have a good day,' he said to Stone.

Stone was hot and tense after a long, uncomfortable journey, but as he took a breath, he felt his hunched shoulders drop. Walking in the slowly moving queue in front of him, within half a minute, he was in the arrivals hall. He felt free – he put his hand into the bottom of his bag to feel the diamonds. No, they don't smell; they are just good lumps of easy-to-carry money.

Today was a big first step in clearing four hundred thousand dollars. He was trusting that American woman, with the long, flowing hair over her shoulders. He would waste no time finding out if these precious stones had real value.

20

It was cold in the early morning; Stone was tired and irritable as he left the taxi at the front of Marine House. He did not see him or hear him until he had paid the taxi driver. He was suddenly stopped at the foot of the steps that led to the front door of Marine House. It was the same large man who had landed a heavy fist on his face in his kitchen. Stone looked up and saw the wispy grey beard, intimidating stare and menacing eyes as they glared at him this cold morning.

'Mr Xavier told me to keep a look out for you. We don't want you to run away, like, because there's the large number of notes that you owe.'

'Get out of my way – tell your trash I haven't got it and I'm not paying anything.'

'No, it don't work like that. Mr Xavier says to remind you about Electric Motors Inc. There's money there for you, he says. So don't gamble with your luck anymore. Some people out there are getting very grouchy. If I don't see your money very soon, then me and me mates'll be around to deal with you. We'll show you the knife first before we use it and you'll know what that means, Harry.'

The thug leant close into Stone's face as he spoke, and Stone pushed him away.

'I wouldn't do that again, Harry. Because I'm going to be here to watch you until you pay up.'

Stone felt the sudden hard slap across his face, and he stumbled onto the bottom step to his front door. The overnight bag he had carried from Nevis, holding the diamonds, fell onto the path.

'So, what've you got in there? Feels heavy enough of bundles of £20 notes all ready to give to Mr Xavier.'

The threatening man in front of him held the bag in his hand as if he was weighing it. He went to undo the zip that held it closed, but it was locked. Stone reached out to grab the bag, but his back would not let him as he felt a stab of pain stretch from one side to the other.

'What say I let you have this bag back if you give me some notes for my trouble coming to see you this week? Eh, Harry?'

Stone took out his wallet and counted out five £20 notes. He held them out and they were snatched away in one quick move.

Stone watched as Xavier's hooded thug slouched away. As he climbed the steps to the large front door of Marine House, he was cold, angry, wiping his eyes where the hard fingers had slapped him. The inside of Marine House was gloomy and quiet. The diamonds could have been snatched – Stone shivered; he was helpless as he felt the tentacles of a racketeer he thought had been put away for five years squeeze tighter.

In the gloom of his study at the back of the house, he spread three diamonds across his desk. Pain was nagging at his right hip; there was a tiredness after his visit to Nevis; and he felt weak. The whisky bottle was not far away; it was only early morning, but he took a swig.

He knew nothing about glistening pieces of rock and their real value. Were they dud? Was he being conned? And did he really have to give up ten per cent just so that he could handle them? It did not take him long to flick through an old diary from his desk drawer for the number of a contact he had known for many years. It was still early, but he called. With no pleasantries, he arranged to meet Sol in Hatton Garden mid-afternoon, tomorrow.

Even in the early morning, he was unsettled. In the sitting room, he looked across to the sea that had an early morning mist. He felt the growing menace of Xavier and his gangsters; they were pushing, hustling him on Electric Motors Inc. As if it was something he had forgotten about, he quickly opened his laptop to check on its share price. This was just not real; he ran his hand through his hair as he saw a row of red figures and, as if it was mocking him, a red arrow pointing to the bottom of the page. The value of Electric Motors Inc was still going down.

Roger was right – Electric Motors was sinking fast. But Stone's brain worked quickly. An odd logic still gripped him. With the price of the shares much lower, he could buy more of them, and when they went up, he would make more money. It would be a gamble, but the whole of life was a gamble, as he was rapidly finding out. He would deal Electric Motors. Tomorrow, after he had seen Sol with a big diamond, when he felt less tired.

Stone had a lot to do in a short time; his impatience started to make him worried where it was all going to end.

21

Oustide Claridge's Stone felt the tension drain from him as he walked into the sunlight of the day. He vowed that he would have no invasive treatments against this insidious enemy that was attacking his body.

He stopped a taxi and directed the driver to an address in Hatton Garden, London's area for diamond dealing. In the taxi, Stone handled and studied the large diamond he had brought from Nevis. Dug out from deep in the ground, he now dared to believe this glinting piece of rock was not just another jewel to hold and admire. It was the same as a large fistful of notes. Money, its own currency. Usable, tradeable. Anonymously.

The entrance to Sol's office was next door to a sandwich shop in a side street, and Stone was always surprised at this discreet approach to a very valuable item that was traded here. It was unpretentious – for security reasons, wealth was not displayed – it was there, but it was hidden. This was a place Stone felt in tune with.

Behind his brightly lit shop façade, Sol had an office. As Stone came in, Sol looked at his friend with a questioning eye. They shook hands warmly as Sol gave Stone a pat on the back as part of his welcome.

'Feels like yesterday, but it's ten years since we've done business together. So, what are you up to now, Harry?'

'Can't tell you too much, but I'm pushing some cash around which has left me holding a few diamonds. I've got to find their value quickly, and then I maybe want to sell 'em. You might even be interested to buy, so you're the man I need to see this afternoon,' Stone replied.

Stone took from his pocket the small pouch, and a large, round diamond fell onto the table. Sol picked it up and held it to the light. It glinted, and he held it in the palm of his hand as if he was weighing it. For a moment, there was silence. With his jewellers' loupe eyepiece, he studied the diamond closely.

'It's got a laser inscription with its provenance – I like that.' Sol held the glinting diamond in front of Stone and showed him the place where there was a tiny mark on the diamond's girdle. 'So, you have the certificate to go with this piece, I presume, Harry? One from the certification laboratories?'

'Yeah, I can get it, but it might take a few days.'

'That's good because it is a very nice diamond. It feels at least five carats, maybe more, and looks beautifully cut and polished. And the colours shine from it in its brilliance.'

'Just need to find out a value. It's not mine yet, but just give me a ballpark price.'

'I'd like Jake, my cutter and polisher, to have a look first. Another round-cut diamond just like that with similar carat weight sold the other day, and I know it fetched good money. Tens of thousands. Does that sound good?' Sol asked and grinned.

'Yeah, sounds okay, but it's got to be many tens of thousands.'

'Leave it with me, Harry. Yes, it's valuable, but it's safe here rather than loose in your pocket. I hope you're being careful carrying it around.'

'And this small uncut diamond. Any value?' Stone asked, holding the raw stone to Sol.

'That's different; it's small – I'll have to look harder at it but don't expect much. Couple of thousand maybe if it is well cut to shape without losing its weight and size. Do you want to tell me where you got these pieces?' Sol asked.

'Some people in Nevis, little island in the Caribbean. Pay-off for some cash I'm parking there.'

Sol looked away. He knew exactly what his friend was talking about.

'So, are you having it mounted into a piece of jewellery for some lucky lady?'

Stone laughed. He had already decided who should have the raw, uncut diamond that he had in his pocket, but he was not going to tell Sol about that.

'Sol, we'll strike a value first, then the big-carat one is yours. You keep it safe or sell it whenever you want. You take a small cut and give me the difference,' Stone said.

There was silence as Sol again peered at the diamond through his loupe. This was a very special prize and he liked to handle it.

'What do you want? A cheque, somewhere payable in dollars perhaps?'

'I'll get you five bank accounts, split it up over each of them. But I'll need some notes. Can you do me five grand to take with me today? And I will come to get a bigger bundle of notes when we've fixed on value. I'll enjoy doing business with you, Sol, just like old times.'

Sol disappeared into another room and came back a couple of minutes later and handed Stone a large envelope.

'£20 notes. Cash talks when you want something. But I hope you've got good insurance because diamonds like this one are too valuable to leave in your pocket. Even our tight security here with alarms all over the place gets broken into. If I didn't know you as well as I do, Harry, we'd have to keep all the outside doors locked while we talk.'

They both laughed and Sol shook Stone's hand, happy to have the business with such a large diamond. Stone walked towards the door and turned to face Sol.

'Sol, I've not been too well lately, so I'll come around soon to have a cup of tea and collect some more cash. I need to do this business quickly and you haven't seen it all yet. I've got two more rocks, bigger and heavier, which are coming from Nevis. It might take a week or two, but I'll bring them round to show you,' Stone said.

'My friend, I've known you on and off for forty years. Of course, I'm happy to work with you. I still remember how you found someone to lend me money to buy a very big-carat diamond that I needed to be cut into smaller stones. No questions asked. That deal was good – I'll try to repay you. Come and see me again as soon as you can.'

As he left Sol's dingy office ten minutes later, Stone felt more excited. His money from Panama was flowing. With cash in his pocket, enough to pay off Xavier's thugs if he needed to, Stone had an optimistic sense of security as he took a taxi back to Claridge's. In his suite he poured a large whisky, his first of the day.

With cushions at his back, he made himself comfortable on the soft sofa. From earlier that day, he was finished with doctors talking to him about an incurable disease, and he savoured the smooth malt whisky he had in his hand. He was even now closing the wide-open gap to get the £2.5 million he needed for Marine House.

Gradually, Stone became excited that he could now close in on Marine House. Anyone asking for a meeting wanted something, and in the Reform Club tomorrow, Stone would twist the arm of Josh, tie him in, keep the titled family interested in dealing with him.

Stone started to pace the carpet of his suite. Diamonds would help, but they would not finally close the gap of £500,000. His last money-making plans were just a few months ago when he had been looking at converting a large warehouse into flats. But not being able to get the planners to agree to his scheme, he had let it run away. It now left him grasping for ideas and it was then that the words Electric Motors Inc would not go away. He opened his laptop, quickly saw their shares had recovered from dropping just a couple of days ago. For a few seconds, he was tempted still to believe that the whisper from Xavier could be right.

Easy money was dazzling Stone just as it always had done, but something held him back. He ran his hand through his hair.

22

It was only a short distance from Claridge's, but Stone took a taxi to Pall Mall. This was an area with buildings that were solid in their grandeur, and they left Stone feeling intimidated by the place. They smelled of authority, and the reality was that he never trusted what went on inside them. As his taxi pulled up to the porticoed entrance to the Reform Club, Roger was waiting. He walked over to him and, for a moment, forgot the pain that was now incessantly biting at him.

'Before we go in this expansive place, what've you found on those toffs who own Marine House?'

'You may be pleased to hear that there is no Sir Edwin Jackson around anymore. Rumours are that he is a bit foul-mouthed, and eight years ago, he became divorced from Lady Ruth. He was playing around, and she didn't take kindly to it. She got Marine House and then only a small share of his sizeable bank balance and rent-free living in a nice house in Mayfair still owned by her ex-husband. But there was a lot of gossip that even then he had managed to hide a lump away. It made the headlines and I think you're maybe coming in on act two.'

'Is that all you've got? Tittle-tattle?'

'What did you expect? But there's more. There's a son, Josh, the boy we're going to meet, and a daughter, Edith. I found a county court judgement in June last year against her ladyship for £575 in favour of a wine merchant near Cambridge. Son Josh lives at the same address as his mother and, it would seem, likes his drink. And there's a dark family secret.'

Stone had started to walk to the Reform Club entrance, but he turned to listen.

'Just a year ago, Josh was accused of sexual assault of a woman in Hyde Park. Late at night. It never came to trial; the family kept it quiet and damages to the woman were settled out of court. How much was paid to keep Josh free from prison wasn't disclosed, but it's believed to have been substantial.'

'Well, well, well, that could be really useful sometime,' Stone said.

'Between them they're short of ready cash. That's not something a family like that will admit to, but none of them seem to work and that, maybe, is the reason they're trying to sell your large pad, Marine House. But have you got £2.5 million sitting around ready to pay over in the next few weeks?' Roger asked.

'Don't you remember you sent me to Nevis? I'm clearing the Panama deposit. So I'm all ready to go. Sign up tomorrow if I can.'

Stone just grinned. He was not ready to go; he was still £500,000 short, but this was not the time to tell Roger that.

It was just ten minutes later, in the grand building of the Reform Club, that Harry Stone was sitting opposite Josh Jackson, a man half his age. But the high-backed leather chair Stone was sitting in was uncomfortable. With his back pain tormenting him, despite all the medication he had taken that morning, he would not be able to sit there long. This meeting was going to be short.

'It's good to meet you again, Josh. Is this your bolthole, the place where you usually deal with the family business?' Stone asked.

'Only come when I need to meet some important people,' Josh said and grinned widely.

'I like that. Good you think we're key to your plans,' Stone replied with a mocking grin.

Josh hesitated for a moment; he looked unsure as he stared at Stone and Roger sitting opposite.

'I want to talk away from the ears of Mother's office space. And here it's comfortable, with nobody snooping on you. And I trust we can keep this meeting just between ourselves,' Josh replied.

'Let's not waste our time then. Tell me, did I hear right when we met that your mother wants to keep me off the list of potential buyers? Her shopping list for Marine House?'

'Mother's very fickle. Sometime last year you got behind in paying the rent on your lease and she was afraid you would default and have to be evicted. That takes time; it costs money; and she needs the rental income. And there were—'

'Josh, stop. I don't want to hear that gossip anymore if that's what you're about to spout,' Stone interrupted quickly.

Josh looked around the room. Raised voices was not the way business was conducted in this panelled place. He almost cringed into his chair.

'I will tell you as it is, Mr Stone. Can I call you Harry?'

'I don't go in for names and fancy titles, so why not?' Stone replied.

'Mother doesn't think you have the funds to buy the property. She doesn't know where your money's come from, and maybe it's, as she calls it, from dubious sources.'

'That's nonsense,' Stone said and stared at Josh.

'Harry, please, steady a moment – I want to talk about it.'

'I held up paying the rent until they arranged to secure all the locks and bolts around the property. The place wasn't safe, and I'd been assaulted right inside my own bedroom by some vicious snarling dogs.'

There was a pause and Josh looked at Stone with an anxious frown on his forehead. And Roger looked away, as if wary of what Stone would say today.

'You got more to tell me?' Stone asked.

'I can help this deal along for you. Mother owns Marine House, but my sister Edith and myself are left equal shares when Mother dies.'

Josh fiddled with his fingers as he had when Stone met with Lady Ruth. Stone could see that Josh was uncomfortable, and he looked at Roger.

'I advise Harry,' Roger said. 'So first, forget the cheap newspaper reports of a few months back. Harry's not involved in their gossip, never was; the money launderers are in jail where they belong, and we'll get bank references when you need them.'

Stone let the silence run for several seconds. Josh was now perspiring on his forehead. It was obvious to Stone that doing deals behind closed doors, admitting his family problems, was not Josh's scene.

'My sister's the only person who could persuade Mother to sell you the house,' Josh blurted and stared at Stone.

'Let's get straight to it then. Why isn't she here with you?'

'She's too busy today; she has a lot of friends she sees.'

'Too busy to do a deal? Let's get down to it, what are you really after?' Stone asked.

'Something upfront.'

Stone fumbled in his pocket. He brought out one of the small diamonds from Nevis and he leant across and put it on the table in front of Josh. Roger made a grimace – although he had seen Harry Stone do some unusual things, this was something quite new.

'That's worth something; diamonds always are. It's for your sister if she's the one who dictates what happens. Anyway, girls like diamonds – they make them feel good.' Stone's tone was flippant.

Josh leant over and picked the stone from the table. He held it in the palm of his hand and studied it closely. He put the stone back on the table and his face became expressionless.

'Are you prepared to up your offer? Say another fifty grand?' he asked.

'I don't know. You tell me what a small diamond can do first. I want some positive noises of what's going to seal the deal. And I want it done quick, no playing around. Okay?' Stone said.

Stone was still feeling pain as he sat upright in his leather chair. He was not sure of Josh, and every time he looked him in the eyes, Josh turned away. He was wearing a blazer that was crumpled in the sleeves and with a pen clipped into the top pocket. His shirt and tie were nondescript, and he looked as down at heel as perhaps the family was. Stone fidgeted; he was feeling very uncomfortable. He wanted this meeting to finish.

'How much is this stone worth?' Josh asked.

'Don't know. Get it valued and tell me as a surprise. But you listen, Josh, diamonds are all private. You sell it on, pawn it, put it in a bit of jewellery or keep it until its value goes up, which it will. Let's leave it that it's a small deposit on Marine House. Speak to your sister and let me know she wants to talk. But don't leave it too long.'

'The diamond looks good. But, Harry, straight up, I need some money.'

'What're you talking about? Don't push me too far.' Stone's voice was getting loud again.

'Please get me some hard cash. I need some money upfront to clinch the deal. Can you get me £100,000?'

'Part of the price in cash. Is that it?'

'Yeah, that's what'll push this along for you.'

'And your sister's in on this is she?' Stone asked.

'No, but I will tell her. As soon as I get back.'

'I need to be sure this will work. I give you seven days. You call me back that the deal is certain, then I find some cash for you. Okay?'

'Okay, Harry. I won't let you down. But, before we go, there's something else. I'm going to ask you a favour.'

'There's nothing more on Marine House. I've gone far enough,' Stone said.

'No, this is personal.'

'Tell me more, Josh?'

'If you ever need help in your business affairs, I'm always looking for something to do, so can you remember me and give me a call? I'll run around for you. I have time to spend on it; I have wide connections—'

Stone interrupted Josh. He stood as he wanted to finish the meeting.

'We'll meet again, soon. Talk to your sister; remind her where Marine House is, and she can then come and see me any time. And while you're at it, give your mother my regards,' Stone said with a sneer of sarcasm.

Stone left the small diamond on the table. As they got up to leave, Josh picked it up and, by the small grin on his face, was satisfied. £100,000 in cash – if he scraped around, Stone could find it. Josh was the family's dark secret, and as they left the elegant surroundings of the Reform Club, whatever Josh did with that diamond, Stone saw it as putting his foot inside the front door of Marine House.

23

'Funny little island, Nevis. How do you know it's alright?' Stone asked as they walked onto the pavement outside the Reform Club.

'Personal contacts, Harry. That's what you need in this business.'

'I'm trading diamonds from there, stones of big value.'

'I can see that. I can see they're easy to give away too.'

Roger took Stone by the arm and turned to face him.

'How did you know he was asking for a pay-off?' Roger asked.

'It's simple. He wanted to meet away from his mother, out of her shadow. You told me the family is short of cash, and you can't get signals clearer than that.'

'Don't you think that's a dangerous way of dealing with Marine House? He'll go straight back to his mother and crow about another fifty grand added to the price. He'll show up at home as a good boy. And you've never met his sister. How do you know how she feels with a small diamond in her hand? And how do you know Josh will really pass the diamond on to her? I bet he'll sell it and take the money. And asking for a hundred grand in cash upfront is a bit outrageous. Just as him asking for some work, I don't know, but he looks a layabout to me.'

'You still don't know how human nature works, Roger. All I've done is give a guy a diamond. They have a fascination; they're exotic, mysterious bits of rock, and people like Josh will feel grown up at doing such a deal. And that's just as he tried to feel with the sexual assault in Hyde Park,' Stone said.

'Okay, but before we go, Harry, Electric Motors Inc. Shares going up and down like a toy yo-yo. A bit of a dud that one. But your stockbroker account is all waiting for you to pour your money into it.' There was a gibe in Roger's voice.

Maybe insider information emerging from a shadow in prison was a false trail. Just to catch him out. He turned away; he heard Roger laugh, and he felt the taunt. Electric Motors Inc was now left dangling in front of him just as if it was bait hanging at the end of a fishing rod on Brighton pier.

And there was Josh, the son of a titled lady. He too had come close to serving time in HMP Belmarsh right alongside Xavier and his cronies. Stone's time was getting short. He would not forget that.

24

'When I walk around your garden, it always looks so alive with all the colourful flowers, particularly that large red rhododendron bush,' Claire said.

'Ken the gardener does all the hard work; I just add the finishing touches, but this year it has all been good. Lots of sun and lots of rain,' Jennie replied.

'Someday soon, if I again live in Arrow Hall, I'll have all the wide spaces around the house landscaped just as they used to be. There was not much room for flowers, but the dried-out moat is still there, and I have plans to keep it green, make it look like a well-kept lawn.'

'How's it going with Rick?'

Claire sighed and looked to the ground.

'I have growing uncertainty where Rick wants to go with Arrow Hall. He's disappeared to New Zealand, and I can see a rocky time ahead not only with unrest on the site. A few bust-ups coming along which won't help build the place.'

'Don't let your dream stop. It's an important historical site, too good to leave in ruins,' Jennie said.

Claire had just spent a couple of hours with Jennie at her large house in Newbury. Walking round the large, lush gardens left Claire wishing she could stay longer. The mud and dirt, and shouting, on the building site was not an attractive place to return to. By the time Claire said goodbye to Jennie, she felt the stark contrast of the two places.

Driving back to Rick's flat, her journey slow with bunched traffic as she entered the outskirts of London, was not the easiest of times to take an unexpected call from Rick in New Zealand.

'I'm in a hurry. Just about to catch a flight to South Island. I'm meeting an agent. But give me a quick update on the money you're spending at Arrow Hall.'

'Rick. I'm stuck in traffic; it's just not moving. The road report is saying a bomb scare at Marble Arch. And you sound very far away. Can I call you back in half an hour?'

'No. Five minutes and I'm on the flight.'

'James is making mistakes on what he tells me of the money he's spending. All you need to know today is we'll easily go over top of the budget and plus a bit.'

'What's wrong with James?'

'You said he was aggressive and that's an understatement. He is stirring up trouble, and if he doesn't stop bawling at everybody on the site, somebody's going to land a fist on his face and then bury him in the mud that's surrounding the place.'

'Have you taken him off-site for a drink yet? Sit him down; tell him what you think.'

'Yes, we'll have a drink when I'm ready. And that'll be after I've had some serious words with him.'

There was a pause as Claire was now stuck behind a large, intimidating lorry with all the other lanes moving except hers.

'You are going to be back in time for Wimbledon? Just a week away, I'm looking forward to it.'

'I'll let you know in a couple of days. But if I can't get back, you take one of your friends with you for a strawberry and cream tea.'

'Rick, that sounds flippant, and I don't think you're taking me seriously.'

'I'm just telling you how it is, so go and enjoy Wimbledon and then tell me how it was.'

'Your thoughts are always somewhere else, and you've lost interest in Arrow Hall.'

'It's your project – I thought you were really up for it. And that's why I left you to do it.'

'Yes, but it's your money. Your man James is running out of control, and I don't think you want to live in a country house anymore, do you?'

'I've got a lot on at the moment; I'm taking one step at a time. But you're getting ahead of yourself.'

Rick's voice went silent for a few seconds. This was no place to be having a serious call from Rick; she was about to tell him that when he spoke again.

'Ah, sorry, got to end now, we're boarding. But keep your grip on the cash and get an update for me on how the money's running. Send me an email with some figures, can't you?'

Inching forward in the traffic very slowly, Claire flicked her phone off. Her hand gripped the steering wheel; Rick's dismissive call had increased her tenseness. And she could hear the noises rumbling around Arrow Hall – they were getting louder, like a jungle drum shouting out there was something underhand, hidden.

Tomorrow, Claire would see that James could squirm away from the mud no more.

25

'You've got a frown on your face,' James said.

He walked noisily into the cramped container that was the office on the site. He was holding a drawing which he placed heavily on the small, dusty desk.

'All I hear is you shouting your head off at some of the people working on the building,' Claire said.

'It's what happens in places like this. Nothing wrong with that.'

'I hope you've calmed down from the last time I was here because I need to talk to you about money. First, there's £15,000 in cash you've had. You avoided it last time I asked, so where's it gone?'

'I've still got most of it, but I'll scribble something out for you. End of week.'

'No, James. This is not going away – it's urgent.'

James pretended not to hear and started to study the drawing he had just placed on the table.

'I want to know what's going on because there's another invoice you've signed off, just like last time, a duplicate of one that's already been paid. But this one is over £10,000 and for Alison's the plasterers. So, I'm going to check back on everything that's gone out from the account.'

'Show me what you're talking about,' James said, not looking back at Claire.

James scanned quickly the plasterer's accounts, but within a few seconds, he put them back on the desk.

'I've told you later this week. And if a mistake has been made, we'll put it right.'

'No. You haven't done it, so I'm going to call Davies the plumber. Remember £7,500 paid twice?'

Claire's voice was rising, and she stared directly at James for a response. She felt his arrogance and, not for the first time in the past couple of weeks, it was grating on her. This was going too far.

'Give me space; leave it to me. I know how to talk to these people, you don't.'

'There are big mistakes with big money. I'll check the bank account tomorrow to see if it's back there, so get on with it.'

'Remember this place is quite unique. One off. It's always going to have problems as it grows. And that takes money.'

'I don't think you understand what I'm telling you, James. No more flashing your pen across accounts to pay unless you've checked them. And if I keep finding—'

James interrupted Claire again with his dismissive tone.

'The gossip around the site is that a man called Harry Stone owned the old house before it was burnt down. He's a bit of a cowboy. Is that right?'

Just the name of Harry Stone momentarily stopped Claire. She did not want to talk about him; she looked away and she closed her eyes. But the image of Harry Stone in the new building kept on coming back to her. Claire started to close her laptop.

'Before you go, I want another £2,000 in cash. There are some labourers coming to clean up the site tomorrow and they will need cash they can hold and feel,' James said.

'Don't keep asking for money. You're not getting it.'

'If you keep carping on about the petty cash, it'll never get this place built. So please bring some more ready money for me.'

'No,' Claire said bluntly.

A minute later, as Claire was folding her papers, James looked at his watch.

'I've got tickets for the theatre. *The Price* at Wyndham's, revival of a classic play. Next Saturday evening. And what about dinner afterwards?' James asked.

Claire turned, hesitated, James's invite was a surprise. At that time not a welcome one.

'I'll check what I've got on. I'll let you know,' Claire replied but avoided looking at James's face.

The skeleton of Arrow Hall was even more gaunt as Claire left the site. At that moment she felt low and alone. It didn't help that she was going to view a flat in Knightsbridge and maybe take a lease on it. The distance from Rick was becoming wider, and moving to her own new flat was her first step to make a clean break. From here, she was not going back.

But what was James after with his invite to theatre and dinner? Later that evening, with the image still in her head of a dingy, small apartment she had just been to view, Claire could not resist, and she texted James.

If Arrow Hall was ever going to get finished, she had to find out if there was anything but bluster behind James's arrogant façade.

26

It was barely light when Stone woke in the bedroom of his suite at Claridge's. After showering, he dressed, took painkillers and very soon felt fresh to start the day. Room service brought him coffee which was laid out with a white tablecloth.

Stone took the two newspapers hanging in a large suede bag outside his suite door. The business section of a daily paper fell out as he walked to the window. Flicking it open, he looked down a column of share prices as he had done each day for the last week. As he scanned the page, his eye did not miss a headline headed "Electric Motors Inc".

He could feel his heartbeat quicken as he saw that the share price of Electric Motors Inc had moved up to almost double. Xavier had given out priceless information. And the phone call from Xavier in HMP Belmarsh was not a hoax. That extortionist behind bars was not working a scam to prise money out of him. Everybody was now buying electric cars, so there was big demand for electric motors; he should have known that. But he did have a wide grin as he threw the newspaper onto the floor and laid back in a deep armchair.

But Stone swore. What had he missed? Frustration tugged at him – of course he should have looked deeper into the business of Electric Motors Inc. Making enough in one deal to sign off all the money he needed for Marine House, that's what he had missed. It was not only the money that would roll out at the other end, but it was also being part of the deal, the waiting, the expectation. There would be another time and then he would be at the casino for the next roll of the dice.

That, for the moment, turned Stone's grin into a laugh, and he began to feel good. But money was not the only obstacle in the road to buying Marine House. Riled still by the brush-off from Lady Ruth that he did not have the money to buy her big house on Brighton seafront, Stone went to his bedroom. There was a small safe on the floor. Stone opened it and withdrew bundles of £20 and £50 notes. They totalled over £100,000 – Stone could feel it in his hands. And that was just what Josh, in his sly way, had asked for upfront for Marine House. With a sexual assault case against him, paid off and hushed up, it left a tempting thought which he would play out. Maybe the world should know exactly what Josh had done.

His life suddenly had a more positive feel to it. Three times that morning he reread the article on Electric Motors Inc. It left him, for the first time in some days, feeling hungry, and he had some sandwiches brought to his suite. He poured a large whisky from the decanter on the sideboard.

Pacing his suite, again his pain no longer stabbed into his right hip, and he began to hope that Xavier would call again. Ever since he had known this criminal, he had never before wanted that to happen. Another secret leaked from the prison would close off the gap in the money he needed for Marine House. But just pressing his computer buttons to make money was too easy. He did not trust this criminal in HMP Belmarsh, and it left a nagging thought. He was being enticed into something bigger to snare him.

27

Claire and James left the theatre at just past 10.00. It was a warm summer's evening; London was buzzing with people and traffic; and the neon lights around Piccadilly lit the sky in flashing colours.

'It's some time since I've enjoyed the theatre and a play so much. So thank you, James, for the invite. Television really doesn't measure up to seeing a drama on the stage right in front of you.'

'There's more to come. I've reserved a table for dinner at a small place in Covent Garden. If we can find our way through these crowds, we can walk there. It's not far. Are you up for it?'

'Why not?' Claire said and laughed.

This evening, James was different to how she had seen him on the site. Not only was he dressed casually but smart, in a clean white shirt, a contrast to the stained T-shirt he wore on the site, but a deep frown had relaxed from his face. His condescension from the site had died; perhaps he really was a cultured and refined person.

'Tell me about yourself,' Claire said across the dinner table.

'Not much to say. Only family is an older sister in Australia, but I haven't seen her for ten years. Otherwise, I'm on my own. And work is my life.'

'You must have some hobbies, downtime from the site.'

'I can handle the workplace,' was James's terse reply.

'I'm sure you can, but sometimes you look as if you're on your own against everybody else.'

'I'm firm with 'em all.'

'You're a different person across this table to the one I see at Arrow Hall.'

'Which one do you like best?'

'You guess.'

'Why don't you tell me about Rick. I've often wondered, where did he make his money?' James asked.

'He turns around failing businesses and sells them on.'

'So, is Arrow Hall a failing business? Is Rick going to turn it round?' James laughed.

'No, it's never that.'

'Where is Rick?'

'Away on business, back in a couple of weeks. Why do you ask?'

'He called me to take on this challenge, so I might want to talk to him. That's all.'

'We're not here to talk about Arrow Hall. Don't even think about it tonight. And it's getting late.'

There was silence for a few seconds before James finished his food. He then ordered a large brandy, and as he held the glass in his hand, he leant back in his chair.

'Would you like to finish the evening on the dance floor? There's a small nightclub just a few roads from here run by a friend. Someone I was at uni with.'

Claire looked at her watch as if she needed to get away. It was 11.30 and James was enjoying another brandy. Her new apartment was small and cold; Rick's apartment would be cold and empty too.

Claire was not going to let this evening roll too far, but they spent two hours in a packed nightclub, dancing on the disco floor and drinking another bottle of expensive Barolo wine. The place was hot and noisy; it was some time since Claire had felt the buzz of being in a nightclub. James finished another whisky; it was far too noisy to talk; and for an hour or two, Claire forgot Arrow Hall.

The air was cool, refreshing, as they walked out onto the street well past midnight.

'It's getting late. I'm staying at the Savoy. Come and join me to finish the night off.'

'I don't think that would be a good idea tonight, so not this time,' Claire replied. 'Let's just leave it that it's been a fun evening and I thank you for it. We need to split the bill – how much do I owe you?'

'Don't you think I make enough money? No. We'll toss for it when we do it again. Sometime soon.'

James spoke loudly as if he was affronted by Claire's question.

James's speech was becoming slurred. On the pavement, he tried to hold her, and Claire pushed him away. It was getting long past the time to finish the evening.

'I want to tell you something.' James paused as if he was searching for his words. 'Lay off on the site; don't muck around with the money or you'll be finding trouble. You understand what I'm saying?'

James leant into her. His face had a menacing scowl that she had not seen in him before, and his eyes pierced straight at her.

'James, please, this is no time for talk like that. And I don't know what you mean.'

'You heard me. So, are you sure you won't join me at the Savoy?'

She held out her arm to stop a passing taxi to take her to Rick's apartment. James held the door open for her; she could detect coldness as he slammed it shut without looking at her. She doubted James would remember anything but a blur of dancing on the disco floor in the clear light of the next day.

In the taxi, James's threatening words lingered. Money was missing from the site, slipping away into other people's pockets. And that was a menace that Claire had not yet rooted out.

28

To make a distance from James, Claire did not visit Arrow Hall for three days. Work was proceeding but slowly and being uncertain of her ongoing commitment to the place she found made the drive to London more tedious than usual. Inside Rick's apartment, she felt hot and uncomfortable.

Flooding the place with light she hoped would make the emptiness of the large, minimalist rooms easier. In the bathroom she dabbed her face with cool water; she ordered a crab salad to be delivered from the fish restaurant two roads away; and for the next half an hour she sat in the spacious lounge sipping a glass of wine.

On her own in Rick's penthouse, Claire knew this was not the place she wanted to be anymore. Rick was becoming even more distant. But moving on, her lifestyle would change to a small flat; finding paid employment would alter how she spent every day. Claire was going to get this moving – she had to talk to Rick. Later that evening, she called him.

'Claire, you sound very faint. Can you hear me?' Rick asked. The line was indistinct and had an echo on it.

'Yes, just. But no better than the last time we spoke. Where are you?'

'In the middle of North Island, a place called Rotorua. It's very warm and early in the morning. But I've got a full day ahead. I'm seeing a top winery and a hundred-acre vineyard.'

'You haven't called me, so I've decided to call you. This is the first time in eight days that we've talked together so you must listen as there are a lot of things I need to tell you about Arrow Hall. It's not easy over the phone, so do you have a time when you'll be coming back?' Claire asked.

'No. I've got to see this business through. I'm looking for someone to run the place if I buy it, and that's going to take time. So don't expect me for a while longer yet.'

'I've got a lot to say, but you've got to know first that James and Arrow Hall are not working. We're soon to run out of money.'

'I had hoped you would have sorted that. Just tell me quickly. My driver is already waiting.'

'James is up to something. It's getting serious. Money is draining away fast. And we're going to run over the budget by a lot before it's all finished,' Claire said.

'How much?' Rick's question was sharp.

'Don't know yet but completion date will get pushed back at least three months. It's not even half built and we're already spending nearly up to the top figure. That's where we are.'

'What's going on? What's causing this overspend?'

'It's James making mistakes, like signing off the same bill twice for payment. And something more sinister. There's a strange piece of paper I've found. Cleared for payment by James but it looks just as if it was written up in some scam. And the £15,000 cash James had at the start has disappeared into thin air. He's slinking away; he won't tell me where it's gone. And now he wants another £2,000 to clear the place up.'

'Don't let him have it, Claire. You control the money; you surely know how to do that.'

'That's just what I am doing. But James is flitting around, still arguing with everyone – he's evasive; he's slippery.'

'Sounds like you've lost control of the rebuild. If it goes on like this, I'll call a property agent on site to see what it's all going to be worth when it's finished,' Rick said.

'If you're that worried, I suggest you stop work now. I'll sack James; I'll pull everybody off-site; and you relook at the rebuild without me.'

'No. I want you there. I'm not ready for that. I want the place finished and quickly.'

'I'm tracking and checking everything. James's mouth closes when I talk money; he's hiding from it like a frightened rabbit down its hole. His attitude and arrogance make him dangerous to have around.'

'Push James for a new top spend and completion date. The money's not there for a cost overrun. It can't cost far more to finish than it's worth. Get that for me, then I'll decide what to do with the place.'

'What about your promise that Arrow Hall was to be our country home, a house to have weekends out of London, with parties, dinners, barbecues? We've never talked about it being a property to quickly sell on. What's changed?' Claire asked.

'You sound harassed, Claire. What's the matter? Tell me, but be quick,' Rick said.

Claire hesitated. It was getting late. Her eyes were feeling tired, and Rick was not taking the time to listen.

'I'm feeling uncomfortable on the site. The place is being watched; there's shouting over debts not paid; and James is walking straight into fights that will end nastily,' Claire replied.

'You're painting James in a black colour – are you sure you're right?'

'I don't know what you see in James that I don't, so I took your advice and spent time out with him. We went to the theatre and had dinner last week. That was okay but then on the site it all changes. I need your support, Rick, to see this through.'

'I left you to deal with it all, so try to get it worked out with James, and have something better to tell me by the next time we talk,' Rick said.

'You're still too busy to listen. And please understand I am no longer interested in rebuilding Arrow Hall unless I can live there. So you make time to call me so we can talk properly, and soon,' Claire said.

The line was becoming very faint and making conversation difficult. Claire closed the call abruptly. It left the lingering dream of resurrecting the place, and even living there sometime, draining from her.

Claire shivered, suddenly feeling cold – she nibbled at the crab salad that had been delivered. Her decision had been taken. Money was being syphoned off – she was going to search for exactly where it was going, and then she would clear James from the site.

Claire expected Rick to call back, but it was silent.

29

Claire knew exactly what she going to do today, and on the drive down to the Essex countryside, she was cautious. For a brief moment it was as if the old house was still standing as she approached down the narrow lane with trees that made an arch over the road. But that enticing thought was abruptly blotted out as she drove through the large industrial gates. It was busy; the gardens had been turned into parking for builders' white vans; and there were only patches of green grass to see beyond the ruts of mud. This jarred with Claire.

But that was not all that was nettling her on this bright summer's day.

The office space was dirty and dusty, and it had not been cleaned since the day it had been put on the site. In the corner of the cabin, on a small table, was the usual folder marked by James with another pile of bills to pay. She flicked through them quickly. Had James inspected the work before he signed these off with a sandwich in his hand and a squiggle as his signature? Claire was very doubtful, but it was time to ask her own questions.

Through the grimy window of the cabin, Claire saw a carpenter who had stopped for a break. She knew who he was, and she quickly searched in her bag for a sheet of paper that James had passed to her for payment. The carpenter was sitting on a pile of blocks, sipping a mug of tea as Claire walked over to him.

'Can I talk to you just for a few minutes?'

'Sure. How's it all going, Mrs Watts?' he asked.

'Leave the formality, and I'm not Mrs, so just call me Claire, okay? And you're Darren, aren't you?'

'Yes, this is going to be a posh house when it's all finished. Are you going to live here?'

'Maybe, some of the time.'

'There's talk around the place you must be very rich to put all this together. I mean, this place looks as if it will be something quite special when it's all finished.'

'There's a long way to go yet. Tell me, what do you make of this invoice that I am just about to settle?' Claire handed a sheet of paper to Darren.

Darren paused and looked around as if he should not be seen handling papers. He quickly scanned it, and after several long seconds, he put his mug of tea on the pile of blocks and handed the sheet back to Claire.

'I'm no good at that paperwork. Holly, my wife, looks after all that for me.'

'It's got your business name at the top. Is it about your work here?'

'Look, I can see the numbers on that bit of paper, and they don't add up. So, I don't want to know any more about what you've got there, because it's not mine.'

'Are there any outstanding bills that we haven't settled for you yet?'

'I don't know. You'd better go and see Holly.'

There was suddenly heavy shouting from inside the skeleton of the building. Claire was not sure, but she thought she heard James. It went on for half a minute and then suddenly stopped as quickly as it had started.

'What's that all about?' Claire asked.

'Money, unpaid debt,' Darren replied quickly, and he turned away.

'Why are they shouting about that here?'

'I don't want to know what it's about. But, Claire, you best stay right out of it. And just be careful around this place.'

Darren's reaction was nervous. He finished his tea with a quick gulp and put his mug back heavily on the bricks. Without a word, he walked back into the building.

And Claire, avoiding the mud, walked back to the cabin.

She watched through the dusty window and saw James standing in front of Darren the carpenter, gesticulating wildly with his arms. James stopped, turned and started walking quickly towards the cabin. The forged piece of paper Claire quickly folded and, with her laptop, put it in a bag. This site was becoming creepy; that bit of paper told her a lot. There was little left of the façade of James controlling the work and she was now wary that, when she confronted him, he would get physical, abusive.

30

James came into the cabin as if he had been running and just as Claire was ready to leave.

'I see you were chatting to Darren the chippy. What did he have to say?'

'You were with him – didn't he tell you?'

'We were fixing what he does next. Just keeping this place moving.'

'What's all the shouting going on out there? Something to do with an unpaid debt, Darren says.'

'There's always shouting out there. Forget it,' James said.

'No. I won't forget it. What has this site got to do with unpaid debts?'

'Why do you question it? Just leave it alone. It's nothing to do with you.'

'I don't think you understand – everything on this site is to do with me. And I've found a very odd piece of paper, looks like a forged invoice signed off by you for payment. So you have some explaining to do when I've examined it all more closely.'

'I still don't think you have any idea how building sites like this work. So, let's move on. I've got a lot to do.'

'Yes, you have. And I thought you already knew, but I'll repeat it – this site, as far as money is concerned, works exactly the way I want it to. Not you.'

'I haven't got this under control. Is that what you're saying?' James asked sharply.

'I don't think you have when you clear work for payment. I'm watching it closely.'

'Arrow Hall's a large, complicated job. It's all organised, but if you've got any problems, can we talk about it later? I'm very busy just now.'

James, for a brief moment, looked flustered. He noisily bent over to inspect one of the large drawings on the table. Without looking up, he spoke quickly.

'Have you brought another £2,000 in cash for me?'

'No, I certainly haven't. There's no more cash until I get details of what's happened to the £15,000 you've already had.'

'Claire, don't be troublesome. Can't do that yet, but let's keep this place going with a bit of loose money spread around, oil on the wheels.'

There was a pause as again James fiddled with some papers.

'That was a really good time we had together at the weekend. When can we do it again?' James suddenly asked.

'How much do you remember of it?'

'The play was good; the wine was good. And the disco. What else?'

'You made some demanding comments to me about the building work here. Warning about how I dealt with the money. Don't you remember that?'

'Your memory is better than mine. We agreed before dinner not to talk about Arrow Hall, and I don't remember breaking that rule. But what about dinner tonight?'

'No, James. And you can't dismiss me with a quick change of subject as easily as that. So, where has the £15,000 gone?' Claire demanded.

'Claire, please, give me space. Yeah, I've told you I'll scribble something out for you when I've got time.'

James started to walk from the cabin.

'That's not good enough. So, James, come back. Mysterious accounts which don't make sense? Two more invoices that have been signed off by you twice? It's not small change; it's big money. I want to know how you intend to get the money back. Got that, James?' Claire was raising her voice and James looked away.

'I don't have a clue what you're talking about. Yeah, we'll meet. But what about dinner this evening?' James asked again.

'You're not taking me seriously. Last time, no. Not tonight. And not again until I find out what's going on here.'

Claire was getting hot, angry in the confined space of the small cabin. She started to put on her coat, but she was interrupted by the loud noise as the landline phone on the table rang. It startled her. It had never rung before while she was in this small cabin; it was covered in dust and almost hidden under a pile of disused drawings. For no other reason than to stop the intrusive noise, Claire picked it up.

It was a voice that Claire remembered immediately. She froze. Holding the phone away from her, she looked at it and flicked it off. For a moment, she stood absolutely still, and she was shaking. Claire moved away from the phone as if getting a distance from it would keep it silent and stop it ringing again.

And James said nothing – he left the cabin quickly with his face rigid with lines of tension.

31

The sun was breaking through a misty haze; it was just getting light as James drove his open-topped sports car onto the Arrow Hall site. He parked next to the cabin, and he carried a plastic bag under his arm. His hand was shaking as he went to try the door handle as if somebody should be looking out at him. He looked around – he was satisfied it had not been opened since last night and he was on his own. As he walked back to sit in his car, he stared nervously down the small lane that led to Arrow Hall.

It was another five minutes before a black mini noisily drew up onto the rutted grass. It stopped close to where James was standing. The window was lowered, and James handed the plastic bag to the driver.

'This is the last time. The lady who runs the money is getting onto it.'

'You deal with that, James. Something to frighten her. A little run off the road around one of these country lanes. But this isn't the last time for you, so listen hard. You've gotta get the numbers up. You know how to squeeze a lemon – that's how you squeeze the people helping you out here. So, I'll be down again in two days. Don't forget, James, be on time.'

James had no chance to answer; there was a snarl from the driver of the mini, a look of disdain as he reversed and left as quickly and noisily as he had arrived. The site was still empty, and the sudden quietness left James feeling very nervous. It would usually be a time when he would be motivated to start the day's work, making the building slowly rise. But not today.

Fumbling with the key, James quickly opened the cabin door and sat in a dusty chair. He stared at the plans laid out on the table but did not see them. His hands were shaking, and his mouth was dry.

32

Before accusing James of outright fraud, Claire was going to search in all the dark corners of this deceitful web. Unsure of what she would find, today Claire took a twenty-minute drive from Arrow Hall to a village she knew well.

Turning from the dual carriageway into the narrow country road to the village, Claire looked into her rear-view mirror. A white van was driving up close, too close to be safe. Touching her foot on the brake pedal she saw her rear lights reflected clearly in the van's windscreen. Being closely followed was intimidation, why, she did not know, but it added to her anger at what she was uncovering.

She drove slowly past the well-kept cottages that lined the wide village high street; the van overtook her and was soon gone out of sight. Number fifty-eight was a house fronting onto the road; it had a newly painted, bright-red door. Her knock was quickly answered.

'I'm Claire from the Arrow Hall site. Are you Holly, Darren's wife?'

Holly looked startled for a moment; she was not expecting to see a well-dressed lady from Arrow Hall.

'Yes, nothing wrong is there?'

'Could I come in to talk with you for a few minutes? I'd just like to clear up some questions on your accounts which Darren tells me you deal with.'

'Yes, he has told me about you.'

Five minutes later, with a cup of tea in her hand, Claire passed the sheet of paper to Holly that she thought was a forgery.

'I'd like to know what you think of this.'

'Darren told me about it, but it was not something he wanted to get involved in.'

'Can you tell me more?'

'He says there's talk around the site about an easy way to make money. There's talk about the building costing a lot and taking from the pile that's being paid out will never be noticed. Whoever's working it, Darren wouldn't tell me, but he was asked to join in. He said no and was told to keep quiet or else. It's left him nervous; he just wants to finish the job and get out.'

Claire passed Holly the letter from her address asking for bank details to be changed for future payments of the account. Holly read it slowly and laid it on the arm of her chair.

'What is going on here? That invoice is not one I've sent you – it doesn't even add up. That's not our address – we are Appledore not Appleton – this letter is sham. We only have two bank accounts: one for Darren's work and the other for our personal money. I've certainly not changed banks, so who's signature is this at the bottom of the letter? It's not mine, so this is a forgery too. Should we call the police?'

Holly had a deep frown on her forehead as she passed the two sheets of paper back to Claire.

'I need to find out more first before we decide how to deal with this – I'll call you again when it's become clearer,' Claire said.

'We were talking about the Arrow Hall site – Darren remembers the old building but is not sure if the new one can be finished to be as good as it used to look.'

'When it's all done and we've had the gardens landscaped, I'm sure it will be a landmark again and fit into the countryside round about.'

Claire had hopes that that would be true, but doubts were clouding her remote images for the site. And as Claire left Holly, she had another call to make. It was a ten-minute drive to a small town not far from the motorway. An address for heating engineers and plumbers for an account of £18,000 signed off by James that looked suspicious. She had not been able to locate it in the telephone directory, nor was there any website or Facebook page, although the symbols were on the invoice heading.

There was a tidy row of shops, from hairdressers to grocers, and a couple of cafes with tables outside. Claire drove slowly along Bridge Street, but there was nothing looking like heating engineers or plumbers. Claire parked at the end of Bridge Street and, with paper in hand, walked along the right-hand side to find number twenty-two.

And there it was. The office of country town solicitors, May and Fletcher. Claire entered.

'I'm looking for Biggs and Son, plumbers and heating engineers, and I have your office as their address.'

The receptionist smiled at Claire.

'I haven't heard of them but let me check.'

She turned to her screen and, a few seconds later, said, 'They're not on our list. Are you sure you've got the right street number?'

Claire handed the receptionist the invoice to Arrow Hall from Biggs and Son. She scanned it quickly and frowned.

'I'll have a word with one of the partners to check if it's a new client.'

She returned two minutes later.

'No, they're not a client – Mr May's never heard of them in this town and nor have I. And that's an odd address because the postcode does not match this end of the street. It's a mystery. Sorry I can't help you.'

Claire left and walked quickly back to her car. In her hand she now had vital evidence. It would snuff out the acrid smell surrounding these unsavoury ways to extract money from Arrow Hall.

33

In her car, Claire scanned the sham pieces of paper again before placing them on the passenger seat. They were important – they told their own story, and she would get answers. She breathed out heavily and sat still for a moment. With the car radio on to blot her thoughts, Claire drove carefully from the village high street and into the country lane towards the motorway.

The large, white van screeched in front of her. Claire's reaction was quick – she steered away from the van, and her foot hit the brakes. That reflex movement pushed her sideways onto the thin grass verge. The seat belt held Claire, and the papers she had been carrying fluttered from the passenger seat onto the floor. It was only seconds before a hooded face, heavily shrouded in a scarf, opened her car door.

'What's up with your driving to screech right in front of me like that?' Claire shouted.

'Keep your hands off the money. I gotta warning for you to leave it alone.'

'What're you talking about?'

Claire did not wait for his reply, and she pushed the heavy man away from the door. She hit the button to lock the car doors, reversed in one quick movement and drove at speed away from the van. Her eyes flashed to the file of incriminating papers still lying on the floor.

This was intimidation – Claire had seen how that worked with Harry Stone. Today it raised her anger – she was being conned, and she was going to unravel this swindle.

34

The new morning did not help Claire's deepening feeling that her life was changing very fast. The sky was dark; it was raining; the walk from the agent's office took ten minutes. It was early, just 8.00 when she entered the apartment to view in Knightsbridge. This was her second visit and the rooms looked smaller, more enclosed than when she had first inspected them. She would have to add to the sparse pieces of furniture that were already there, and as she peered from the windows, all she saw were the other apartments close by looking back in.

Claire hesitated. Leaving Rick's apartment was a big break, but it was time to move on. The young associate took her back to the agents' office and she held her umbrella close to keep the rain off. Just half an hour later, she had committed herself to a three-year lease and with a bank transfer she paid a deposit of £5,000. She felt this stark reminder that she had lived for free in Rick's penthouse and from today she would have to settle her own rent. She took a taxi back to Rick's classy apartment, but she was uncomfortable and apprehensive.

This move would only be for a short time – Claire was sure of that. Whatever happened to Arrow Hall, Claire still had this wild dream. She would sometime soon live in the same space in the new Arrow Hall that she had become close to when working for Harry Stone. She had walked away when the fire raged, but now that man was out of it – he was long gone.

But reality hit her as she started to pack some of her clothes to take to her new flat. She took a last farewell as she looked into every corner of every room in Rick's elegant apartment. This seventeenth-storey penthouse Claire had never got to think of as her own home and, looking around as if she was snooping, even now, left an uncomfortable feeling. But she held some of the glass ornaments of antique cranberry on a window corner of the sitting room, which reflected a soft, reddish glow as she held them to the light. She liked them very much. And every window she went to had a view, from the sweep of the Thames to the tall buildings that almost reached the clouds in Canary Wharf. It was captivating; she would miss it.

White vans tailgating her had left her nervous, but today Claire drove quickly to Arrow Hall. The first words she heard made her stop as she drove onto the muddy field surrounding the half-finished building.

'Before I finish with this place, you'd better pay me and my boys what we're owed. I can see through what you're up to with your fancy money tricks, but don't come near me with them trying it on. So, Jimmy, I've had enough listening to your flaming arrogance and your poncing around in that shiny red motor car.'

Claire watched, stunned as the builder walked up to James's car and dragged a large knife alongside the driver's door. The sharp grating noise echoed back into the momentary silence of the site. The red-faced builder, full of anger, got into his van, slammed the door shut and churned up mud as he quickly left.

As she walked into the cabin, Claire again felt the undercurrent that was running through this place. There was a drawing spread across the table; Claire folded it and opened a file of accounts signed off by James and still to be paid. She started to thumb through them, but she was interrupted as James came in.

He never looked smart, or even clean, on the site – today he had on the same stained shirt with sleeves tightly rolled up that he had been wearing for longer than the past week. He stood looking over her shoulder at the papers as if he had not seen them before. He leant closer to her, and as Claire turned round to look at him, he put his hand on her arm.

'Whatever's happened to you?'

She pushed him away and peered more closely at his right eye.

'You won't believe this. I fell off a chair in my new flat as I was putting a bulb in the spotlight. It was in the kitchen, a bit difficult to get to.'

James's naivete showed with a glazed look in his eyes as he was talking.

'Don't give me that story – you're right; I don't believe it. So, what's going on here?'

'Just a little discipline around the place. It won't do any harm. I know him – it's bluster, and he'll be back.'

'How much do we owe him? What's he arguing about? Is there a dispute? And a large knife scratched into your car?'

'I said don't listen to him – I'll deal with it.'

'You've been thrown to the floor and now knives. This place is becoming unsafe. And just yesterday I was run off the road by a large white van. What do you know about that?'

'Nothing. What do you expect me to know about your lousy driving?'

'You know more than you're telling me. But I'm going to find it all. And loud arguments round this site doesn't help.'

'Okay. You're right – you've told me that before as if I'm a kid.' James's raised voice echoed in the small cabin space.

'James, I'm not taking any more of this. Sit down now. I'm going through every payment we've made, every piece of paper, and I want to know exactly what work they've done for it. £15,000 has gone into thin air, and the money's not yet back in the bank for the two bills you signed off twice. Davies the plumber and Alison's the plasterers. I'm going to lock the cabin door – turn your phone off so no interruptions.'

Claire moved towards the door, but James stood in front of her.

'I can't stop now. I've got a visit in ten minutes from the planning office – you remember that pernickety man with the bald head and oversized glasses. But you're being too fussy. Leave it to me – next time they're on site I'll talk to them. But if you think I've got names and addresses of all the itinerant labourers I paid out some cash to, you're in cloud cuckoo land – that's not a detail I find they ever give away.'

'Right. Get your diary out. As long as it takes, next Tuesday, midday. If I don't get answers I can believe in, I'll close all bank accounts until I'm sure this place is under control. That'll mean nobody will get paid, and next time there's a fight here, I'll call the police to investigate,' Claire said. 'You've overspent and you're not looking into a bottomless money pit you can keep clawing it from.'

'Why are you questioning it all? Arrow Hall is a very difficult job. It's a listed site, and you've got to understand it's not like building your usual urban semi. And don't you dare call the police – I'll deal with overpayments…'

James's voice trailed off; he straightened as he was talking and walked to the other end of the desk. Staring moodily from the small cabin window, James was suddenly distant. But Claire needed answers from James. She moved to tap him on the shoulder to interrupt his reverie. He suddenly recoiled from his vacant stare. *His face flushed red*, Claire thought with anger. He almost ran from the cabin without a word.

A few seconds later, there was a small knock on the cabin door. Claire turned as the door opened. She put her hand to her mouth as if to stifle a scream.

35

Claire put her head in her hands. Just for a moment it was quiet.

'Claire, hello, can I come in?'

Claire looked up. Harry Stone was standing facing her. He was smartly dressed – polished shoes with a crisp white shirt – and he had a grin on his thin face. Claire steadied herself, not sure what she was seeing – she was shaken by this sudden visitor. Two years since she had seen him, his hair had turned a silvery grey, but his face was weak. The skin around his eyes was loose, showing none of the staring determination she had known before. His arms too, hung loosely from his jacket.

And Stone saw Claire's stare as he walked further into the small cabin.

'We haven't met for a while; I knew you were working on the rebuilding of Arrow Hall so I thought I might call by. A bit like old times.'

'What on earth have you called here for?'

Claire poured the words out. She could read Harry Stone like a book – he had come to get something, and he was trespassing on her space in this small cabin.

'I've just come to say hello; I was passing, so why not?'

'I don't want to talk about the past. Whatever has happened is now out of my life; I've moved on.'

'That's good, Claire, let's not look back. I don't want to rake up all that led to the burning down of Arrow Hall. But you now look well, and that's good to see.'

'Yes, and you look better than the last time I saw you. Being beaten up in this very place by those drug-crazed hoodlums. Have they gone away, have you paid them off?'

'No, I didn't pay, but that's all finished now,' Stone said.

Stone gritted his teeth. A thug thumping him round the face in his own kitchen, phone calls from a man serving five years for money laundering, drug-pushing and even GBH, but that was not what he could talk about with Claire.

'You do know Rick bought this site, don't you?'

'Yeah, of course I now know that. But he wanted to hide from me – one of Rick's property companies bought it; I never knew it was him. But tell him I wouldn't have sold to him if I had seen his name on the contract. And tell him I sold too cheaply; he got a steal. I should have got a lot more before signing it off.'

'I'm not going to talk about that. But give me the truth. What have you come for today?' Claire asked.

'I need help. I've got a lot of business that needs sorting.' There was a pause from Stone. 'You remember Panama, the bank accounts you set up?'

Claire looked away. 'Of course I remember. But I cleared it from my thoughts a long time ago. And now I don't want to hear about it again. But you've got more to tell; you've got a furtive look on your face.'

'I'm into some big stock market deals – I'm buying a big property and I want you to come and tidy everything up for me. Just as you used to do.'

'No. That's not something I ever want to go back to. I'm very busy on the site here,' Claire replied.

'You haven't seen Marine House. My big place on Brighton seafront. It's where I've lived since I left Arrow Hall.'

'Yeah, I've heard about Marine House. Not the best of stories either. I met someone on the site here searching for you. I told him to explore Brighton. He didn't look too friendly to me, so I hope he found you.'

'Forget all that, I'm getting something special lined up. I'm trying to buy Marine House.'

'Why don't you get on with your big deals and leave me out of them?'

'This is special, Claire.' Stone paused for a moment and moved closer into the tiny cabin. 'It's the vendors of Marine House. A lady with a title. I don't find it easy to deal with people like that.' Stone spoke quickly, almost in one breath.

'Have you been civil to them?'

'The lady got too excited, trying to rake up my past, so I had to tell her how it is.'

'What I remember is you talking too loudly, and too quickly, in Arrow Hall. You were often full blast into the phone. I'd never want to hear that again,' Claire said.

For a moment, Stone looked at Claire – he knew exactly what she was saying, and he did not know how to answer it.

'I need Marine House, and when I've bought the place, I'm going to convert it into apartments. How would you like to live there? Have one of the apartments, low rent in an upmarket place by the sea? And it's an easy drive down from London,' Stone said.

'I'd need to think very hard before getting into anything like that,' Claire said forcefully.

Stone fumbled in his pocket for a small velvet pouch tightly tied, and he laid it on the desk with his business card for Marine House.

'I never really said goodbye when you left Arrow Hall after the fire, but you didn't stay around for long. So I've brought you a little present, Claire, for all that you have done for me over the years. Give me a call when you've had time to think about coming down. But make it soon, please. Oh, and before I forget, I don't expect you to come for nothing – I'll pay you well for your time as I always have done,' Stone said.

Without looking back at Claire, Stone left quickly. It was suddenly quiet in the small cabin. But this visitor left Claire shivering; she sat on the only chair and put her head in her hands. Seeing Harry Stone, looking older, thinner, was all too sudden. It was returning memories that would haunt her if she let them.

Claire untied the small pouch that Stone had left and held it over the table. A rough raw diamond fell out and landed on her laptop. She picked it up and held it to the light. This would never be a gift; if anything, it would be a bribe. Yes, that's what Harry Stone really did well, she had seen it many times.

36

For a few minutes Claire sat still. The ghost of Harry Stone was suddenly implanted right inside Arrow Hall, just where she never wanted to see him again. She was going to get out of this cramped cabin and back to London. As she was closing her laptop, James noisily bustled back to the small space and interrupted her. He stared at Claire as she quickly placed the diamond back in the velvet pouch.

'What have you got there?'

'I'm not sure what it is. But a present from somebody I knew way back,' Claire said.

There was a pause as James hovered, uncertain. He stared through the dusty window to the site.

'Looks like a diamond. Do you know him?'

'Why do you ask?'

'Just curious.'

'It's Harry Stone – don't you remember you called him a bit of a cowboy? But when he owned Arrow Hall, I worked for him for a few years,' Claire said.

'Lucky you.' There was dismissive sharpness in James's voice and his arm was shaking as he flicked over a plan lying on the table.

'What's the matter, James? Are you alright?' Claire asked.

'Yeah, I'm fine.'

'You look flustered. Unusual for you.'

'Does your mate Harry Stone often give away diamonds?' James answered, avoiding Claire's gaze.

'Don't be inquisitive – you don't need to know any more about him.'

Claire put the diamond pouch in her pocket and placed her laptop in her bag. James stared at her as if he was expecting her to say more about this sudden visitor. But Claire stood – she wanted to get out of this place. The site was empty – it had been for a couple of hours – and Arrow Hall, in its half-built state, Claire was finding spooky, something sinister in the gaunt outline shielded by scaffold. She had felt it before.

James looked at his watch and stood for a moment in front of her, blocking her exit.

'Move away.'

Claire shouted at him and pushed him aside. James did not resist, but what was he trying to do? The drive back to her new flat was slow, tedious, and as she let herself in through the front door, the sparseness of the small space made her unsettled. In the tiny kitchen she sat for a minute, poured a glass of wine. There was something about Harry Stone calling in at Arrow Hall that did not quite add up. She handled the small diamond he had given her, and her future suddenly stared her in the face. That man was intruding into her life again.

What was it about Harry Stone that would not let his gaunt image fade away?

37

When Claire woke in the early morning in her new flat, it felt claustrophobic. She looked around the bedroom – it was not a place to linger. She dressed, and, in the kitchen, she made a breakfast of muesli and yoghurt. As she carried it into the small lounge, she wondered what she had done in renting this space. It was even tinier than when she had seen it on the first day.

But she had to deal with moving away from Rick, and the question of earning money would not go away. Claire stood in the small kitchen and methodically made a list of the basic things she needed to fit out her new place. And for the next hour, she sat uncomfortably on a wooden chair revising her CV. The last three years looked bare. And whichever way she worded it, even after adding some exciting times with Rick's property deals in Valencia, Madrid and London, it remained a skeleton. She closed her laptop, uncertain any employment agencies would want to read it.

Late afternoon, Claire drove into the underground garage of Rick's apartment and, even before she reached the seventeenth floor in the elevator, she sensed its coolness. Inside, Claire inspected that the cleaners had dusted the ledges and tables, and she was happy that she was going to leave the large rooms tidy.

From his letter box on the landing, Claire bundled up the post; she checked through it as Rick had asked her to and placed it tidily on a ledge by a wide window that overlooked the Thames. Claire then spent a short time packing the final few clothes still in the wardrobe and she removed personal items that were in the guest bathroom she had been using. There would not be space for everything in the small bedroom of her new flat, but from today, that was how it was going to be. She was moving on.

It would be very early morning where Rick was, but she held back. Claire was still angry from the last long-distance call. In her frustration, she shouted his name. But in the large space of his apartment, her call bounced off the vaulted ceiling. Sinister problems at Arrow Hall were growing; she was no longer sure of her own safety around the site; and Rick was ignoring her.

With a mug of strong coffee, and with her laptop, she sat at Rick's large desk. Methodically, Claire spread papers across the wide area and started to scan through all the invoices from contractors and tradesmen right from the beginning of the rebuild. She turned the television on just to kill the total silence that pervaded the place. A dance show, with as much shouting as music and dancing, she kept on a low volume.

There were at least seven changes of banks from contractors giving new details for payment. As Claire studied them, she noticed that the changes were to three banks, and when she quickly checked, she found they were all within a short distance of each other in London's Canary Wharf. That could be no coincidence; it was where James had his own apartment. So, what else had he lied to her about? It left her uncertain that she had paid any of the accounts to the right bank. Where that money had gone, she did not know. As she sipped her third cup of coffee, her suspicions were complete.

After a couple of hours finding more blatantly fake bits of paper with wrong spelling, wrong figures that just did not add up, Claire closed her laptop in frustration, her eyes aching. It now amounted to at least £100,000 lost through this scam, as easy as the tap being turned on and money flowing freely to waste down the drain. That was what had come from trusting James, and it left her riled by the underhand fraud running round the site, a colony of ants colluding together. It was right under her nose, devious, squalid, almost petty.

Alone in Rick's large penthouse apartment, Claire changed for bed, her brain still buzzing. She turned off the light – she had purpose to sort this mess before it grew any bigger. It was that thought alone that would keep her determination alive to live in Arrow Hall again.

But tonight was the time to finally seal the end of living with Rick and all that would mean.

It was a long while before Claire went to sleep.

38

The ringtone on his mobile was a car hooter. It was grating in its loudness. But that is how James wanted it. It was the only way he would ever notice it was ringing when he was on a building site and often high up on scaffolding. For almost a minute it rang before James woke. He flicked on a light and stared at his phone. The time was 1.05 in the morning – anyone calling at this time had to be a wrong number. James flicked off the light and his phone and turned over back into his bed.

But something jarred – he put the light back on and stared at the ceiling for a few minutes. He was unsettled; he felt hot and now very wide awake; it would be impossible to go straight back to sleep. It was just two minutes later that the klaxon noise penetrated the room again. He picked up his phone and touched it to speak. But he said nothing and listened for a voice.

'It is you young James, and we gotta talk for a minute.' The voice was rough; James knew immediately who was calling.

'No more. I've got to keep that site working and little scams don't help. A couple of the boys on site are getting nasty – they think I'm not paying enough, using their name for hiding the money. Kicked to the ground, a big scratch on my car, that's enough. And leave the lady on the site alone. Running her off the road just makes her look more closely. So, you leave off calling me,' James said, his hand trembling as he held his phone.

'Yeah, you be careful, you've got to win this one, because you can't run away now.'

'I'm doing nothing more – I'm finished.'

'I'm not listening to that. Take it as a little reminder of what we talked about a couple of days ago. Double up. Usual time, I'll call six in the morning, nice and early. And you won't forget this chat. People never do when their phone rings in the darkness of the night. But for now, James, sleep well.'

"Sleep well" rang in his ears as James left his bed and walked to the balcony that looked out to the Thames. His apartment was small, and he sat on a chair for the next few minutes just staring at the water. Alone in his flat the previous evening, he had drunk too much; he was trying to bury what he had let himself get dragged into. And now he did not feel good.

He feared what might follow from that phone call.

39

It was precisely midday; it was raining as Claire drove back into the Essex countryside. Her patience stretched, she was angry as she entered through the old, rusting gates at the end of the lane to Arrow Hall. James's shining red sports car was standing next to the cabin and rain was splattering heavily onto the seats.

But Claire was here to stay for as long as it took. One thing she had learnt from Harry Stone was how to keep meetings eyeball to eyeball, sharp, short, just long enough to say what was going to happen. She was going to frighten James. Unless she got answers, the police fraud squad would scour the site. His perfidious dealing, thieving directly from Rick's bank account, would be brought right out into the clear light of the day.

Of course, James would argue. For a very brief moment, Claire's memory jerked back to the evening at the theatre and dinner, which could have ended differently had she not said no to staying on. She had kept her distance then, and today she would coldly cut James out from Arrow Hall as if he had never been there.

But as she drove onto the site, she sensed what she had to do this morning would not run as she had planned. There was shouting. Loud, coarse, top-pitch shouting, bouncing off the walls of the unfinished building.

It was still raining and, sitting in her car, Claire stared across to the edge of some newly erected scaffolding. She put her hand to her mouth and gasped. James was squaring up to a large brickie on the first-floor level. James was small against this six-feet, muscular body, waving a builders' trowel at him. This was only ever going to be a one-way contest unless James walked away. But James took a pace forward and lashed out with his right fist. It missed any contact with the brickie, who instantly charged back at him. James ducked, but he was caught as two fists in succession quickly smashed into his face. He fell onto the scaffold boards with a groan.

He lay there for a few seconds before he scrambled to his knees and coughed loudly as if he was choking. The brickie was standing over him, holding his arm high and waving a long-bladed knife in the air. James lashed out at his legs. It was a futile move. A glinting knife was glanced across James's back. It came down, tore into his shirt; there was blood and James yelled with pain.

'Don't play games with me, Jimmy,' the brickie shouted. 'You owe me a couple of grand from your fancy scheme, you devious little dickhead.'

There was uncontrolled rage in James's face as he stood and arched his back against the pain of the knife wound. The blood stain on his shirt widened and he tried to stand square to the brickie. But another fist landed straight into his face. He toppled backwards, missed his step, his shoulder hitting hard between two scaffold uprights. With a growl into the now still air, James fell thirty feet, hitting the ground with a heavy thud.

The brickie ran down the ladder and looked at James, who was lying on his face with no movement. He turned, ran quickly to his van and, within a few seconds, drove at speed from the muddy site.

It left Claire shaking. She was stunned but quickly walked over to James and knelt by his side. She tried to talk to him, but he gave her no reply. Claire gently moved his body over so he was not facing the ground. His eyes were closed; he was unconscious, but he was breathing. Fumbling with her phone, she called 999 for an ambulance. The rain had stopped, and she covered James with her jacket, feeling helpless at the sudden quietness around her.

For ten minutes it rained heavily, but James remained inert on the grass. Lights flashing, an ambulance arrived in the small lane just fifteen minutes after her call.

The paramedics quickly examined the casualty and Claire stood back.

'Who is this?' a paramedic stood and asked Claire.

'James, fit thirty-five-year-old. In the rain he slipped and fell from the first-floor level of the scaffold. Onto his head and right shoulder. And he might have a gash in his back as well as he hit one of the scaffold poles.'

Claire knew that was not true. She had seen a knife slashed at James's back – this was a fight with a brickie, an argument about money.

The paramedic returned to assist as James was groaning on the wet grass. He did not respond when the paramedic started to talk to him. Claire was still feeling the shock at what had happened, and twenty minutes later, she could only watch as James was carefully laid on a stretcher. They put his head in a securing brace so he could not move as the trauma slowly unfolded. He was now silent, barely conscious and Claire turned away as he was lifted into the ambulance.

It took just five minutes to give her personal details and James's as far as she knew them. She left her mobile number and address in case they wanted to talk to her again.

Claire now wanted to get away from this place and she drove very slowly to her small apartment. Later that evening, she thought to call the hospital to get news of James, but she left it. From fists to his face, a thirty-feet fall and a blade flashing over his back, with serious injuries, he would not be good. She did not want to know.

In the confined space of the kitchen, she felt her hand shaking as she scrambled a quick email to Rick. With a few unfeeling words she told him of the fight that James had just lost. But she left out James as being part of the growing sinister undercurrent running through the site, a flashing blade form the brickie and threats to herself. An email could not say that as it was and she wanted to tell it direct to Rick's face.

Her determination from earlier that morning to confront James with his corruption was now boiling over. But she would leave her anger at what had happened hanging in the air until he came out of hospital, just like a spider's web waiting for its prey.

40

To get some air from the closed space of his suite in Claridge's, Stone stood for a moment on the busy pavement outside the hotel. The nagging pain in his hip and back was constantly with him; this morning he was feeling tired. His phone buzzed in his pocket. This had to be Josh with agreement to selling Marine House. Stone momentarily forgot his pain and eagerly pulled it out.

'Harry, my friend. How're you doing this bright, sunny day?'

It was Xavier. He had a bounce in his voice, and for a moment, Stone thought he must have got out of jail. His tone was light, flippant, free for a while from the daily confinement of his liberty. Perhaps it was that he had been smoking something. Stone stood on a street corner for a moment, just listening. His eye quickly attuned his brain to the image that would never leave him. His brain saw Xavier's ugly, shiny bald head and rippling square lump of neck. And how close was he?

'What do you want?' Stone's loudness was lost in the air.

'Where are you, matey? I can hear people talking. I hope they can't listen to what I'm saying.'

There was silence for half a minute as Stone crossed the road. The flashing image he held was as if Xavier was walking by his side. Stone even looked over his shoulder, thinking he might see this racketeer, with his grinning face, walking with him.

'Did you check on Electric Motors Inc? How much did you put in, matey? How much did you make?'

'I didn't go for it, and you're just gambling.'

'Listen, Harry, don't talk like that because I got another big deal for you. Don't stand off again; you'll find it's real money. My man is sharing what he knows; he likes to spread it around but only to a few select people. And you're one of them. Because remember, matey, you still owe a quarter of a million and some of my boys are getting all over a bit fidgety about it. This'll help you make it up so you can repay that pile. Have you got a pencil handy?'

'I'm listening.'

'Goldnight. Runs a couple of casinos and a couple of nightclubs. All right in the middle of London. They're spreading into high-street bookies, and an American outfit from Las Vegas is going to buy the whole business on the stock market, and it's going to happen by the end of this week. My friend I enjoy dinner with says to get onto it, this one's a cert.'

'Never heard of Goldnight. I don't know what they do, so why should I want to get in on it?'

'Harry, don't sound stupid. You're not following this closely enough are you, matey? You don't need to know all that stuff about what they do. Just go and press the right buttons on your shiny new computer, and it'll come out right at the other end,' Xavier said.

'How much are you gambling with this time?'

'The thirty grand I made on Electric Motors. That sound good? Do you trust me now?'

'You're a thieving con. Who is this other crook with you, guffing out this stuff?'

'Don't get nasty, Harry. We'll both want to keep these deals running, won't we?'

There was a pause. Stone held the phone away and looked at it until he heard it speak to him.

'And there's something you gotta do, Harry. My mate who shares the next room to me needs to spread some backhanders around. There's a few little inducements that need paying to some of his close contacts. For services rendered by those boys who work in the big buildings by the tower of London. Do you know what I mean?' Xavier said, his voice still floating easily and not with his usual croak.

Stone said nothing as he walked slowly along a quiet backroad of Mayfair.

'I hope you're still listening, Harry. Because this is important. My business partner in here needs to oil their greasy hands. So, please, matey, gather five grand in notes. And do you know your way around central London, places in the City?'

'What're you after?'

'Trust me, Harry this is good. There's a pub in Leadenhall Market, right in the middle of the City, called the Lamb Tavern. There will be someone there waiting to see you at the bar. He's tall; he's a city gent with a light-grey suit and black briefcase. Tomorrow morning, midday. Okay?'

'Give away five grand in notes to one of your mates, who do you think I am?'

'Harry, it sounds from your voice you don't trust me. So, matey, listen, that goes both ways, and I gotta get the quarter million back from you that you squandered. So, do what I say, and you keep safe.'

'I'm not taking five grand anywhere, so stop…'

The phone suddenly clicked off. Stone looked at it and put it in his pocket. Of course he knew Leadenhall Market; he knew it well. Nearly a century ago, his dad worked there. He swept up after horses that had trampled through the place on their deliveries. But that was before he took to drink and left home for good. Stone had a familiarity with Leadenhall Market, though today it gave him no comfort that he should take cash there to oil some greasy palms for Xavier's mate in the next cell.

For a few minutes, Stone stood still on the pavement – he took out his wallet and wrote on a scrap of paper the word "Goldnight". He felt a tug, a lure to get onto this. Electric Motors had been good; he had missed joining the party. And now, with his life expectancy quickly draining away, what had he got to lose by using insider tips from the middle of HMP Belmarsh? He put his wallet back in his pocket and laughed.

Something was holding him back, and he was hesitant. An inmate convicted for fraud with a contact in the City would soon be traced. A lot of money flowing to buy into these deals just before the leaked news became public was asking for somebody with a search warrant to knock on his door. Last time they came, it was 6.00 in the morning; they trampled all over the house. And Lady Ruth had got to hear about it. And where was Josh with his promise that he would talk to his sister if he could get £100,000 to him upfront?

Uneasily, Stone looked around. He had a growing fear that this racketeer, who had blackmailed him into corners, or his cronies, could still find him. He walked slowly back to Claridge's, and he began to feel better. It was obvious. Get the name of the City gent at the Lamb Tavern, then he could get insider feeds direct. And at a stroke, wipe Xavier inside HMP Belmarsh right out of his life. Forever.

41

Stone poured a whisky; his old confidence was coming back as he now had work to do. But what to do with Josh? There was something creepy about Josh; he had seen it in the way he slouched in his chair, the disdain in his eyes when he looked at his mother as they met in the stuffy Mayfair office. The Reform Club meeting just gave him a thin veneer of competence and respectability. Like a spoilt child not getting his own way, Stone suspected he was cheating on the family. And probably other people too.

But carrying a bag of cash? Could he be trusted?

He called Josh and the phone was answered after the second ring.

'Do you know Leadenhall Market? It's in the middle of London, in the City.'

'Yeah, of course I do. I go to see my insurance friends at Lloyds right next door. The Jackson family has been a name for a long time on top syndicates of underwriters there. But profits have been a bit slim in the past few years. Yeah, and I always get a good lunch when I go there,' Josh replied with a childish eagerness.

'There's a pub in the market called the Lamb Tavern. Josh, I want you to take an envelope there for me and give it to a guy, a tall man standing at the bar of the pub. Clean shaven, your age, light-grey suit and carrying a black briefcase. I want his name, where he works, and then give him the envelope and say it's from Xavier. That's important – have you got that?'

'Harry, yeah. It'll be good. So, when?'

'Midday tomorrow. Collect the envelope from the concierge at Claridge's. I'll leave a couple of hundred with it for you. Is that okay?'

'A small touch of pocket money. I'm always short. But who isn't?'

'What about the diamond? Remember your promise at the Reform Club? What did your sister say when you gave it to her?'

Josh hesitated as if he had not heard what Stone was talking about.

'Harry, sorry, no, not yet. Haven't had a chance to tie her down, but I haven't forgotten.'

'Time's now getting short. But I'm still very interested to talk about Marine House, and I'd like to meet your sister.'

'I can arrange that. But have you been able to find the hundred grand in cash that we talked about? That money will do the trick. It'll deal the right cards for you.'

'One step at a time, Josh. I'll find it when I know I'm having a serious conversation, like making me the preferred buyer for Marine House.'

'I could come to Brighton to collect it and give it to my sister when I give her the diamond.'

'Have you told your mother about the money and the diamond?'

'I don't see Mother very often these days. She's too busy playing bridge with her friends.'

'You know what I want, and I know what you want. So we'll talk again. But first you pick my envelope up, keep it carefully and let me know you've delivered it.'

After filling his whisky glass, Stone put £5,000 in £20 notes in a large envelope – he scribbled on the front "Mr Josh Jackson", and he sealed it with tape. He walked down to the hotel foyer and left it with the concierge.

Stone's tiredness from earlier that morning was ebbing. He began to feel a freshness, even growing excitement that Josh was now the pawn to lead him straight to the front door of Marine House.

42

Stone paid off the taxi outside the sandwich shop next door to Sol's office in Hatton Garden. As Sol greeted Stone with a double handshake, he looked into Stone's face as if he was detecting that his friend was not a well man.

'How are you today?' Sol asked.

'I'm seeing my way forward. But the doctors keep telling me what I don't want to hear.'

There was silence between the two men and Sol again examined Stone's face.

'I need a few things in place to buy a big property. Like, I now need some big cash urgently for the diamonds.'

'Well, I'll give you some good news that might help you with that, Harry. We've checked out that big stone you brought to me. Heavy, beautifully cut and polished, you get me the official laboratory certificates and we then owe you some serious cash,' Sol said.

'How much?' Stone almost rasped back.

'Allow me a little commission on it, and I can give you eighty grand. It's that good.'

Stone was sitting heavily in his chair, and he let his head drop in mock surprise.

'You really do bring me good news. I'm dealing with the right man.'

'I've got a contact coming in next week. A man over from St Petersburg doing a bit of Harrods shopping. He's seen a picture and he's very interested from what I've told him.'

Stone passed to Sol the details of his five accounts in different banks around London.

'Spread the money around and keep it secret; you understand how the world is these days.'

Sol did know what the world was like – a lot of his business was done that way, and people from the Russian city, like his client, were as up with it as the rest. He put the bank details from Stone in his pocket as if to shield it even in his own office.

Stone sat more upright in his chair to help the stabbing pain in his back.

'I trust you, Sol. I've got two more big diamonds coming out of Nevis. But the doctor's telling me I'm not too good, so I'll need to take my time to go and get 'em.'

'If you bring me more diamonds like the first one, Harry, I'm sure they will be very valuable. I can find a good home for them. My Russian client will be very happy. But, Harry, you take care of yourself.'

'Yeah, I'm doing that.'

'Do you want to stay for a while and have a drink?' Sol asked.

Stone followed Sol into his private sitting room on the top floor. He needed the company of a man like Sol, and they drank whisky for the next two hours. Sol never asked again how Stone was, but he did look at him as he got into a taxi. And he wondered if he would ever see his old friend again.

Half an hour later, Stone was back in Claridge's sitting on a deep sofa in his suite. He was still tasting the whisky shared with Sol and he poured himself another glass. Today was a big step to get the cash for Marine House and, spurred on by his excitement that diamonds were worth real money, he opened his laptop on a low table.

The Goldnight page had a glossy picture of a nightclub in the seedier parts of Soho, and for a few minutes, he stared at the screen. Just the name had a certain lure to it, but what was Goldnight all about? He did not know. The only casino he had ever been into was in Monte Carlo. A mate came out with a couple of thousand euros, his winnings on the blackjack table, and Stone had just watched him play in the dimly lit room.

With the whisky, he started to mellow. He keyed into his new stockbroker account. Sprawling more deeply into the sofa, he scrolled through the screen for five minutes, not really seeing it.

Casinos, nightclubs? No, they were never his type of place, but what did that matter if there was money hidden right inside that name, Goldnight? And now was not a time to hold back – Electric Motors had come good, and he had stupidly missed it. And alone, sipping from his glass, suddenly he felt the excitement of a quick deal. Satisfied, he pressed the button on his laptop and £150,000 worth of shares in Goldnight were his.

But he stopped and stared at the screen. His money had gone into a glitzy business based only on a tip that had come from a sinister criminal serving a three-year prison sentence. The same man who had sent his goon to threaten and intimidate, to collect from him a quarter of a million pounds he was never going to pay.

Stone's hunch was that, this time, everything was going to be very different. He was certain of that.

43

Claire led her close friend Jennie up the narrow staircase to the third-floor landing of a red-brick building two roads away from a bustling shopping area in Knightsbridge. As Claire unlocked the door, she looked at Jennie's face. It was blank.

'Come in – there's not much to show you; it's very small.'

They walked into the kitchen; it was bare. The whole place in the bedroom and sitting room was cold. Jennie took Claire by the arm.

'Yes, I see what you mean,' Jennie said. 'It is small.'

'It's all I could find at a price I could afford in London.'

'You're in the most expensive part here. Do you have to live in London?'

'I need to work. I need to earn money. I'll doubt I'll get anything outside of London.'

Jennie had seen enough. Claire saw the uncertainty in her eyes.

'I'm moving on from Rick – I'm going to find my own independence again and this is the first step.'

'I'm sure you're right, but where does that leave you with Arrow Hall?'

'There's been a stabbing on the site, a fight leaving James, the project manager, badly injured in hospital. I'm uncovering a fraud that's leeching money, and I'm uncertain how safe it is for me to be there with all that going on.'

'You've told me enough. Walk away. Forget it – get on with something else in your life,' Jennie said.

'I've always wanted to see the new Arrow Hall completed, and I want to live in it again just as I used to. It's leaving a very nasty, sour taste in my mouth.'

'You've got more to tell me, haven't you?'

Claire closed the door of her very small apartment and, twenty minutes, later sitting in a noisy coffee shop just off the high street, she told Jennie.

'I'm going to do something I never thought I would ever want to be involved in again.'

Claire looked uncomfortable with a deep frown, and Jennie put her hand on Claire's arm.

'Take it slowly,' Jennie said.

'I've decided I'm going to do some work for Harry Stone,' Claire said as she looked away from Jennie.

'That does not sound a very sensible thing for you to be doing. Do you think it's wise after all the unhappy memories he left you with?'

'He came onto the site at Arrow Hall, two days ago. He looked very frail, just a shadow of how I knew him. His face was gaunt and grey; his hands were almost skeletal.'

'You're curious, aren't you? You want to see what's happening to him.'

'That's what concerns me. I don't want that to be the motivation that drives me to go and work with him again.'

'Does Rick know about this?'

'No, not yet. But it'll be the first thing I tell him when he comes back from New Zealand.'

'You're doing all this in a hurry, so be careful.'

'Harry Stone lives alone in this seven-bedroom mansion on Brighton seafront; of course I want to see it. I think he's an ill man; I want to find out what is really happening to him. And he'll pay me – I need the money.'

'You sound determined to go and see Stone again, but my advice is: don't do it. Your bad memories will flood back; Harry Stone's a shark just like the scam you've found circling Arrow Hall. I'm sure you can easily find work somewhere else,' Jennie said, finishing her coffee.

'I've made up my mind. The Arrow Hall fire was two years ago; it's history now – I've moved on from that. And I don't owe him anything even though, trying to lure me in, he gave me a diamond the other day. If it doesn't feel right when I get to Brighton, then I just walk away again.'

Claire left Jennie later that morning certain of what she was going to do. She planned her visit to Marine House would only be for a short time. But Claire did not plan for everything, certainly not how her short time visiting Marine House would turn the indelible memories she had of Harry Stone upside down.

44

Stone sat completely still as he faced the urologist.

'Mr Stone, I have studied the detailed images from the MRI scan. The prostate cancer has spread to your lower spine and towards your right shoulder. And that is where you are likely to feel the most pain. We should continue to monitor that, and from here, we must plan how to manage your pain. There are several things we can look at, like radiotherapy and hormone therapy, and as it progresses, there are stronger drugs we can use, such as morphine and steroids or even chemotherapy.'

The urologist spoke in a matter-of-fact way as if this was just another day's normal business. He looked closely at his patient as if he would find signs as to how much this disease was really hurting.

'I want to keep it all simple. I know exactly where the pain is around my body, and it moves around my back. I'll take drugs, but I'm not on for treatment like chemotherapy where I have to come to the hospital to get it administered and then suffer all the side effects that brings.'

'I understand that, and perhaps I should refer you to a pain specialist to help you control the next few months.'

'No more specialists, thank you. I said I want to keep this simple. Send a note to my doctor in Brighton about the MRI results and I'll take it from there.'

'Yes, of course I'm happy to do that, together with a recommendation for your treatment. You should also think of contacting your local hospice where you will find great advice on managing your pain.'

Stone was in no mood to ask questions; he already knew more than any doctors; he already knew where the pain was – he could feel it – and he knew how it was spreading. And the urologist continued about how radiotherapy and hormone therapy might help, but it was getting technical, and Stone only half listened. And a short while later, as he left the hospital, the news was still ringing in his ears, and he wondered why he had bothered to spend his valuable time having a scan.

He walked back to Claridge's and even felt the sun on his face as, for a short while, the ache in his back was held in check with strong painkillers. But they made him tired, sleepy, lethargic and with an odd feeling that his body was just too heavy to carry around. And that was even though he had lost almost a stone in weight in the past three months.

There was a note under his door as he entered his suite, discreetly reminding him that he had run up a bill well into the thousands. He called down to reception, gave his credit card details and told them to clear his account. His consultation was finished; London was finished – it was time to go back to Marine House.

With a full glass of whisky in his hand, he sullenly opened the *Financial Times* that had been delivered to his suite. A small headline on the front page made his eyes light up. It was an article on Goldnight Casinos. They had agreed a merger deal with a large American casino operator in Las Vegas. And the price which was being offered by the Americans was nearly double the current price of Goldnight on the stock market. Stone at last was onto something big, and the hassle of the MRI scan quickly left him.

Within a few seconds of opening his laptop, he had flicked to his stockbroker account. It was all there. Chancing £150,000 into the shares of Goldnight had nearly doubled his money. This was like picking notes up as they floated down from the sky. Helicopter money. Even his nemesis Xavier behind bars for the next three years, for a moment, seemed benign.

With just five weeks left on his lease, and daring to think he could close in on Marine House, Stone quickly counted the money. News from Sol on the first big diamond, and now clearing the jackpot on Goldnight, he could see that he was now only £270,000 short.

From the coldness of the hospital earlier that morning, a smile crept across Stone's face.

He was becoming more certain that he would close the gap further in his chase to buy Marine House. And Stone could often judge character. Like anybody else, Lady Ruth would not care where his money came from as long as the cash landed in her bank.

His mood lifted, but his pain persisted.

45

Ignoring Jennie's advice was not something Claire would do easily – she trusted her friend – but this early morning there was something driving Claire. A couple of lines, something solid she could put on her CV, stark curiosity to look into Marine House, a fanciful dream of having a flat living by the seaside, so much better than a small, pokey flat in Knightsbridge, were all bits of it. But perhaps there was more than that.

Harry Stone answered his phone almost immediately.

'Yes?'

It was the tone in Stone's voice that caught her, and for a moment it jarred.

'Harry, it's Claire.'

'Claire, great to hear from you. I hope you've brought me some good news. I need it at the moment,' Stone said.

'You caught me by surprise when you called at Arrow Hall. I'll come to Marine House. But I've got to be quite certain before I come that those drug-crazed criminals who always circled around Arrow Hall have gone and they haven't just moved to circling around Marine House.'

'Take it from me, I've cleared them all off. No more police raids – Marine House is different; it's safe; it's why I'm living here.'

'I am going to finish off Arrow Hall, that's still going to take my time, so to start with I can only come for just a few days. And I'm going to remind you, I'll need paying. That's in cash, please. I'll give the diamond back to you when I call.'

'Yes of course I'll pay you in cash if that's what you want. And I'll give you a raise on what you were getting at Arrow Hall. But the diamond is yours to keep. I insist.'

Claire heard Stone laugh as if he was being generous.

'I'll be down Monday afternoon. Two ish.'

'There's a lot to do. I want to show you around Marine House; I want you to help me buy the place; and I'm making big plans with what to do with it. I've got stock market deals running; my money in Panama is coming back; my study's a bit untidy; and my papers need sorting,' Stone said. 'So, I look forward to working with you again. It'll be like old times.'

The thought of "old times" from Harry Stone was not the easiest of greetings Claire could have heard as she closed the call. This visit had to be the start of something new, not going back to the old circus that had seen the destruction of Arrow Hall.

Just for a short while, working for Stone would help her break from Rick. And Claire was not deterred. That early morning, she believed there was still a new Arrow Hall to be built, and she could see it through, out of the dark hole it had fallen into, even if Rick was becoming a distant memory.

46

Stone wanted to open the doors of the sitting room of Marine House, stand on the balcony and smell the sea air again. The limousine had brought him from Claridge's – he stood on the front steps and searched the street. There was nobody lurking outside his front door or across the road, but one day soon his paranoia told him there might be.

He poured a large whisky and took up what had become his favourite posture of reclining on a chaise longue in the sitting room. Stone drooled as he thought of his fistful of Panama dollars waiting in Nevis. And no authorities knew what he was doing; that added the edge for Stone. It made him satisfied; it perked him up, even though grabbing diamonds he was not sure would have any lasting meaning for him. His time was now short.

Stone sat in silence. Sweating again in the torrid heat of the Caribbean to collect diamonds was not something he could face again. For a moment Stone closed his eyes. He took another sip from his whisky, and he quickly knew he now had another job for Josh. And it was within an hour and a half after calling that Josh was knocking on the door of Marine House.

In the hallway, Stone stared him directly in the eye. But Josh did not look back. Josh had an air of being shifty, looking around, looking down at the floor as if he had something to hide. In the Reform Club just a few days ago, Stone had seen the same blazer with crumpled sleeves, a tie with food stains and ill-fitting shiny black shoes. And today, Stone could see that Josh had not shaved for several days – he had a stubble growth – he was growing a beard. It did not suit him; his face was not serious enough for the sophistication of a beard. Perhaps this Jackson family were really hard up.

Stone led him into the brightly lit kitchen, and he stood still in the middle of the room.

'You did that little run to Leadenhall Market okay?' Stone asked.

'Yeah, he was waiting there. We went to the same school, but he's a bit younger than me. We had a beer, but he didn't want to stand and talk for too long.'

'Did you get his name and telephone number?'

'No, he said it was top secret. Undercover stuff about shares. In the City it wouldn't be anything else. That's just what they do there. And he wanted to get away back to his office.'

Stone quickly let it pass. Cutting Xavier out of the line for insider leaks was a good idea. A few years younger and his health restored, he would have pushed it. He poured coffee from a percolator and handed a cup to Josh.

'I've got another job for you,' Stone said.

'I've got some time to spare, so what goes, Harry?'

'Have you ever been to the Caribbean?'

'We spend Christmas there. Done it for the past five years. Barbados. Mother likes it there. She says it's the same as being at home but a bit warmer.'

'No need to tell your mother about it, but could you go tomorrow?'

Josh looked at his watch as if time was running away.

'Why not? Haven't got much else to do tomorrow.'

'A little island called Nevis. I want you to collect a parcel. I'll pay economy class fares and an overnight if you need it.'

'What's in the parcel? Not drugs or nasties like that.'

'No, this is okay stuff. But something valuable that needs to be collected quickly. And safely. Are you up for it?' Stone asked.

He almost felt sorry for Josh, someone reduced to being an errand boy for him. And a mother with a title. It was wrong.

'Give me the details, Harry. But can't you stretch to paying club class? I don't really travel at the back, and Mother always travels right at the front.'

'No,' Stone said sharply. 'You upgrade if you want, and you pay. Got it?'

It took two minutes for Stone to write out the details of the American in Nevis. Josh did not need to know any more. Stone walked into the hallway; Josh followed, and Stone saw in the glint of his eyes that he was eager just to do something. This son of a titled Lady must live a poor, idle life.

'Did your sister get the diamond I gave you?'

'I haven't seen her yet; she's very busy and always around London with her friends doing something,' Josh replied.

'That's exactly what you told me last time I asked. So get on with it please – call her and tell her you've got a diamond for her. When you've done that, we'll talk about the hundred grand advance you asked for. You are trying to get Marine House for me, aren't you? Don't you remember?' Stone kept his voice level low, but it was time to push Josh beyond his shifty response. He led Josh to the front door.

'Harry, don't worry – I will give it to her as soon as I'm back. Yeah, I'd like to talk about the hundred grand you promised, and I can deliver Marine House.'

Josh was being evasive. Stone had seen slipperiness before, and this time he was certain Josh was telling a downright lie. And so was his amazement that this man in front of him had been accused of sexual assault – he did not look big enough for that. In his febrile mind, Stone would not forget that, but for today, he would use Josh. He did not trust him; he might well walk away with more diamonds, but that would slowly draw him right in. Josh was becoming a pawn for Stone, a bargaining chip to get Marine House.

Quickly, he sent an email to the American woman in Nevis with the long, blonde hair. A man in a scruffy jacket was going to call to pick up the diamonds was all that was needed. On handover, she could draw down the balance of Panama dollars and send lab certs separately in the post.

He was now in a race; his money was growing; and Marine House would one day be his if he could fight this menacing illness eating away at him. But sitting alone, he naively had not understood that Claire could soon disrupt that thought.

47

Stone's mobile rang. He did not recognise the number, and he stared at the phone for some seconds before he picked it up.

'Yes?' Stone snapped in his usual, offhand manner.

'That is Harry Stone, mate of my boss Xavier?'

'Who are you?'

'My name's Chad. I've got a message for you from the man himself, yeah, right from his comfortable little cell. He says he can't call you today and he asks me to be friendly and tell you something that'll make you rich.'

'Get on with it. I've got better things to do than listen to you all day.' At that moment Stone could not control feeling irritable at anything he had to think about.

'Give me a minute, Harry, and I'll tell you of a big money-making swoop about to bounce out. Xavier's insider mate has had another top tip, a mega deal going to break out from backroom privacy in some big bank and right onto the stock market.'

Stone reached for a pad and a pen on a side table.

'Okay. I'm listening, but be quick.'

'This jumbo money grab'll be spread to the world by the end of the week. So, he says you gotta act fast if you want to get in on it. Do you know what I mean?'

'I'll decide that when I've checked it out,' Stone said.

'Yeah, but first you got to understand you're not to let it out to anyone else, this one is too valuable.'

'Why can't that thug Xavier call me? I want to hear about this direct from him.'

'He's had some human rights taken away. No television, no talking to his mates. He hit a warder who was getting a bit narky, and they searched his cell and took his phone before he could hide it. Putting it in a pocket under his pillow was not good enough to keep it away from the screws. You must know what it's like, Harry. Poor man, he'll be in solitary soon. And that means all alone.'

'What you got for me?' Stone asked abruptly.

'How much do you want to put in it, Harry? Fifty grand, seventy-five grand, hundred grand? Remember you're going to double your money in the next few days.'

'I want to know what Xavier's putting up,' Stone said.

'Don't know that. He keeps his money secret. Like we all do.'

'What's the name of the deal this time? I'll need to look into it – then I'll let you know,' Stone said.

'Harry, you just listen for a minute because this deal's got to be different. Mr Xavier's prison mate is getting worried that we'll all get found out if there's too many people buying it up before it's announced to the world. We don't want that, do we?'

'You're not talking to a schoolkid – what have you got?' Stone felt immediate tension in his stiffening neck.

'If you want to come in and join the party, Harry, you've gotta deal through an account in Geneva. The man on the outside who's feeding us this valuable stuff has set up a bank account in that lovely Swiss city in each of our names and that's where we will put our money. Then this deal is done in one big buy from there. Anonymously.'

'Don't give me that. He can't set up an account in my name without my ID. He needs passport, place of birth, where I live, where the money came from, all that stuff.'

'Harry, don't be naïve. A man with your experience will know how these things are done.'

'What's this business all about that somebody wants to buy it for big money?'

'Before I give you the name, a final warning, Harry. You run away and do this on your own, then our mole in the high-rise building in London will catch you and spill you right out onto the doorstep of the police crime squad who look at these things and somebody officious will come knocking on your door.'

'I want the details.' Stone was not sure where this was leading; he sipped his whisky and sat forward in his seat.

'Sapphire Holdings Inc. Deals in precious stones. Do you know what a sapphire is, Harry?'

'Leave it, I'll find out. Give me the Geneva account details,' Stone demanded. He was becoming annoyed at the increasing hustle coming from Chad.

'I'll email a letter from the people running this Swiss account, guaranteeing your money is safe. They take fifteen per cent commission on your profit. But we've got to close it today. Time limit is 5.00. That's enough time for you to move your money into Geneva. Now's the time to deal – you're either in or out,' Chad said, and Stone heard the phone click off.

Within a minute, account numbers, passwords, ID and names, PIN numbers, everything came through on an email for the new account in his name. And there was a letter headed Minted Money Investments, Rue Paradis, Geneva.

Dear Harry Stone,

We look forward to working with you in this special stock market investment. Your money is safe with us, and we guarantee your capital and profit on this transaction will be repaid to the same account from which you deposit with us your funds.

Confidentiality is assured by us at all times.

Jean Roche
Principal
Minted Money Investments

Stone read it through twice. He had never heard of Minted Money Investments. Then he knew he never would if it was a business run from the edge of Switzerland. He quickly checked the name Minted Money Investments on the internet. It showed Lake Geneva with a clear blue sky and a picture of Jean Roche, founder and Principal of Minted Money Investments. He looked no older than twenty-five.

Between indecision mixed with excitement, Stone started to pace the elegant sitting room of Marine House. He straightened his back, but it hurt him with a stabbing pain. It reminded him that his days were limited. And it increased his determination that Marine House was where he was going to spend that time.

But this Chad who knew too much about him was suspicious, jostling him with tight deadlines. He scanned again the account with bogus details but enough to be in his name in Geneva. And he admired the slick, almost frightening, way, using his fake identity, that had been done. He stood and stared across to the sea. His memory was still very sharp – he had closed the gap to buy Marine House in one easy deal in Goldnight Inc.

But Stone, in his years with many property deals, had often smelled when something was too good to be true. And now, was dealing in Sapphire Holdings Inc just too easy? His sense was guiding him, but would it close the gap of chasing £500,000 even further?

48

It was just after 4.00 in the afternoon – Stone's indecision was weighing on him, and time was moving past him quickly. He called Roger. There was something dragging him towards this deal, and he wanted to hear what Roger thought of this leak from a fraudster in prison. But what had he now to lose?

'Did you check out the price of Electric Motors Inc? It doubled. Did you buy into it?' Stone asked.

'No, I've told you before I don't work on tips. They can be wrong and mostly they are,' Roger said.

'Okay, but you listen to this one. It's another big deal coming off. Sapphire Holdings Inc. Going to be taken over just like Electric Motors Inc was.'

'I don't think you should talk to me about this, Harry,' Roger said.

'You sound as if you know something.'

'There's been a mountain of gossip about Sapphire Holdings for a long time. And a few months ago, I splashed out and bought a bundle of their shares.'

'We can watch them together then when they double at the end of the week.'

'Be careful, Harry. Don't be caught in the middle of these deals, and as I've told you before, some regulator'll tear you apart if they catch you at it,' Roger said.

'They'll never know where I get my information from, and I'm never going to become a snitch for the police to find out.'

'Okay, we'll open a bottle of champagne at the end of the week. Give me a call then, Harry.'

Stone felt the note of confidence from Roger on Sapphire Holdings Inc. He again walked to the balcony window and looked across to the sea. Marine House was now very quiet again and it somehow mesmerised him. Stone topped up his whisky glass and ran his hand through his thinning grey hair. He opened his laptop and found the web page for Sapphire Holdings Inc. It had glowing pictures of a deep-blue sapphire stone mounted on a white gold ring. He flicked to the financial page of the business – he noticed that it did have a pile of cash in the bank and was not borrowing, and he liked the look of that.

Stone slumped back into the chaise longue, but he could not find a comfortable position. For a minute he stared at the ceiling. When the price of Sapphire Holdings Inc doubled at the end of the week, he could make another fifty grand to put to his Marine House purchase. With diamonds from Sol, Goldnight safely scooped and a bundle of notes stuffed in his safe, it would leave him just short of £170,000 to get. And he still had two big, glinting, diamonds to come from Nevis.

He reread the email from Minted Money Investments. It was uncanny, spooky, the email was personal to him – they knew who he was, where he lived, with ID and passwords all set up ready to go. Roger too had bought into Sapphire Holdings Inc and that allowed Harry Stone a few moments of optimism.

Stone looked at his watch. It was just before the deadline of 5.00. He poured a whisky; he felt excitement as if he was in the chase, but he let the clock tick for the next ten minutes before he stirred.

49

It was Claire's early call that lifted Stone from his gloom for a short while. Marine House had to look as if he cared for it when Claire came, to show it as if she would want to live there when he had bought it. He quickly called the local florist and arranged for a large display of flowers for the entrance hall to be delivered.

He had not yet cleared the hoodlums away from the front door of Marine House. His promise to Claire was false. He had already felt a fist into his face, that was the gentle stuff, and of course they would be back chasing for money he was never going to pay. But, when the house was his, he would have security patrols, CCTV cameras installed and alarms over all the doors. Claire's visit was very important to him.

With his bathrobe over his shoulders, he started to walk around the sitting room and hallway and then to his study. He opened a letter from a brown official envelope. It was an aggressive demand from the revenue. Pay up £25,000 now on account of back tax or face penalties, fines of hundreds or even thousands of pounds. He tossed it aside – they could whistle for their money – he no longer cared. Agitated, restless, he ran his hand through his hair.

His phone buzzed in his pocket, and he stopped his pacing around the large rooms.

'Mr Stone, could you be available to meet Lady Ruth at her Mayfair home in two days' time?'

Stone saw the number – it was the agent for Marine House.

'Is she in the mood to sell to me now?'

'I'm not sure about that. But don't call her would be my advice. I don't think you should get too eager as she wants a meeting to talk about the end of your lease and, in particular, clearing up the final payment of your rent.'

Stone breathed out heavily. That talk was the first thing that would make him angry, again questioning if he had the money. But he kept his reply steady.

'Yeah, I'll be there. Tell her to put the kettle on.'

Stone liked the quick sneer. Whatever Lady Ruth wanted to talk about, drawing Josh into his web, running errands, Stone would stay on top of getting Marine House. He slit open an airmail letter from Nevis. There were certificates from the grading laboratory in Antwerp for three big diamonds. He scanned them and, satisfied, tucked them back in the envelope to take to Sol. Panama was now swapped for big-carat, glinting lumps of rock worth thousands. He would maybe, one day, thank Roger for his insight.

The air was fresh early in the morning as he walked very slowly for a while along the side of the beach across the road from Marine House. Sitting on a bench, the sun warmed his face – he stared out to the sea, and he gradually felt the warmth ease the pain in his back. There was no hoodlum with the wispy grey beard lurking around the front door; probably his name was Chad, trying a con with Sapphire Holdings. That made him angry, with growing suspicion of insider leaks from an inmate of HMP Belmarsh. But, inevitably, there was his eagerness waiting for another call from Xavier.

Staring at the horizon, he was afraid of what the next few months might hold. The reality of his lifespan was closing in, but he was going to face up to how he would spend that time amassing the money to get Marine House.

50

Stone crossed over the road back to Marine House. He was going to pour his first whisky of the day and take the palliative medication prescribed by his consultant. But as he was climbing the steps to the front door, his mobile buzzed in his pocket. He knew who it was; this was a call he would answer.

'Harry, I have to clear something with you, mate. We've been giving you nice tips, and my boys are getting angry; they're ready to follow you up if you don't pay a lump of the outstanding money. A solid quarter million is the debt. Remember?'

It was Xavier who sounded distant just because he had not raised his voice.

'Can you hear me because this is getting important?' Xavier persisted.

'Why don't you listen? I've told you many times that I don't owe you and your thugs, so forget it.'

'No, mate, can't do that. This is not how this is going to work out anymore. And do you know what? I'm being harassed in here by some of my partners who had earned that cash with some tight deals out there on the pavement. Dodging the cops, looking out for knives with long, sharp blades being flashed all around them. Some shooters too. It's safer in these walls. So, for starters, a down payment of £25,000 is what they want; all in notes'll do.' Xavier's voice was unusually light, and his words ran easily off his lips.

'Have you got something good to tell me before I finish this call?'

Stone held the phone away and sat down heavily in the chair next to his desk in his study.

'Next Tuesday, one of my boys'll knock on the door of your big pad in Brighton, so if you want to keep out of trouble, do what I ask and give him the cash. Then we all live safely. Until the next time.'

'There won't be another time. Don't push me. And tell your thugs to keep away from Marine House.'

'That don't sound like you, Harry. What's biting?'

'Your money's dirty from narcotics, street heroin dealing, extortion, GBH. I don't want any part of that.'

'Hold it, matey, how much have you made out of my tip for Electric Motors Inc and Goldnight Inc? And how much of that money have you used to repay the quarter of a million you owe?'

'For the last time, get it into your thick, ugly head – I don't owe you anything. You tried to ram that money on me, I didn't play with it, so don't place your sticky fingers around me, trying to lever away fifty grand on Sapphire Holdings with fake IDs in Geneva. Keep that con man Chad away. Got it?'

Stone spoke quickly and put his elbows on his desk. There was a pause – Stone grinned to himself – he'd got one over this thug.

'Sounds like you've nearly been conned, matey, from one of my boys being dirty, a bit tricky. You know what I mean?'

Xavier laughed, followed by a guttural cough.

'Yeah, I'm warning you, don't try that fancy stuff again. I can smell a rat and your mob stink like vermin,' Stone said.

'Okay. Some words of advice, matey. First, never listen to any voices but mine. But look out, Harry, for when one of my boys knocks on your door for some readies. Twenty-five grand in Bobby Moores on account'll keep you safe just for a very short while.'

Stone held the phone away and it left Xavier shouting into the air. He grunted. Was this man still in jail? He sounded so close.

'Don't keep spouting that nonsense. You can whistle for twenty-five grand because I haven't got it.'

'I'm not listening to that. So keep your back covered because someone'll come and deal with you for the last time, and you know what that means. But before we go, just one other little thing, matey. I don't know who you got to deliver the five grand to my mole in Leadenhall Market, but when it was counted up, there were five hundred of the readies short. A little man who spoke posh. Seemed to know my mole so I hope you're keeping our insider deals tight. We don't want everybody poking their finger in our pie, do we? Harry, you take it yourself next time.'

There was a pause. Stone did not reply; he did not know how to. But he soon heard Xavier's gravelly voice.

'So, ta ta, I gotta go now, matey. I'm ready for my elevenses. But we'll talk again, soon I hope.'

Stone clenched his fists and walked quickly into the sitting room. He poured a large measure of whisky and paced round the elegant room. Stone's foul mood deepened.

It was the sinister, threatening face of the crook behind bars in HMP Belmarsh, shouting for phantom money, that made Stone fretful. Xavier and his hoods were still very close; he could smell their hostile menace wafting in the air, and that would never mix with Claire calling at Marine House.

51

Claire took her time on the drive to Brighton. A mile before Marine House on Brighton seafront, Claire left her car. She walked along the wide path by the side of the beach until she reached Marine House where she stood and stared across the road. Its size made it an imposing building, three stories high; she admired the impressive Regency façade with its second-floor windows, each with wide balconies. The stark contrast with Arrow Hall, a house surrounded by green fields, immediately hit Claire.

Calling on Harry Stone was something she had thought would never happen again. On the drive to Brighton, she already felt today that she was running from Arrow Hall. She sat for ten minutes on a bench by the edge of the beach. Her curiosity rising to see the inside of this imposing property, she walked slowly back to her car and drove round to the garage at the rear of Marine House. But she was going to call at the front door. As she walked up the few steps that led to the wide entrance, Claire had a moment of doubt. What was she doing here?

Just a very few seconds after she pressed the bell and looked into the video link, the familiar voice of Harry Stone answered.

'Claire, as always, you are right on time. Come on in and welcome to Marine House.'

'I've only got an hour today, so my visit'll have to be quick.'

Stone grinned as Claire stood and looked for a moment at the large arrangement of flowers on the hall table, even leaning over to savour the scent of the roses. For some reason, Claire knew that

Stone wanted to impress her. He led her quickly into the elegant Regency sitting room that looked across a road to the sea.

'Sit down. Do you want some tea, coffee, something stronger?' Stone said, and he gestured to a deep sofa with cushions arranged around the edge.

'Another time but not today. I just want to see Marine House and find out what you want me to do.'

'Do you like this room?' Stone asked, again looking for Claire's approval.

'It's very imposing; it has an air of being refined but it doesn't look comfortable.'

'I've started talking to the people who own Marine House, but they don't want to sell to me. Don't think I've got the money. But it's a Lady Ruth Jackson, with an idle, layabout son who had a sex assault case against him hushed up.'

'If you have the money, that will always talk for you. You know that better than most people.'

'Yeah, I've got it all. You remember my money in Panama? That's moving back to London. Diamonds, some big, some small, is how I'm carrying it all home.'

'Does Lady Ruth Jackson know that's where your money's come from?'

'I dunno, but she doesn't like the way I talk, and she thinks I won't look after the place. She wants a meeting tomorrow, in her Mayfair office. Could you go, talk to the family, charm them so they can't say no?'

Claire hesitated. She looked at Stone's lined face. There was tension there, it was thinner than when she had known him before.

'Yes, but what can I say to them that you can't?' she asked.

'You know by now that it's not always what you say but how you say it that counts. Her Ladyship wants to be sure that I will keep the house tidy when the agent brings another buyer to view the place, and she also thinks that, with just four weeks left, I will slip away without clearing the last quarter's rent. And you can tell 'em that whatever happens, I'm going to buy this place.'

Stone started to pace the room. This was what he did when he was unsure of something, as if he could find an answer stepping in circles.

'There's something else you must know. I gave a diamond to the son, Josh, to buy him into the deal, and he was to pass it to his sister. I wanted to get them all excited that dealing with me would be different. Maybe it's time to remind them about that.'

Stone sat facing Claire and again ran his hand through his short, silvery, hair.

'I've got cancer. Prostate. It's spreading, the doctors tell me I don't have long to go.'

Stone blurted the words as if a dam had been broken. He could no longer hold it back and he looked at Claire, uncertain if he should have told her.

A frown immediately spread over Claire's face. Her intuition had told her there was something wrong just as soon as he surprised her when he walked into the small cabin at Arrow Hall. His face was gaunt; his arms were loose in his jacket; and he had an ashen colour to his skin which was still there as she looked at him today.

'That's awful, Harry. How long have you had that?'

'Don't know. Probably some time. It's eating up my bones, spreading around; it wasn't caught early enough.'

'That surely changes everything. Why on earth are you chasing such a grand property as Marine House?' Claire asked.

'It'll be my one last big deal. I'll be around long enough to see it remade into fancy apartments and then I need somewhere to live. So why not?' Stone said.

There was a pause as Stone sat on the chaise longue. He closed his eyes and Claire saw the pain being etched into his face.

'Show me quickly round this big house, so I know where I am next time I come to look through your papers for you.'

Stone took Claire into a dining room, into the kitchen and three of the other rooms on the ground floor. Upstairs, he quickly showed her his bedroom opening onto a balcony with views across to the sea, and he then led her into the study.

Claire frowned at the piles of paper littered around the room. Tidying this was not something she was going to do; she had done it before for Harry Stone and never again. But Claire saw how big Marine House was. And with all its chintzy Regency furniture, there was nowhere she had seen that looked easy to live in. This was not Harry Stone as she had known him, and it left Claire still unsure of the motive he had for buying this huge mansion and why he was in such a hurry to do it.

'How are you being looked after in your illness? Who comes in to help you?'

'I haven't made any arrangements yet. But I'm never going into hospital. I get medication from the consultant I see at the urology clinic in London. The rest I'll take as it comes,' Stone said.

Claire had seen enough. Stone did not look well – he moved slowly, and his voice was flat. It was time to go. This visit was not what she had expected, though. Nobody ever got close to Harry Stone. Claire was no exception. But she felt him looking at her with almost pleading in his eyes. Was this a time when he would want her to know what he truly thought each day?

'Call in again soon, and have this key so you can feel at home here. And will you visit the Jackson family tomorrow? You know what to say; you know what I want. Any of the technical stuff about buying the place is in this envelope,' Stone said.

'Yes, I'll call on them. But from what you've told me, don't expect answers.'

As Claire said goodbye, she felt his stare, and she walked quickly from the elegant Regency sitting room. Closing the back door noisily so he would hear, Claire did not look back. The garage at the rear of Marine House was dark and gloomy, and Claire sat in her car for many minutes. She suddenly had the overwhelming feeling of being squashed in the middle of the sinister problems developing with James at Arrow Hall, leaving Rick and Harry Stone a pitiable sight, sitting alone, lonely in Marine House.

On her drive back to London, Claire was tense, stunned by the dire news she had just heard from Harry Stone. Calling on Brighton again would be hard. All that had once seemed certain in her life was now evaporating as easily as an early morning mist. Claire doubted that tomorrow, a new day, would be any better.

52

In the morning, Claire woke early. She quickly came to. The ambulance, lights flashing as it drove away, Claire had not dared to watch, and the memory was still too vivid. Sitting at the kitchen table, Claire phoned the hospital. James was receiving attention for a broken right leg, several broken ribs and smashed right arm from his shoulder and a gash in his back. But he also had a more serious head injury. There was a bleed on the left side of his brain which had shown up on a scan, and that would need emergency surgery.

That was the stark message – his injuries were serious. And it left Claire with the certainty that sitting at the bedside of James in hospital was not something she could face. It would raise her antagonism against him to a new level. Scraping the money back that had been raked off came first, and then the time would come to silence his aggression for good.

Her phone rang as she was preparing to have a bath. Sitting on the end of the bed at that moment, Claire was not sure she wanted to answer it. But after thirty seconds, she gave in. She stood, walked to the window and thumbed it on. There was no "hello", just a burst of words.

'What on earth's going on?' Rick asked.

Claire felt her arm tremble and she held the phone away from her ear. Rick's voice was sharp.

'You know James, you brought him on the site, news from the hospital is he's lucky to be alive,' was all Claire could say.

'How can this suddenly flare up? Most contractors and tradespeople around the site just want to get on with their work; goodness knows we're paying enough for it. Hope you're being serious about rebuilding Arrow Hall.'

'I stood and watched James's aggression flare, not for the first time. He's gone, and I don't ever expect him to come back. And I'm going to take a few days off from the site,' Claire said.

'How long will James be in hospital?'

'He's not good, surgery for bleed on the brain, broken bones – it's too early to know.'

'I don't think you should be staying away from Arrow Hall at this time. It's already a high-cost building, and where's that going to end?'

'Lay off please, Rick. I've spent a lot of time on the site getting the building to where it is. I've dealt with testy planners, architects who think they know it all and I've been controlling James. His arrogance alone put him in hospital. I didn't; he did it himself,' Claire said.

Claire was now seething; her arm was shaking; and her voice was rising to a level which was very unusual for her.

'I'm having to spend a lot more money than I expected to complete the wine estate down here. And that's going to make a difference how much I'm going to lay out for Arrow Hall. I now urgently need the update on exactly what has been spent and what's still to be done to finish it all off and what the new completion date will be.'

'I can't do that without James; I've pressed him twice but he was not cooperating, just dodging away from every question. And now you know where he'll be for several weeks. And I've tried to tell you, if only you would listen, that because of James, there's some fraudulent and forged invoices, overpayments, accounts paid twice. Getting the money back is not going to be so easy.'

'Rebuilding Arrow Hall is running away from you all. And how's it all going to work while James is in hospital and you're taking a rest from the place?'

'I'll talk to each of the builders, and they've all got my phone number. I can be back in an hour if I need to, but the site'll run on for a few more days, and more easily without James,' Claire replied.

'You know what I'm feeling about it all; you know the money is tight. And I gave you Arrow Hall to rebuild but I didn't think it would turn like this. But I'm in a hurry now; I'll have to go. I'll call again soon to get an update.'

Rick's voice was distant and, as ever these days, his time was short.

Holding the phone from her ear, Claire pressed it off and sat on the edge of the bath. She felt the cold distance that had been growing between them. This was not how she had ever talked with Rick in the past. Perhaps those days were gone. Forever. What had come between them to make that happen she was not sure. But it left Claire very unsettled; she did not like it.

Living in her own flat, this confined space, and spending time in Brighton with Harry Stone – how could she ever tell Rick about that?

53

After Rick's early call, Claire tried to calm down. She was in a cold place. Rick's interest in Arrow Hall was hanging by a thread. In the quietness and confined space of her new flat, Claire quickly drank two cups of dark coffee and nibbled at a croissant. Wherever Arrow Hall was going, killing off the fraud on the site and the people dealing in it was becoming urgent.

But today she had agreed to face up to Lady Ruth Jackson. Later that morning, she scanned the few papers Stone had given to her about Marine House, this large, seafront mansion, and she was unsure how easily Lady Ruth would meet her. Dressing smartly, she took her time in front of the mirror; she had to feel right, but her confidence was always there, having met many antagonistic, even plain rude and shifty, characters. She had tidied up many messy deals for Harry Stone and Rick. And what made it easier today, tempting her to this meeting, was a tinge of curiosity about the titled Jackson family.

The distance from her new flat to the Mayfair house of Lady Ruth Jackson was only a couple of miles, and to unwind further from the dark and devious legacy with James and Arrow Hall, Claire decided to walk to the meeting.

Claire was shown to the same third-floor room, just as Stone had been. As she was staring at the full-length portrait on the wall, the door noisily opened. A woman, who had grey hair and who was very upright, as if she was facing up to someone she did not like, came in. She was followed by a man some years younger.

Claire knew who they were. But, in these very formal, unsmiling surroundings, talking about Harry Stone's future was very unreal.

'Please sit down,' the woman said, pulling her own chair noisily from the table.

'This is my mother, Lady Ruth Jackson. I'm her son, Josh.' The man spoke quickly as soon as they were seated.

'I'm pleased to see that Mr Stone is not with you. I had told him last time he so rudely stalked out of this room that we would not sell Marine House to him. That hasn't changed. We wouldn't want to be accepting laundered money in payment for that lovely property. But there's more than that. I hear from the letting agent that he intends to sit there after lease end for as long as he likes. Well, we'll see about that. And now I want the strongest message taken back to him that we will have him evicted very quickly, and I will hound him for trespass and costs until my property is restored to me in good order and with vacant possession.' There was a pause as Lady Ruth looked at Claire. 'So, after that, what have you come to say that won't waste our time?' Lady Ruth asked, eyeing Claire closely.

'I will pass your message back to Mr Stone, but I'm sure he already knows what he can legally do. May I move on, because his interest in buying is still there. I can confirm he has the money, it's all ready to pay, he does not need to borrow anything, and he can move very quickly to finalise a contract. And he will not only pay all rent due to lease end, but he will also be ready to pay rent right up until completion if that runs beyond lease end,' Claire said in one breath.

'Why does a well-spoken, nice-looking lady like you get to do business with a man like Harry Stone? He's rough, and he's vulgar; he has no manners. So, where do you fit in? But I haven't asked your name yet,' Lady Ruth said, suddenly remembering her omission.

'Claire, Claire Watts. I've known Mr Stone for some time – I've kept his business affairs tidy for him, and he's asked me to help him with everything at lease end with Marine House.'

'So, where's he got the money? Where does a man like Stone

suddenly find £2.5 million? Honest money I mean, not from some laundering scam.' Lady Ruth asked.

'Let me be firm, please, in saying that Mr Stone has the money. I am collecting all his investments into his one London bank. The price will be ready to pay over as soon as a deed of sale can be signed,' Claire said, slightly raising her voice.

'Coming from you, Claire, I perhaps can convince myself to believe that.'

'Thank you, and I hope that gives you confidence to reconsider his offer to buy the property.'

'I'm still worried about that man's consorting with criminals. The raid on Marine House was in all the papers, you know. So, don't get too close, Claire, would be my advice.'

'Those problems are all in the past. In all his dealings, he has never been convicted of any offences or even charged with them. Though the police visited Marine House, they found nothing to connect him to any money laundering,' Claire said, her voice again getting louder.

Josh stared at Claire, and his face was blank. It was as if he wanted to say something to her but not in front of his dominant mother. The door of the room noisily opened. A middle-aged woman entered. Her hair was windblown, untidy and her round face showed a pout at her mouth. She gave Claire a sullen look and then moved towards Lady Ruth, who had slumped back in her chair. Lady Ruth put her hand up to halt the intruder.

'Mother, I don't know who this woman is, but this meeting has got to stop. And I will deal with Marine House my way and only when I'm ready,' she said.

The intruder was talking very loudly; it surprised Claire, and she sat more upright in her chair. She looked at Lady Ruth, who had closed her eyes. The meeting had lasted less than ten minutes but was now finished. This was a family warring with each other – Claire had often heard Stone lose his temper, and she did not want to hear more like that today. Claire picked up her papers, and she stood to leave as the woman advanced more into the room.

'Thank you, Lady Ruth, for seeing me. I'm sorry to take your time, and I had hoped for a more positive response that I could report back to Mr Stone,' Claire said.

Lady Ruth did not reply but glared at her daughter. Josh, the son, said nothing but looked angry at the interruption from his sister. And without looking at Lady Ruth, Claire left the room. As she was starting down the circular stairs to the front door, Lady Ruth's daughter caught up with her.

'I'm Edith. Mother doesn't know how to handle these things, so anything to do with Marine House you deal with me. Tell your Mr Stone that too, please,' she said.

'I've come to find out if the offer from Mr Stone is going to proceed. And your mother was not able to give me an answer. So, if Mr Stone should only deal with you, why don't you ask your mother to confirm the position to me so that we don't waste any more time together?' Claire said.

Claire felt hostile to this very aggressive woman, and she stood square to face her.

'Here's my card – call me sometime,' Edith replied sharply.

Edith looked at Claire with eyes that glared. She did not know what to make of this well-dressed woman facing her. But Claire turned away. And as Edith stalked off noisily down the corridor, Lady Ruth called out to Claire.

'Claire, please would you come back for a few more minutes.'

As Claire turned, Lady Ruth looked directly at her as if she was seeking somebody to confide in.

'I don't normally have to apologise to anyone, but I'm sorry for this interruption. Please remember this, I own Marine House. It is mine to sell, but what you have seen is the children expecting to share in the proceeds. They're trying to jump in front of me.'

'Mr Stone knows you own it. But we do need to know who to talk to about Marine House, if only to discuss end-of-lease matters.'

'Claire, please listen to me because I am the only one who will deal with all this.' Lady Ruth paused and again looked directly at

Claire. She had more to say. 'You look like someone who understands how families work, so let me tell you, Edith is just going through a divorce. She's a bit upset at the moment. She married below herself. A man nearly twice her age, worked in the City. It fell apart last year as we all thought it would. He left her with nothing, and now I have to support her. Silly girl. But, Claire, don't take any notice of her outburst this afternoon.'

Claire listened out of politeness as Lady Ruth spoke with a tone of authority. Dealing with this disjointed family was like trying to hold a plate of jelly, and Claire could now see clearly that Stone would have been hostile to meeting with her. Lady Ruth's scorn for him would have shown too much, and he would not know how to deal with her. The daughter Edith's intrusion with a loud, booming voice was perhaps the sort of person Stone could argue and bargain with. In their loudness, they would almost respect each other.

But today's meeting had wasted valuable time. And Stone did not have much time left.

54

Once in the street outside the elegant town house in Mayfair, Claire started to walk back to her flat. The family squabbling annoyed her, and she was anxious she had not come away with something positive to take to Stone. There was a tap on Claire's shoulder. She turned quickly. Josh was standing right behind her.

'I've got something for you to give to Harry. He told me he wanted this urgently.'

Josh handed Claire a small leather bag. It was closed with a zip along the top.

'What's going on in there with your mother?' Claire asked sharply as she took the bag.

'I'll come to Brighton to talk to Harry. I can help him finish this,' Josh said with a vacant stare in his face as if he had only just met her.

'I told you at the meeting, I don't think you should come to Brighton again to see Harry. He's not too well at this time, and I will now be dealing with anything to do with Marine House. But as a family, you'd better decide what you want to do with that big place in Brighton. And then perhaps let me know, because Harry is a committed buyer.'

Still with a vacant stare, as if he was thinking of something else, Josh pointed to the bag he had just given to Claire.

'I think there's something valuable in that bag. I've been to the Caribbean to collect it for Harry.'

Claire had taken an instant dislike to Josh. His eyes and mouth were in a sneer. And this was not the place to stand to talk to him.

She left Josh standing alone and she walked quickly back to her small flat. Once inside, sitting at the bare kitchen table, Claire unzipped the bag that Josh had given to her. One small diamond fell into her hand. It was just the same size as the one Harry Stone had given to her when he surprised her calling at the Arrow Hall site. She examined it, but it meant little to her. Then she spilled into her hand one large, glinting, blue diamond. It looked very special. Just the size and sparkling colours made Claire look at it again.

What is Harry Stone going to do with these? Claire wondered. Claire called him.

'Harry, as you said before I left, a family not talking to each other. It's worse than that. It's going to be very difficult to tie that lot down; it's like a dog fight, with the puppy Josh cowering in a corner and daughter Edith showing her sharp canines and growling at her mother, the Great Dane.'

'Let 'em fight; I don't care. But, Claire, keep trying. I need this place – tell 'em again and again I'm not moving from here until I've got it.'

'They're going to hawk Marine House round the market, so I told her you've got the money and you're ready to go. I hope that is true. But what's all this about diamonds?'

'Josh owes me some. Collected from the Caribbean.'

'Yes, he gave me a bag with diamonds inside. All a bit undercover from his mother, I don't think he wanted her to see them.'

'What did he give you?'

'One small one like the one you gave me and one big, lovely glassy blue in the light.'

'Are you sure that's all you've got?'

'What are you expecting?'

'If you want to know, I was expecting Josh to thieve something. But check what's in the bag.' There was a low growl in Stone's voice.

For a moment, Claire fumbled in the zipped bag that Josh had given her just an hour ago. The contents clattered onto the kitchen tabletop.

'Only one small one and one big one. There's absolutely nothing else in the bag.'

'There should have been two shiny, polished big diamonds. Josh has already thieved £500 in notes from a bundle I asked him to deliver for me and a diamond he didn't pass to his sister. But take what you've got to my friend Sol in Hatton Garden,' Stone said.

'Why did you send him to collect from the Caribbean?'

'Claire, don't ask.'

'After the Jackson family I need some fresh air. I'll go straight away.'

'I'll tell Sol you're coming.'

After noting the directions to see Sol, a diamond dealer, Claire held the phone away. A determined tone was in Stone's voice, just as she used to hear it in Arrow Hall. His belligerence was rising, and she sensed a fight with Lady Ruth Jackson and her thieving son Josh was not far away.

The moment at the end of the lease in just three weeks' time flashed in front of her. It would not be good to watch, and until they dragged him out, Stone would just sit in Marine House and laugh at the Jackson family. And unless it could be stopped, Stone's health would drop quickly.

Claire held the large, blue, glinting diamond up to the light. It sparkled. She could become part of Stone's hostility, and there was now only one way to deal with this light-fingered son of the family.

55

Claire parked her car in the garage at the rear of Marine House, and it was gloomy in the shadow. She leant back into her car to pick up her bag, but a large hand suddenly held her arm in a pinch. Her reflex response was to scream but another heavy hand was held over her mouth. The more she struggled, the more tightly her arm was pinched.

'Do you bring money for Harry?'

'No, I don't have money. What are you after?'

'Let me look in your bag, lady.'

Claire went to close the car door, but she was roughly pulled back and her bag was grabbed from the car seat.

'I'm nothing to do with Harry, so leave me alone. Take my purse but get out of here,' Claire shouted.

Without a word the vice grip on her arm relaxed, and with one quick movement, she was thrown to the floor.

'Tell Harry I gotta have the money. Remind him twenty-five grand in readies.'

The attacker quickly left the gloomy garage space and Claire scrambled to her feet. Her bag had been thrown to the floor, still open. She quickly searched inside, and her purse was missing. Just a few notes, nothing more had been taken.

Claire was shaken. But it was now quiet, and she walked out into the warm summer air. There was nobody there; she was on her own. Walking quickly to the safety of the rear door of Marine House, she fumbled with her key and let herself in. Claire had carefully chosen her time to visit – today, Harry Stone was away in London and, alone, she could search around his large, empty home.

With tenseness in her frown, she made a coffee and stood staring through the rear door of Marine House for several minutes. The quietness of the high-ceilinged kitchen was overpowering, and she almost expected somebody to jump out on her from a cupboard. This place had a sinister feel to it. She crept slowly and warily across the hall to the Regency sitting room where the light was flooding in through the two wide balcony doors. For a moment she stood outside and breathed in the sunny air as if it was a tonic.

For the next hour she walked around Marine House, opening doors, peering into rooms, opening cupboards where the dust had settled long ago. Some of the tiny, cramped rooms on the top floor, servants' quarters, were creepy, quiet; there were too many spaces with histories of long-gone families living there. Even on a summer's day, the rooms at the rear were dark and cold. There were two staircases (one for servants), and most of the rooms were musty, with windows that surely had not been opened for many years. The grand Regency sitting room – comfortable in a formal way and now with crumpled cushions – Stone's study and bedroom, were the only spaces that she could find any trace of having been lived in.

It was easy to see how this large building could be converted into apartments. With views across to the sea, some rooms with spacious, high ceilings, momentarily the thought of living here made Claire excited. But the moment did not last. Just half an hour ago, in the dark garage, Claire had found this place was tainted by money Stone was never going to pay to extortioners, just like Arrow Hall had been.

The bell rang on the front door as Claire was gathering up her papers. The noise startled her; she walked to the video camera and saw the round face and unruly hair of Edith, the daughter of Lady Ruth. As she stared into the video again, Claire saw the same fiery red eyes, just as she had seen them jumping into a meeting in London. This was Edith's desperation; she was demanding attention.

Claire stopped and, without thinking, let the front door open. Edith almost fell into the hallway and stood glowering at Claire.

56

'Is that man Harry Stone around?' Edith asked. There was menace in her eyes and her tone was demanding. 'No, Mr Stone's in London. If you want to see him, you should have called before you came here.'

'Claire, that's who you are, isn't it? You listen to me. You tell Harry Stone that I need £75,000 and all in cash. Tell him I want it quick, a payment upfront to show that he really wants to buy Marine House. If he won't pay, I'll see he doesn't get into talking with Mother anymore and it'll be put to another buyer. There's plenty of them out there, you know.'

'Does Lady Ruth know what you're here asking for? After all, a large sum of cash upfront on a property deal is a bit unusual to say the least.' Claire's voice echoed with sarcasm.

'It's nothing to do with Mother or Josh. And anyway, Mother does what I say.'

'Where is Josh? He's walked away with a very valuable diamond, and Mr Stone's anger is growing at what is happening with Marine House.'

'Josh is nothing to do with me; that silly boy finds trouble as he runs around with his loose friends. But he won't be too far from his mother's apron strings.'

Standing in the wide hallway, Claire stared hard at Edith. Her upper lip was in a sly grin; it gave an open sneer of arrogance to Edith's face. Claire was not going to be intimidated by this woman. With her arm outstretched, Claire tried to usher Edith back to the door; she wanted her out of this place. But Edith had come for a purpose; she pushed past Claire and walked to the end of the hall.

'Where are you going?' Claire shouted to her.

'This is my house, and I shall go where I like.' Edith spat the words back.

'You shouldn't intrude and roam around the house, especially as Mr Stone's not here,' Claire said as she walked towards Edith.

'I've told you I own this house; it's mine not his.'

Edith turned away from Claire and opened the door to the Regency sitting room. She walked in quickly and closed the door behind her. It left Claire in the hall, hesitating but angry. How was she going to stop this arrogant interloper? She should tell Edith of the health condition Harry Stone faced, but she stopped. Harry Stone's illness was still private.

And there was Stone's study. Entries in diaries, emails, Panama bank accounts and diamonds from Nevis would give Edith a wide, gloating smirk on her face and the last say on Marine House if she saw all that. Claire walked quickly up the stairs, locked the open door and put the key in her pocket.

A short while later, Edith made heavy noises on the stairs walking to the top floor. Claire's anger was rising, but there would be another time and place to deal with her and the whole family. Claire had already decided where and how that would be. She let today run on. With a mug of tea, she sat in the sitting room and left the door to the hallway open. Resting on the edge of the chaise longue near the window, vacantly she stared towards the sea. But there was the clamour of doors opening and closing and then heavy footsteps on the stairs.

A few minutes later Edith came back into the hallway. She had a half smile on her face; she looked satisfied. Under her arm she carried a small frame, but she held it away from Claire.

'What have you got there?' Claire asked.

'Just an old picture. Not valuable. It's something I remember being in the house. I liked it so much, so I'm taking it with me.'

'Let me see it,' Claire asked.

Edith half turned the picture to Claire. It was a small oil painting, a scene which looked like the grand canal of Venice.

'You need to ask Mr Stone before you take that.'

'I doubt he even knew it was there going by all the dust on it. But you can tell him it's mine now if you like.'

'It is still part of the house, and you have no right to take it. Don't think you can harass Mr Stone like this; I can tell you now, it won't work,' Claire said.

'Well, we'll see. But let's meet again, Claire. Soon. And to make sure Harry gets this lovely place, make sure you bring me a large bundle of notes adding up to £75,000.'

Edith was being facetious and the arrogant smirk on her face was still there as she walked quickly to the front door with the looted picture. Was the picture valuable, too valuable to be left for Harry Stone to keep if this house was ever sold to him? Claire did not know, and she doubted Harry Stone would know either.

But Edith roaming freely around Marine House would make Stone's temper simmer. It left buying Marine House from the Jackson family like a casino with counters on the roulette table which would be lost in the turn of a wheel.

The heavy front door closed with a thud.

A few minutes later, as she locked the back door, Claire tried to calm her anger. Her call to Marine House had left a scar. This was not a place she ever wanted to come back to.

57

After visiting Harry Stone's Regency property, Claire was very tense the next morning. She walked round the small rooms of her flat and peered out of the window onto a courtyard. Her space would fit easily into two of the grand rooms in Marine House.

The bathroom in her new apartment was tiny but a shower fitted into a corner was tighter still. She stood under the spraying water for five minutes and it lifted her feeling about the place. Claire dressed slowly, and with a cup of strong coffee, her tension lowered. It was time to call the hospital where James was being looked after.

The news from the patients' information office was brief. James's condition was stable – he was now fair and still in intensive care after surgery for the bleed on his brain. He also had a broken thigh bone and his right arm had needed surgery to reset bones which had been mangled in the fall. James would not be discharged for a while yet, and it was suggested to Claire she call back in a week.

That was not what Claire wanted to hear. She wanted to see James here, now; she wanted to deal with him and squeeze every last penny from him that had flown out from Arrow Hall. As she ended the call, it left her feeling hot and frustrated.

In that angry mood, later that morning, Claire made a call to Stone.

'I was at Marine House yesterday, but I soon found you lied to me about it being clear of thugs searching for money. I was thrown to the floor and had my purse snatched. So, what's going on?'

'Claire, leave it. It's people coming out of nowhere making fancy demands. Make sure you let me know when you're calling again, and I'll make sure it's clear.'

'£25,000 a fancy demand?'

'The world's like that these days.'

Claire held her tongue. But anxiety about Stone's dealing with Marine House was rising in her.

'You'd better know what else happened when I was there. Lady Ruth's daughter, Edith, called. I opened the door, she bounced in and pushed past me, flouncing off, roaming around the house. I couldn't get rid of her for nearly an hour.'

'You didn't let her near my study, did you?' Stone asked, his usual blunt sharpness back in an instant.

'No. I locked it; she didn't get there. But she did walk out with a small oil painting. She said it was in one of the back rooms, covered in dust, and she didn't know if it was of any value,' Claire replied.

'I know exactly what it was. I was going to take it to an art dealer in London to get it valued. I'm not giving it away to her or anyone else until I've had somebody have a look at it. It stays with the house.'

'There's something else. That woman is demanding £75,000 in cash. Upfront to her. She says that'll seal Marine House; it'll show her that you're serious and that you've got the cash to complete the purchase. So, you need to make up your mind quickly, otherwise she says she's talking to other buyers. What do you want to do?'

'I'll pay her,' Stone said without hesitating.

'Can you find that sort of money? Quickly and all in notes?'

Stone paused and stared across to the sea. He had money, dirty notes stashed in a safe in his bedroom. They would cover it.

'Yeah, I've always got bits and pieces of money sitting around. But it's not to give away. Get something in writing from her.'

'I'll take it to her, and I'll call when I've fixed a date to hand it over.'

'Yeah, and when you meet her, tell her straight, unless her thieving brother Josh comes to me with a very valuable diamond he's pocketed, then the Jackson family name will be dragged right down into the dirt where it belongs. I've got a buyer for that diamond. It's big money. That lot are as slimy as rancid butter. Probably smell as bad too,' Stone said.

Finishing the call, Claire felt the enmity that was growing inside Harry Stone. But she had her own rage with that man to deal with. The bruise on her leg from the thug throwing her to the floor in his garage demanding £25,000 was turning black. And where did he find £75,000 in bank notes, as if it was waiting to be handed out as a bribe?

Running away from finishing Arrow Hall was no longer a rational choice of where she needed to be. At midday, Claire left her apartment to walk to her favourite Michelin-starred restaurant in Mayfair. She had a date for a long, late, relaxing lunch with Jennie. Harry Stone was blundering his way forward, and she was ready to admit to Jennie that she had made a big mistake talking to that man again.

58

A low mood had not left Stone that day. From the sitting room he spent some time staring across to the sea; Claire's call had been difficult. That family were devious, paying the sweetener to Edith was all just a game, but he was becoming more certain he was going to win against them. Even if he could not clear the money they were demanding for Marine House.

There was, though, another much louder ringing in his ears. The demand from Xavier for £25,000 in notes. Just to keep his gang of druggies and extortionists at bay and to buy precious information to make Marine House his. He searched along the road and across to the sea, but he saw no hooded druggie with a grey wispy beard lurking around the place. Their confining closeness was an invisible iron ring around Marine House, and now Claire had felt their brute force.

But to get Marine House he needed another big insider deal from Xavier. It left him inevitably being drawn, sucked into the eddy of a whirlpool that spewed out money.

Stone poured a whisky and slumped onto the cushions of a sofa. He momentarily closed his eyes and was interrupted as his phone buzzed. It was his diamond dealing friend, Sol.

'Harry, I had a visit the other day from an attractive lady, says her name's Claire. And she's brought me another beautiful diamond. I hope you've got these stones insured. A lady walking around London with some valuable jewels in her bag is a sitting duck. I put her back in a taxi to her apartment, but tell her to take care, Harry. You never know who's out there picking off people like your nice lady.'

'What's the price, what do you give me for it?'

'Ninety grand. How does that sound?'

'That sounds right on, Sol.'

'How do you want it, cash to your banks, money in your hand?'

'I need some notes. Can you do me twenty-five grand in Bobby Moores? I'll come in the next couple of days to collect them. The balance, pay into my five bank accounts. Split it up and make it all look like normal money flowing.'

As he said it, Stone sat more upright on the sofa. The cockney slang for that bundle of notes for a moment lifted him. They would be his insurance to clear the heroin and narcotics dealers that he saw circling around Marine House.

'I'll get that for you, but come and see me soon,' Sol said.

'I've got three laboratory grading certificates. Came the other day. But tell me, Sol, if a diamond is lost, could it be sold without those bits of paper?'

'Doubtful if it's been engraved with its own number. But you could find a cutter, pay enough and the diamond could be sliced up into smaller pieces. Then they would be sold on, no trouble.' Sol laughed. He had been there himself before.

'Thanks. There's one more big diamond still to come, and it'll be with you very soon. Okay?'

'My Russian friend tells me he'll be in London in two weeks' time and that big-carat diamond he'd like to handle and take back with him. When can you get it to me?'

Stone hesitated. Where was that little man Josh?

'Claire's collecting it. It'll be a day or two,' Stone replied.

It was from this top price from Sol of his big-carat diamond that Stone thought he had earned another glass of whisky. Without the pain still nagging in his lower back, he would have gone straight to London, to the Mayfair house, and confronted Lady Ruth about her son with the sticky fingers stealing his valuable diamond. He went to his study and totted up his money; he was still over £80,000 short. Today he would keep his final card on the table; he would let them sink further before dealing it.

And as he sipped from his whiskey, he could not know how Claire would artfully intimidate this family to do that dirty work for him.

59

Claire watched as the locksmith removed the two padlocks on the large, industrial gates at the entrance to the site. He gave her two sets of keys to the new locks.

As they walked towards the cabin that was the site office, Claire again felt how this place was unfinished business. And now it was eerily quiet, just as it had been when a wide-shouldered man with a wispy grey beard had asked Claire where to find Harry Stone.

'I hope you don't keep anything valuable in there,' the locksmith said.

'No, just a few bills to pay, plans, nothing else,' Claire replied.

'These places are too easy to get into, doesn't matter how many locks on the door, somebody with a large axe can easily smash their way in.'

The lock in the door was quickly drilled out and again the locksmith gave Claire two sets of keys to the new lock. Now satisfied with the new security on the vacant site, Claire cleared all drawings and three files that James had left and put them in the boot of her car.

The whole site was now hers to control, and she was not going to let James smear her dream of once again living in Arrow Hall. The punch-up, with a flash of a blade that sent James to intensive care, was only delaying the big fight looming when she finally got rid of him.

60

As Claire was closing the lock on the cabin door, a large four-by-four with mud spattered over its windscreen and sides drew onto the site.

'Hi, are you Claire Watts?' the driver shouted even before the car had stopped.

'Yes,' Claire replied.

'I've had a call from Rick. He tells me you're his partner.'

Claire nodded. 'I'm locking up. I have to be away. So, what's this about?'

'Rick tells me there's some problems around this place. The surveyor supervising the building has had an accident. He wants me to run through the place and let him know how much and how long it'll take to get the site finished.'

'I'm doing that. I'm working on it,' Claire replied, feeling tension in her face rise.

'Just give me a list of the contractors and tradesmen you've been using, together with a detailed schedule of the work done and what you've paid out so far. And then I'll get on with it. Oh, yes, before I forget, can you give me the keys to this place so I can come and go as I need to?'

'Rick's said nothing about this to me.'

'He called to say it was urgent – he needs my report by the end of next week.'

Claire was by now feeling belligerent at this intrusion on what she was doing. Harry Stone and James was enough to deal with and she did not want anyone looking at the costs she had paid out until she had got back every penny that had been creamed off.

'Please leave the site until I've talked to Rick.'

Claire spoke sharply. She got into her car and drove to the large, industrial gates at the entrance. She was going to close them, lock them with the new set of keys, keep everybody out until she was ready. She knew that time may never come.

The visitor drew alongside Claire.

'Don't waste my time, Claire. My time's expensive and Rick's paying.'

He drove off noisily at speed.

It was still early in the morning, sitting in her car, that Claire called Rick. It would be late evening where he was, but it was becoming vital that they talk. Her call rang for a minute but there was no answer, not even voicemail inviting a message to be left. Rick was not answering texts, she was not sure he was even receiving them, so she sent an email.

Rick,

What's going on? Why didn't you tell me that you had asked another surveyor to come into Arrow Hall? I'm sorting the money, so leave me to finish what I've already started.

Claire

It was blunt, terse; it was how she felt. She reread it once again, prodded the send button and it was gone. She breathed out heavily. £120,000 worth of fraud money was missing. Where was that money now? To be sure that Arrow Hall would one day soon be finished, Claire felt the growing pressure to trace it to every last penny.

Claire threw the new keys to the site onto the car seat. Her fury was bubbling – nobody was going to push her around as if she was incapable of dealing with this corruption.

61

Josh arrived in Bangkok in the evening just as it was getting dark. For the flight he had booked himself into an executive seat. He had paid for it on his mother's travel account with an agent in Cambridge. He did not expect his mother to check on the account any time soon, and his trip could then be kept just to himself. Sitting comfortably on the flight, he took his time on his phone to search for the likely addresses where he could spend his short time there.

He kept off alcohol, ate all that was offered on the long flight and drank plenty of water. He took a taxi into the centre of the city; his briefcase was light – he had brought no papers – but he did have a large diamond in a pocket in the side. He was over dressed for the humid heat that hit him.

The window of the first address he had was glinting full of shining jewellery, many pieces with diamonds embedded boldly in them. Rings, necklaces, earrings, and he even saw a watch with more diamonds than bezel face, were stretched across the brightly lit window. He walked in slowly; the lights were very bright; the shop had other people browsing; and he noticed several security cameras in the ceiling of the shop. His mother had told him to show confidence in whatever he was doing, "look people in the eye and don't stutter", but this evening he didn't feel able to rise to that in these foreign places.

An older man with short grey hair approached him. 'Can I help you, sir?'

'I see you have some very nice pieces of jewellery in your window, but what I am looking for is to trade a diamond.'

'Yes, sir. We do trade. And are you looking to buy or sell?'

'I have a big-carat stone for sale.'

Josh felt uneasy. He did not know how to do this, and he was sweating under the bright lights of the shop. He fumbled with his briefcase. He brought out the large diamond that he had carried from Nevis and held it in the palm of his hand. The assistant, or more likely the owner of the business, Josh thought, peered at it closely across the display cabinet.

'May I hold it?' he asked.

Josh passed it to him and watched the face of the elderly man. He weighed it in his hand and studied it closely.

'I see it has an identity number engraved. So do you have the laboratory certification papers to go with it?'

Josh felt the gaze of the man standing opposite. His ignorance was being exposed.

'No. I don't carry it with me. For security reasons, you understand,' he added but did not know why.

'It's heavy; it's finely cut with nice colour and clarity – it's a very nice stone.' He paused and looked at Josh. 'But we could not discuss a possible purchase without seeing the laboratory certificate of grading and authenticity.'

The man handed the diamond back to Josh and turned away. Josh could read the signs about this man's face. He had no interest in talking to Josh further. Josh kept his briefcase shut and placed the diamond in his pocket. He left the premises quickly and he was breathing heavily as he entered the humid heat of the noisy, evening time street.

He had a similar experience in another shop in a large shopping centre. He was not being taken seriously, and he wandered aimlessly through two very busy roads, with the smell of food wafting closely in the air. It made him feel hungry. It was then that he saw a brightly lit sign to a gem factory. Inside it was milling with tourists, but it was air-conditioned, and Josh welcomed the coolness of the place. He walked slowly round the large space; he stopped and looked at a row of benches where experts were making jewellery from rings to necklaces. He stopped and browsed at a counter with diamond rings in brightly lit showcases.

He was showing interest and a smart Thai man with a buttonhole approached him.

'I'm looking to sell this diamond,' Josh said.

He showed the rough, uncut, small diamond that Stone had given to him in the Reform Club for his sister. It had no markings on any of the facets and he just hoped he would not be asked about a certificate. The man took the diamond and examined it under a magnified light for a minute. He weighed it and again studied it closely.

'$500. That's all I can give you,' he replied at last.

Josh did not know what to say; he thought it would have been worth more than that. His memory told him Harry Stone had said in the Reform Club a few thousand sterling. But Josh hesitated no more.

'I'll take it. In dollar bills please.'

Josh now knew he had enough for a hotel for the night and he would get the first flight back tomorrow. He was sweating heavily; he was very uneasy. He had a large diamond still in his pocket. It was to pay the £100,000 that he thought Stone had promised him for getting the Marine House deal. And he had hoped to take a cut from selling that diamond, but now how would he tell Harry Stone where he had been? Or his mother?

There was also the small matter to explain of what had happened to the diamond that should have been given to his sister, the one he had now sold for a song in Bangkok.

Josh thought he could ride this out like he always did, but he could never have known that he was soon to be found out in front of the family.

62

'Claire, what's going on? I've had a message from my surveyor, Tom Hardman. He says that you wouldn't cooperate with him on site. And your email was a bit sharp.'

'I'm surprised you've decided you've now got the time just to call and ask what is going on.'

'Claire, please, I'm extremely busy down here and I do need to know how Arrow Hall stands. I haven't got a bottomless purse to throw at it.'

'First, I seem to remember I was going to sort out the money. Don't you think I can do that?'

There was silence for several seconds before Claire continued.

'And it would at least have been courteous if you had taken the trouble to talk to me before sending somebody to see what the state of the place is.'

'Don't sound so angry; you don't need to.'

'I've changed all the locks on the site and told that very officious man not to come back until I call him. And I'm not going to do that until I've cleared up a nasty fraud run by James who you appointed. Remember him?' Claire's sarcasm was spoken forcefully.

'Where is James?'

'I'm glad you ask. He's in hospital still. Emergency operation on his brain. The site is empty and today I'm the only person who can change that.'

'I want you to let Tom Hardman back on the site. Tom's the right person to dig all this out for me. I hope you understand this is all very urgent. So please cooperate with him so it can all be finished.'

'Not yet, Rick. I know what you want, and I'll get all the costs sorted and detailed lists of what is still to be finished in the building and gardens. But I'm not going back to the site at least until I have dealt with James. That won't be until he is discharged from hospital, and I can promise you won't see him again after I've told him how close he's come to being shoved into jail.'

'This all sounds a nasty mess with Arrow Hall running out of control.'

'If you had taken time out to listen to me, this wouldn't be happening.'

There was an audible sigh from Rick.

'I'm meeting some more people from the wine estate who have just arrived. We'll speak again soon. Give me a call, Claire, before you go to bed tonight.'

'I suggest we leave everything now until you return to London. You let me know when and I'll be ready.'

There was a sharp and demanding tone from Claire which she had never used when talking to Rick before. But she was digging her foot deeper into the just open door of Arrow Hall, and she was not going to let it close on her easily. Claire was tense and the call ended, leaving her very irate.

63

The previous night Stone had rested well; he was not sure why, but it left him feeling more positive than he had done for a while. He had taken a large dose of diamorphine and the pain in his right hip was subsiding. As he was pouring his first whisky of the day, he was interrupted by a long ring on the front doorbell. Swearing loudly, he walked into the hallway.

In the video to the front door, he saw Xavier's heavy. The same thug with a large face, wispy grey beard and wide shoulders who was always lurking around Marine House as if he had nowhere else to go. Just the sight of this gangster made Stone wary; it raised his hackles – he immediately became irritable. He called into the speaker.

'Clear right off, right out of my sight, before I call the cops.'

'I got a message for you, Harry. Can I come in?'

'No. You stay right there where I can see you.'

'Listen then. You owe Mr Xavier money. Big money. And to start you gotta find £25,000 in notes, like quick. That's to show you want to be friends. And I'm here; I've come to collect it. So where is it?'

'You tell that thug he's getting no money from me, so get off my steps.'

'Now just think hard, Harry, before someone gets right up close when you're not watching. One of the boys on the street will visit with sharp knives, meat choppers, and they'll work on you so that you don't forget the money you owe. So just twenty-five grand is what I need to start it running, and I want it now. So which way, Harry?'

'I don't listen to crass threats,' Stone said.

'One day soon this bit of wood that is a door won't separate us; we'll both be close together and you won't like that – you'd prefer a picnic in the sun over on the beachside of the road.'

'Clear off back to your squat.'

There was a pause as Stone heard the minder laugh.

'Well listen to this, matey. I've got another important message for you from the man himself. Xavier wants to see you. He needs to talk to you, privately, says it's urgent.'

'Has he been let out?'

'Not yet, but soon. His phone's been taken away again.'

'So, where does he think we're going to meet?'

'Belmarsh.'

'Me visit Belmarsh? Do you think I'm going there? That's a sinkhole I'll keep clear of,' Stone replied.

'Harry, you need to go to see him. Don't argue – do it.'

'No. What's he after?' Stone asked.

'The time is fixed. 10.30 in the morning. That's next Wednesday.'

'Tell him, no. Visiting that place is too dangerous. I've never been in a jail, and I'm not going to find out the smell of it any time now.'

'Let me remind you how it is. The quarter million you owe is now getting too hot, and twenty-five grand in notes to show us you're not running away from your debt, will keep you safe. Just for a few quiet days. And you won't forget Xavier needs some personal words with you, like looking right up close into your face. Nobody else to hear. And before I forget, there's a bonus for you, Harry. He says to tell you one last big deal coming soon. But you don't get in on it unless you cough up twenty-five grand and then sit right in front of him. Belmarsh next Wednesday.'

The noise was sharp – it was a heavy kick at the front door of Marine House. Stone stood back and then watched through the video link as Xavier's minder glared closely, silently, into the camera for half a minute. Stone saw the squint from his forehead and the whites of his eyes; he closed the camera and heard the clatter as he quickly walked back down the steps.

Inside the walls of a prison was a space Stone had never seen before – he had never been taken into one; he had never dealt that far on the edge. Stone had always kept his distance from the physical, raw stuff of enforcers, and he had no doubt that Xavier would be just as lethal when he came out in three years' time as the day he was taken in.

Slouching back into the sitting room, Stone did his usual thing when confronted with something he immediately did not know how to deal with. He poured another whisky from a carafe and sank into a deep sofa facing the balcony windows.

There was £25,000 to collect from Sol. Stone was realistic that it would never clear these thugs away, but would it buy him the secrets of another big insider deal? There was, though, the nasty thought of penetrating inside the high walls of HMP Belmarsh to get at it. It made his heart beat quicker.

64

Claire parked in the garage behind Marine House, and she hesitated. It was gloomy; she was wary. This was not a place she could ever feel safe in, and she walked quickly to the back door.

Stone was sitting in the kitchen as Claire entered. He looked frail – his lithe build was diminishing; his hair was uncombed, it needed trimming; and his face was gaunt with a hint he had not shaved for a few days. Claire could not see any trace of food on the table or that he was eating properly; he was drinking too much whisky, and Marine House, even on warm days like today, was cold. Stone had a mug of coffee in his hand, and he looked up. He squirmed in his chair to get comfortable.

'I've got a lot of pain in my right hip and back today. I don't feel good.'

Harry Stone's blunt words bothered Claire. She stood, uncertain, by the door.

'You should surely go to the hospice? Just some respite care. Would you like me to arrange it?'

'No, this is where I'm staying.'

'But do you really need this big house? And you'll only be comfortable here if you get a lot of help.'

'Housekeeping for Marine House is all I'll need. Laundry, somebody to go buy another bottle of whisky. And I'm never going into a hospital or anywhere else like that. The smell of the places put me off. And nobody out there is going to tell me what to do,' Stone said.

'You must listen to your doctors. They know how to deal with your illness.'

'Let's move on, Claire. I've put seventy-five grand in £20 notes in there.'

Stone pointed to a holdall bag on the kitchen table. It was heavy. Claire lifted it and Stone, for a moment, looked satisfied. Manipulating money was an art, still like a game to him.

'That's a lot of money. Where did you suddenly get it all from?'

'You don't need to know. But here and there. Just take it. And before you give that bag of money to that woman, I want a sheet of paper in writing and signed by her that she's had it. No unreadable squiggles but the real thing. You watch her do it. And then we deduct all this upfront stuff from the price of the deal. The daughter sounds just like her brother, grasping, wriggling idlers. I can feel it even sitting here.'

'Yes, I'll deal with that. But you decided very quickly to pay Edith what she's demanding. Are you sure you're doing the right thing here?'

'Give them enough rope and they'll hang themselves. That's why I'm letting them have some more of it.'

Claire then heard a grunt from Stone. He hesitated for a moment as he watched Claire handle the bag of money.

'Any news of that idler, Josh?' Stone asked.

'Probably still running.'

'There's a glinting diamond jewel missing. That boy has run away with £100,000 in his pocket.'

Stone clenched his fist. But his reaction was to be more subtle than that. And as Claire reached the door, Stone stood. He put his mug of coffee on a low table and took a step towards her. Claire watched as a thin smile crept over Stone's face.

'I want you to come back soon,' he said.

His snappy voice showed how very fractious he had become with the Jackson family. His innate distrust, the large bag of his money she was holding, missing precious diamonds, in all was a heady mix. Claire could see a tipping point looming in his anger towards them and, in his present state of health, he would soon erupt like a volcano letting off a lot of boiling, dangerous invective. Yes, Claire would come back soon.

Harry Stone was standing in the middle of the stark kitchen as she left. His gaunt, ashen face was a pitiable sight. Whatever he did in the last few days he had left, no money could now ever buy him extra time. Claire suddenly wanted to get away, out of Marine House.

65

In her car Claire put the bag of money out of sight. Last evening, Edith had responded to her call to meet as if she wanted to be friendly. Edith's voice was calm, slower and softer than when she had floated around Marine House. And even when she shouted with a raucous sound at her mother.

Claire was dubious about this meeting, and she drove carefully to London. As she entered the busy bar lounge of a large hotel on Park Lane, Edith was waiting for her at the entrance. She was smartly dressed in a dark business suit, and her hair was neatly combed. With little greeting they sat in a quiet corner of what was a busy space. Claire put the holdall on the floor and a waiter laid out coffee on a low table between them. Claire purposely left it to Edith to speak first.

'I've never met Harry Stone. I don't want to. Mother tells me he's very brash, vulgar, and he walked out of one of their meetings,' Edith said.

'Does that matter? He wants to buy Marine House. The Jackson family want to sell it. You wanted money upfront in notes, so here it is. And the deal now needs to be closed quickly. You do know he's not a well man, don't you?' Claire asked.

'I don't care how he is. That's nothing to do with me.'

Claire pointed to the holdall on the floor.

'I don't expect you to count it in this place but there's £75,000 in notes. And before you walk out with that money, you must write a note confirming that you've had a bag of cash from Mr

Stone totalling £75,000. And more than that, Harry Stone wants it confirmed that this upfront money is part of the price that you are asking for the sale of Marine House. It's a lot of money. It can't now just disappear into thin air. So, it's up to you and Lady Ruth to finish the deal. That is quite clear I hope,' Claire said.

'I'll send a note to Marine House when I get home, when I've counted it,' Edith said.

'I'd like to take something back with me, please.' Claire's voice was insistent.

Within a few seconds, Edith got up quickly. Her face scowled as if she was offended at what she saw as a demand inferring she was not to be trusted. Without a word, Edith stalked away with a swaggering, jaunty stride across the large room. For the next few minutes, Claire wondered why she had come here to be part of this madness, unsure where it would lead.

Five minutes later, she watched as Edith returned with a large sheet of paper. It had the hotel letterhead at the top. Edith sat down and scribbled a note, folded the paper and gave it to Claire. There was silence as Claire purposefully unfolded it, took her time to read the scrawl and, satisfied, she put it in her bag. She sat back and looked at Edith, who now had a smug grin on her face.

As Claire passed the bag to Edith, she felt conspicuous, although the lounge was too busy for anyone to be interested in looking at them. But Claire was again uncomfortable with Edith. As with her mother and brother, there was a certain conceit in expecting their demands to be met. And today the family were clashing with Harry Stone. They would soon find that he would make the money he was dangling in front of them talk loudly for him. It could be no other way with Harry Stone.

'I'll talk to Mother. She doesn't have to know about this cash yet, but I'll tell her to instruct the lawyers to get on with the Marine House agreements.'

'Mr Stone gave a small diamond to Josh; he was to give it to you. Have you had it?' Claire asked.

'Diamond? No, I've had no diamond. But that would be very like that small boy who is my brother. He thieves lots of things and we even had to bail him out a couple of years ago to prevent a prison sentence for him. You'll understand that was only to save the family name, otherwise he'd have got locked up just as he deserved.' Edith pulled the holdall up from the floor.

'Somebody needs to find your brother. He's walked away with serious money; as a family, you'll be bailing him out again soon as Harry Stone's going to start action against him by the end of the week,' Claire said.

'Don't be silly – Harry Stone won't do that while he still wants to buy Marine House from us. But, Claire, I think you and I could get along. I'd like to talk about having an apartment in Marine House if Harry Stone gets it divided up. So, can you please keep me informed of progress.'

'I did say that Mr Stone is not a well person. He has cancer, so his plans for that could take a little longer than you might think.'

Claire sat still for a minute as Edith defiantly strutted across the floor of the hotel lounge with the bag of cash. Claire had not taken to this arrogant woman. She did not work, what did she do with herself all day? Of course, she would inherit the title from her mother. Lady Edith. That did not sound real to Claire at that time as she was watching Edith take money from her family without notice. And Claire's doubts were growing that Edith was ever in control of what happened to Marine House.

Doubts, yes, but at least Claire now had Edith's own signature on a piece of hotel paper. One day it would be shown to Lady Ruth. The day of reckoning with this family was coming very soon.

66

The sharp noise of the shattering glass woke Stone. He jolted alert from his early afternoon nap in a comfortable chair in the sitting room of Marine House. Almost at his feet, there was a large brick lying amongst the splinters of glass on the carpet. He felt his heartbeat suddenly rise in his neck.

Almost in one move, he left his chair and was at the balcony doors. But the sudden jolt tore at the pain in his hip. And, yes, the man with the wispy beard was there staring at him from the pavement by the side of the road. Stone stepped back to the sitting room and picked the brick from the carpet. His impulse was to hurl it back with force against the face leering at him from below. But he stopped as the pain seared across his lower back. He sat slowly again into the chair.

It left him breathing heavily for a minute, uncertain what to do with the persistence of Xavier and his crooks surrounding Marine House. Perhaps it was time to call the cops or even arrange his own security. He knew enough people who would find great pleasure in working around such a place and dealing with the cocky arms reaching out from an inmate of HMP Belmarsh.

Heavy thuds suddenly filled the room from the front door. Stone's fury was rising. He stalked into the hall, flicked on the video camera and looked into the thin, sinister face of the man with a wispy beard staring back.

'Give me the twenty-five grand that we agreed. Where is it, Harry?'

'If you're not gone in two minutes, I get the police down. You're getting nothing from me.'

'This don't look good for you. You don't pay the debts what you owe. And the gentle tap on your window is to remind you Mr Xavier's expecting you to call on him. In his new home. Tomorrow. The time is fixed: 10.30 in the morning. For a friendly chat.'

'Tell him loud and clear I'm going nowhere near him.'

'Harsh words, Harry.'

Stone started to walk back down the hallway. His anger was rising.

'Yeah, and I hope he rots away behind those high walls,' Stone shouted over his shoulder.

'You remember the top-secret stuff, stuff he's been squeezing out for you. Stuff that could make you rich. Stuff to buy an even bigger pad than this one. What about that then, Harry?'

In the hallway, Stone reached into a cupboard and grabbed a thick cudgel that he had kept just in case somebody like Xavier with a slobbering dog got into Marine House again. But he was not up to the physical stuff. These hoodlums were younger, perhaps half his age, and fitter. He swore as the pain in his back stopped him.

Within a few seconds a heavy banging started again, noisier than last time. Stone carried the cudgel with him as he walked to the front door.

'Last chance, Harry.'

Stone heard the words just as if the door was not there.

'If you don't visit Xavier tomorrow like a good friend would then I'll be back, Harry. That's every day until you do. And I need my £100 from you for this week.'

Stone took his wallet from a back pocket and grabbed five £20 notes. He looked through the intercom at the man with the wispy beard sitting on the top step with what looked like a cigarette in his mouth. He shoved the notes through the letterbox, unsure why he was doing this, but he liked to think it would make him less vulnerable to the physical hits that would surely come.

He peered into the video camera and saw the wide back of the visitor slouch off down the front steps and across the road, carrying a sledgehammer with a long handle. A minute later, Stone opened the front door. There were deep marks where the wood had been split and on one side the frame had been badly damaged.

His rage at the intimidation from these racketeers simmered as he slumped back into a chair in the sitting room and closed his eyes. Half an hour later, with a glass of whisky in his hand, Stone gradually calmed down.

Stone was not going to let Marine House slip away from him. He was short of £80,000 and there was still the lure out there towards another money-making deal with secret information, seeping like a calm stream, flowing from HMP Belmarsh. He sipped his whisky, and he could feel his heartbeat quicken at what he might one day find if he ever went inside the high walls of HMP Belmarsh.

67

5.30, early morning just as it was getting light, Stone was up – as usual, he had not slept very much at all. Waking left him with the grim, persistent thought of HMP Belmarsh with its high walls. In his dreamlike state in the dark of the night, he was intimidated by the frightening claustrophobia in the jail, and he was there for life, never going to see the outside again.

He opened the large stand-up fridge in the kitchen. There was only enough milk for one cup of coffee, and there was a loaf of crusty bread but hardly enough butter to cover a slice from it. His appetite was waning fast, but as he looked at the empty food larder, Stone knew this was a crazy position to put himself in. He saw a half-full whisky bottle in the cupboard, and he wondered for a moment why it was there and not in the sitting room where he normally drank from it. But he had the strength to resist it. Pouring a tot this early in the day was no answer to the growing problem.

The arrangement he had with the local delicatessen to keep his larder and freezer stocked had come to a halt. He thumbed through a pile of papers on the kitchen table; he found their account of two months ago – it was still unpaid. He also found an account for the local garage which was also unpaid. Reluctantly, he admitted to himself he needed help and he needed care.

But his determination to corner Marine House was relentless. If he could not get from that racketeer, money launderer in HMP Belmarsh the leaked secrets for making money, then he would twist the arms of the Jackson family to reduce the price. He had enough on them – blackmail was the only way to bring them up short. He was even beginning to relish the thought.

Later that morning, Vlad, his driver, took him into Brighton. He called on the deli, paid their account and they agreed to come to stock his kitchen again. Next, he called on his doctor Sean where he had an appointment. He was seen promptly.

'I have all the reports from the London urology hospital, and we should discuss more treatments.'

'I'm not going to have the patience for more hospital visits,' Stone replied.

'What we are talking about won't cure your cancer, but it could keep your symptoms under control and probably prolong your life.'

'If it's chemotherapy it's still no. Going to the hospital every day for a month. Hair loss, nausea, side effects. No, not for me.'

'It's your choice, Harry, but think about it. In the meantime, to control your pain, we'll up your prescription for morphine which should make you more comfortable.'

This disease was rapidly eating away at his body. Stone knew himself that his cancer was very advanced; he knew how the pain worked in his body each day; and he knew that there was likely not much time left.

'I'm going to make arrangements for a private nurse to call, perhaps just twice a day to start with, and then see how you are in a few weeks' time. She will also be able to help with your medication.'

'Do you think I have more than a few weeks left, Sean?' Stone asked.

'The scan showed several secondaries of your cancer so now it's important to make yourself comfortable. Are you alone in that big house on the seafront?' Sean asked.

'I have a lady coming back who used to work for me, keep my deals tidy.'

For a moment Sean looked away.

'I doubt you'll feel much like doing any big business for a while. Take it slowly,' Sean replied.

Stone sat with Dr Sean for just short of an hour, and the doctor insisted the nursing agency would call later that morning. But Stone did not tell his doctor that there was only two weeks left on his lease of Marine House, buying the place had run away from him and he had no plans to move anywhere else.

As he left the surgery to walk a short distance to find a taxi to take him back to Marine House, his thoughts were taken up by the prognosis. But whatever Dr Sean said, he was still chasing big insider deals and trading diamonds with Sol. He was so lost in his own thoughts that he did not even look along the street for a shadowy figure with a wispy beard.

Outside the wide façade of this fine Regency building, there was a fresh breeze coming off the sea with imminent rain. He stood for a few minutes breathing in the air as if this was something he had just found out was an invigorating thing to do. But it was just two days ago the thug had tried to knock in the front door of Marine House and Stone stood at the bottom of the steps and saw the damage. The window still had shards of glass and rain was gusting against the curtains in the sitting room.

A side street led onto the rear of Marine House and Stone wandered slowly to the back door, an entrance he rarely used. It was cold, it never got the sun, and he fumbled for his door key. It was silent; it was quick. A heavy metal bar crashed onto Stone's right shoulder. He did not see it coming or the hooded attacker who had hit him. Stone fell into a heap against the door. He tried to look up – his eyes blanked out, and he hardly heard the shouts of the hooded face standing over him.

'Mr Xavier's very cross with you, Harry. You don't pay your debts, £25,000, due now. Remember? A gentle tap on your shoulder'll do today. But you don't do as we tell, there's more to come. Okay?'

'You trash get out of my way.' Stone tried to shout but it only came out as a whisper.

'Not so fast. You didn't go to see Xavier in his safe house in Belmarsh yesterday. So, one last chance. Tomorrow. 10.30 in the morning. You don't go, I'll be back, and you get busted. Remember that, old man?'

Blood was spurting freely from a gash on his shoulder and, waving his arm limply, Stone tried to push the hooded face away as he loomed over him. The staring eyes with a stubbly grey beard did not move. And the shouted demands rang in the air as Stone tried to stand. But he was just too fragile, and he quickly lost consciousness. He slumped like a sack of coal noisily against the rear door of Marine House.

68

Nurse Carol was on her way home after visiting a patient earlier that morning. She was driving along the seafront just two miles from Marine House when she received the message. Would you please call on an elderly man, Harry Stone, and deal with his case on an emergency basis? Dr Sean was very concerned about his patient, and he had emailed full details of his progressive illness.

It was thanks to Dr Sean's quick action that, a few minutes later, Nurse Carol saw the blue and gold sign to the side of the front door, "Marine House". Most of her patients were housebound in small, terraced houses, just a few on the outskirts of Brighton in detached houses with a garden around them. She looked at the wide façade, with its portico entrance – who was this patient who lived in this very grand property on Brighton seafront? Nurse Carol was intrigued to find out.

She parked in the road behind Marine House, and as she walked up to the back door, she thought she saw a drunk sleeping it off on the steps. At first, the nurse took little notice of a scene she had seen far too often, but as she moved closer, she stopped. It was beginning to rain heavily and the body, lying inert, with head on its chest and eyes closed, was already getting wet from the downpour. It was not a down-and-out, and she knelt to hold the man's head up. Opening his eyelids, there was a flicker which looked back at her with desperate pleading.

'What's happened?' Nurse Carol asked.

'I fell.'

Stone's head again dropped to his chest. He was drifting out of consciousness and the rain was now falling heavily on him as the nurse tried to hold his head up again. There was a trickle of blood staining through his light jacket from his right shoulder, and he did not reply as she tried to talk to him. She could only guess from the note from the doctor describing the patient that this was Harry Stone.

As if he did not know where he was, Stone opened his eyes again and immediately tried to stand up. But he was uncertain on his legs, and she held his arm as he again fell back on the step.

Carol put her cloak around his shoulders trying to shield him from the rain.

'You are Harry Stone, Dr Sean's patient in Marine House? Do you have a key so we can get you inside out of this rain?' the nurse asked.

Stone fumbled in his jacket, but he could not find the key. He was confused and it left the nurse with no option but to call for an ambulance. As she waited, she tried to talk to Stone, but he only responded with grunts, and it was a long fifteen minutes before the ambulance was at the back door of Marine House. The blue lights were flickering strongly in his eyes and Stone held his hand up.

'I don't need that help,' he said in a low growl, almost to himself.

But he did not try to stop the paramedics as they examined his crumpled body on the doorstep. They found his pulse, which was strong; they looked into his eyes, which gave a flicker back, but he put his hand up as they tried to undo his coat to inspect the obvious bloodstained wound on his shoulder. The nurse told them all she knew about his terminal illness and soon the paramedics were retrieving a stretcher from the ambulance.

Carol took her coat from Stone's shoulders and watched as he was lifted into the ambulance. Stone still had his eyes closed, and all the nurse heard, again, was a low noise as if he was trying to say something. Within a few minutes, the ambulance drew away to

A&E at the nearest hospital where he could be examined properly. This was not what the nurse had expected to find on a first visit to an ailing patient.

It was suddenly eerily quiet as Nurse Carol knocked hard on the back door to Marine House. She looked through the windows – there was no movement; no lights were on; and there was no sign of the key that Stone could not find in his pocket.

She called the doctor's surgery to leave a message. The man who lived in this grand Regency house had received a heavy blow to his shoulder; there was no smell of drink on his breath – surely this was much more than a mere fall on the back doorstep. As she walked to her car, Nurse Carol thought it would be some time before she came back.

But she was not to know what was running through Harry Stone's head at that time. That he was now going to face up to a money launderer in prison who had been taunting him with a promise of stolen, secret information that he could turn into money to buy this large property.

69

'This is Harry Stone, a sixty-four-year-old found by the care nurse lying unconscious on the back doorstep of a large house on the seafront. We understand he has other health issues than a gash to his right collarbone, but we don't have those details,' the ambulance paramedic told the A&E doctor.

Stone came round from his semi-conscious state soon after arriving in the hospital and lying on a bed in A&E.

'So, Harry, this wound to your shoulder, how did it happen?'

'I fell on the back steps to my house – it was wet – I slipped.'

The doctor looked at the nurse standing by him. They did not believe what he said – had he got concussion that was clouding his memory?

'We'll make you comfortable, do some X-rays of your shoulder and collarbone to assess the damage.'

His shoulder was throbbing with an ache, and he made a grunting noise as the nurse tried to remove his shirt which was torn into the wound. A morphine drip eased the pain as they cleaned the wound and applied a dressing. Stone soon felt much easier.

What was he doing here? What had happened? He tried to sit up from his prone position in the flat bed. But the nurse gently coaxed him to stay still until they had carried out necessary X-rays. He laid back with a sigh, his eyes now wide open and fully understanding where he was. It was then that he felt an immediate need to get out of this place. After fifteen minutes, left alone in a small, curtained-off area, Harry Stone again tried to sit up. But the porter and a nurse came to take him to X-ray and Stone reluctantly quickly slumped back in the bed.

Half an hour later he was back in A&E, and he clenched his fists and closed his eyes. The examining doctor told him that his shoulder blade was very badly bruised but not broken. He would need to rest, and it would be painful for some time. That was enough for Stone. It was all he needed to hear – he took the pain relief canula feed from his hand and tried to lower himself to the floor from the bed. But the nurse watched aghast, unsure what this patient was trying to do.

'Mr Stone, we do need to monitor you for the next few hours. You have a nasty wound on your shoulder, and you were unconscious when you came in here. Your blood pressure is racing away, so please relax and we'll do our best to make you comfortable.'

'I'm okay. Good enough to get out of here – I don't like hospitals and I'm leaving. Where is my jacket?'

Stone again felt dizzy, and he rested back on the bed. He put his head on the pillow and, for the next few minutes, heard no more than the buzz of people around him.

'Mr Stone, can you hear me?' the doctor asked.

Stone nodded and again closed his eyes.

'We've had full details of your underlying health condition from your doctor, and we think you should stay with us for the next twenty-four hours so we can make you comfortable and do a full assessment before you are discharged. We are going to transfer you to a general ward upstairs.'

His eyes were closed, and Stone took little notice of what was going on around him for the next hour. He became alert when a porter wheeled his bed to a lift and up two flights to a brightly lit ward with a flickering television high on a corner wall. He became more alert, and he again started to feel that he was being taken somewhere he had no wish to go. It was a new space; it was noisy; it was enclosing him; and he could not stop it.

The ward was small, just six beds, and he again began to feel the stabbing pain in his shoulder. Suddenly he thought he saw, as if he was next to him, the wide-shouldered hooded man who had stood over him at the back door to Marine House. But this reverie drifted away as he rested again on the soft pillow of the bed.

There were visitors sitting by two of the other patients' beds. Stone suddenly felt conspicuous; this place lacked basic privacy that Harry Stone always tried to find wherever he was. Blue curtains were drawn around his space; he was helped to take his torn shirt and trousers off and dressed in hospital pyjamas. But Stone was agitated; he closed his eyes and sank lower into the clean, white sheets of his new bed.

'Where are my clothes?' he asked when a nurse came in five minutes later just to check on him.

'In a small, curtained place just over there.'

The nurse pointed to a gap just into the corridor at the entrance to the ward. The space was open, and the curtains were not pulled across it.

'But you won't need those tonight, and we'll see in the morning how you are. Anything personal, valuable, place in the drawer by the side of your bed and please make sure you lock it.'

It was a matter-of-fact statement the nurse had probably made a few hundred times in the last few weeks alone.

He would need to visit the toilet in the night, but in this curtained-off space his privacy was gone. It was with his thoughts racing that Stone, two hours later, tried to close his eyes. He was going to blot out everything that had led him to be in this crowded, noisy place, and the heavy pain relief he had been given made that easier.

He slipped into a light sleep, and it was some four hours later that he looked at his watch. He roused himself, wondering where he was. There was just a night light in the ward, and it was 2.30 in the morning. The place was quiet except for a deep snoring sleep in the bed next to his. He tugged at the bedclothes and stood by the side of his bed. The pain in his shoulder and his back both hit him, but that is how it always had been for the past few weeks.

Irrationally, Stone now had just one intention, one way to deal with his illness. He was never going to die in a hospital. Or anywhere else except Marine House. He had growing faith that Claire would see to that for him. He walked quickly to the small, curtained place that held his clothes.

Within five minutes, Stone was dressed in his bloodstained shirt, trousers and jacket that were still damp from lying on his back doorstep. He fumbled in his jacket pocket with a torn sleeve for the key to the back door of Marine House. He held it firmly in his hand; his body was fragile, but his mood was now defiant as he walked past the empty nurses' station in the corridor at the end of the small ward. He passed nobody; there was no security presence as he walked down the two flights of stairs to the ground-floor level and followed the signs to the hospital fire exit. When he walked into the air, the rain had stopped, but his pain had increased. It was just after 3.00 in the morning, and the road was very quiet. He could not walk much further, and he sat on a bench in a park just across the road from the hospital. A startled Vlad, his driver from the local garage, answered his call five minutes later.

It was still dark when he arrived at Marine House. Without even saying goodbye to Vlad, he let himself in by the keypad on the front door and shut it securely. The house was cold, very dark and quiet; his shoulder was starting to ache with a throb. Within a few minutes, Stone was in his study and pouring a glass of malt whisky.

Time was just a blur, but when it got light, he had urgent business to attend to. And nobody was going to stop him.

70

Sitting in the kitchen, Stone sipped his whisky, but it did not taste good. He would try to sleep for a couple of hours, but persistent pain was again returning to his hip – it left his shoulder just numb. He quickly changed for bed; he threw his torn shirt into a waste bin; and as he found it impossible to settle down comfortably in the bed, he knew the night would be long. Within half an hour, he was walking around the bedroom; he walked around the sitting room, and what was left of the night passed very slowly.

It was just past seven that he began to feel restless about the unknown of what he had to do and where he was going today. In the kitchen, he started a small breakfast. Sitting in a bathrobe before his shower, almost for the first time in his life, he was suddenly feeling lonely. There was a stillness of early morning and there was no one to talk to.

He looked up to a noise at the window in the back door. He froze. There was a policeman staring back into the kitchen at him. Stone could not hide. Coffee cup in his hand, he opened the door tentatively. There were two officers, lacking in smiles this early in the day.

'Mr Stone, Harry Stone?'

'What do you want?'

'We're calling to see if you're okay. You walked out of hospital in the middle of the night and, as we're told you had been admitted as an emergency with a nasty gash to your shoulder, we thought we should call. Just to make sure everything's alright with you.'

'My shoulder's fine – I had a fall, no real damage. And I thought I would be better in my own bed, that's why I left the hospital early.'

'The hospital told us they thought your shoulder was something more than just a fall. So, is there anything more we should know about your accident?'

'No. I'm okay.' Stone spoke quickly and stared at the officers as he took a step back into the kitchen.

'The hospital would like to follow you up. Your wound in your shoulder will need attention so you should call back to see them. In the meantime, we'll alert our patrols to keep an eye out on Marine House for you. We don't want you blacking out on your back doorstep again with another hospital visit, do we?'

The officers turned away. Stone felt his heartbeat quicken. One of the officers was a face he recognised. He had been part of the six-strong raid on Marine House just a year ago. What did he know that he was not saying?

Stone stared through the back door as the officers left. This was not how he had wanted to start the day, with urgent business to complete. Questions were unwelcome. Time was rapidly running out. But today he would never have a better chance to get even with the gangster who had held a snarling, slobbering dog over him in his bed just a year ago. He felt for the scar, a wound on his ankle that was written like a tattoo, deep into his skin.

71

After his shower, Stone dressed slowly; just buttoning his shirt was laborious. His shoulder was aching from the assault on his back doorstep, and a deep-black bruise was still there on his neck as he looked in the mirror. He stood on the scales and stared at the dial by his feet. Last week he had lost three pounds, and in the past month it was now seven pounds. He was becoming frail; he was feeling tired through lack of sleep leaving his hospital bed in the middle of the night, but his innate antagonism was driving him to get even with this thug Xavier.

Stone finished his breakfast with his third cup of black coffee. He called Vlad. He brought the car round to the front steps of Marine House. As they drove into London, Stone wriggled in the car seat to find a comfortable position. His patience getting shorter by the mid-morning, Stone was braced to face up to this visit.

But it was difficult not to be intimidated as he saw the high, brown brick façade of the building that was HMP Belmarsh. The visitor entrance in a side street, where there was already a queue, mainly of women and some with young children, left Stone's tension rising. He had to get this over – he joined the slow-moving queue.

Once inside, he stood at a desk with a middle-aged female prison officer.

'Your name please,' she asked without looking up.

'Stone, Harry Stone.'

The officer searched down two sheets until she found his name.

'Your ID, please,' she asked again without looking directly at Stone.

Stone handed over his passport. The officer flicked it open at the photo and for the first time looked directly at Stone's face. She looked twice at the photo and his face and then handed it back to him. He was waved forward by a large officer with a sniffer dog just as he had seen at the airport just a week back. He was then patted down.

It was over half an hour before he was directed into the visit room, his patience being stretched as the pain in his right hip from standing too long was increasing. Inside the gleamingly lit, glowing day room, it was stark, with glistening paint on the walls; it even had its own clinical smell of humanity. The place was full, with a cacophony of sound.

For a moment, he had to stand in the growing noise. He leant against a wall. Across to the far corner of this wide, lofty, noisy meeting room, he suddenly saw the large face of Xavier with his round, wide head, completely bald, shining as if it was newly polished. The ripples in his neck were still there and visible. This intimidating image had not grown older.

Stone was taken to the table with four chairs, and he sat opposite Xavier and tried to keep his arms away from the small, thick plastic space that separated them. The sweatshirt Xavier was wearing looked as if it had not been changed for at least the last year since they had met. Stone stared at the ashen pallor of Xavier's face; it told its own story of where this man had been living for some time. Stone suppressed a smile.

'Harry, my friend, it's good to see you've taken some time out to make a call on me. I like that, mate, it shows you're a true friend, shows you still got some respect.'

'I don't like the look of this place, never been in one before and I'm never coming again. So make it quick. What've you got to tell me that I'll want to listen to?'

'Relax, Harry. This is a friendly, safe house and we've got plenty of time. I've not had many visitors since I came in. Some of my mates just don't want to be seen in here. They're all hiding, keeping their faces out the way. Do you know what I mean?' Xavier laughed. But the noise was short, muffled in the growing din of the place.

'You keep your drug-filled gangsters away from me,' Stone quickly replied.

'Ssh, Harry. We've done some good deals together. Haven't I given you information and stuff that has made you rich, enough to repay everything you owe?' Xavier said as he leant closer to Stone.

Stone felt fractious; he started to get up; he was going to walk out. He suddenly knew what was biting at him. It was claustrophobia from the high walls surrounding this place. But he was here until he was allowed to go. This bright sunny day, he was incarcerated, just like Xavier, within the confined space and tight security of this place.

'No, sit down, not time to go yet, you've only just come. And we've got all day to talk.'

'Get on with it. You've already spouted enough.'

Xavier hesitated. He placed his large, clinched hands on the table. An officer was standing just a few feet away and he looked at these two men as if he was expecting trouble. Xavier knew the signal of a straightened body from the warder dangling his keys, and he took his hands off the table and folded his arms. What he had to say, the officer should not hear.

'There's a buzz around a few of the nicks. Some of the boys who were working for me when the cops intruded on our freedom are getting a bit anxious. They have no money and they're looking to do some very serious damage to you. It'll be a bit more than roughing you up on your back doorstep. So last time, Harry, you owe money, my money, quarter of a million; it's now long past paying up time, mate, and that's not a good place for you to be in.'

'Are you threatening me? Right inside this jailhouse?'

'No, Harry. That's not what I do to friends.' Xavier's sarcasm was again said with a smile over his wide face.

'How many times. I owe nothing.' Stone spat the words.

'That's not good for you, Harry.'

Again, Xavier paused. He took his time to pull his large, obese body upright. The warder close by looked straight back at him.

'Now you listen to this. I've got a bunch of officious bloodsuckers pressing me to tell 'em where I got my cash invested. Proceeds of crime is what they call my money. Nasty, eh?'

'I don't want to hear any more of your drivel. You deserve what you get.'

'Harry, please. The only money I have is my hard-earned savings. But these proceeds of crime people think I pinched my money from somewhere. Stole it in some dirty drugs dealing. These bean counter plods have been right in here in my new home to question me. And do you know what? They threaten to double my time inside this pokey if I don't tell 'em exactly what they think I've got. Like where it's hidden in some offshore place I've never even heard of. Then they want to snatch it from me. I don't know about you, Harry, but I call that sort of deal stealing. Yeah, it's ransom money, racketeering.'

Xavier's voice was full of sarcasm. He spoke in a soft torrent and Stone had to lean in to hear.

'What're you after?'

'Well, it's like this. The quarter of a million you had in crisp used notes to wash to legit money for me is part of what these proceeds of crime people are trying to get their greedy hands on. So, if they ever call, you gotta tell 'em you know nothing of it.'

'Get it out of your fat head – I've never had your quarter million; I haven't got it now, and I don't do deals with you lot of thugs trying your usual tricks of blackmail.'

'That's not very helpful, Harry. You want to get another top secret from the stock market then you remember this. They can't keep me in here forever; I'll be out one day and, Harry, I'll come to collect my money. Just like one of my boys who has just called on you in your mansion. He knocked hard on your shiny front door to collect the twenty-five grand in notes. Down payment on what you owe. But you wouldn't pay up. Right, Harry?'

Xavier paused, looked at the warder standing close by and spoke in a low whisper.

'But if you wait a minute, right inside this nick, we can do a deal. We can't shake hands in here like gents do when they agree, the screws won't like it, but just give me a nod that you won't grass on my quarter of a million if the cops call on you. You'll remember it was at 6.00 in the morning and they searched in every cupboard of your place.'

'Forget all that rubbish. I don't like this place and I'm going in two minutes if you don't give what I've come for, an insider secret I can trust.'

Stone was distracted by the noise in this hot, crowded room. He took a furtive look around and shuddered. Just being right inside HMP Belmarsh suddenly made him feel guilty. Guilty of what he was not sure. It may be that for the next few minutes he had to listen to Xavier dishing out money, just like the teller across the counter in a bank. But this time it was from a stolen source.

'You're too jumpy, Harry. You're going nowhere until we've finished our little chat.'

Ignoring the attention of the warder, Xavier leant towards Stone across the table and looked at him with unblinking eyes as if he had not seen him before. He was looking at a changed man since they last met, someone who was now only a shadow of himself. It was age taking its toll, he thought. And for once, Xavier was not sure of Harry Stone.

'My mate in here, who has some friends who live in those high buildings round the stock market, 'll be let out soon, and he's leaving this big goodbye present.'

'The dirty hands of your money launderers and sharks'll be all over it; I'll need to double-check it before I touch it,' Stone said, keeping his voice low.

Xavier had a pleading look in his closed eyes as he sat back in his chair and again folded his bare, hairy arms.

'Well, right, now you listen, Harry. You remember calling on me in my luxury pad in the East End a year ago? I've a lady living in looking after it for me, lovely Lynda, and I want you to call again but this time with twenty-five grand in notes what you owe. She'll be looking forward to your visit; she'll give you a cup of tea for your troubles.'

'That squat of yours in the East End is a grimy place, stinks of dogs. And that's the last place I'm ever going near.'

'Don't get personal, and some advice, matey: think hard. Because it's like this. You don't look the kind of man who'll want to miss out on this last big mega deal, and what I hear is that it's really big. But, last time, Harry, you first take a bag of twenty pounders to the East End for me.'

'You're where you belong, you fat bit of scum. I've wasted my time coming in here and I don't care what you and your lot of thieves want. You're getting nothing, and I'll tell the cops when they call all about your sordid life.'

Stone was getting anxious; this is not what he had come to listen to and he could feel the tension in his back and shoulder. He was unnerved, sitting tethered to a plastic chair in this prison. But he pushed his seat aside and it fell back. His fists were clenched, and in one quick movement, he leant towards Xavier and landed his right fist hard on his wide, red nose.

'That's for your venomous thug trying to frighten me with an iron bar and futile threats on my own back doorstep. You now keep them away.'

Blood immediately spurted on Xavier's face. He tumbled back into his chair and fell to the floor. He let out a low growl and glared up at Stone. His eyes were widened as if he was about to jump up and land his own bare-knuckle fist right into Stone's face. But Xavier was too heavy to get up quickly; he knelt on the floor in a praying posture before he finally climbed back into his chair.

In an instant, two warders were holding Stone's hand high behind his back. It hurt the bruise from the iron bar to his shoulder; he yelled; he tried to struggle, but it only increased the tight grip that propelled him quickly to the door of the crowded room. Another two warders were square on to Xavier. He was going nowhere and the whole large room was reduced to a hush with a low murmur of voices. And Stone felt the glare of all the eyes in the room directed at him.

But Stone was held tightly, and as he tried to turn, he was not given a chance to face Xavier. He wanted to see the blood still spurting from his face. He wanted to see the venom in his eyes. And he wanted to see that this man was now going to be restrained and returned to a small cell for the next three years.

Stone was soon facing the two warders in an empty side room. They released their grip and Stone sat in one of the two wooden chairs. For a moment it was very quiet, and he felt none of the usual tight pain over his right hip. Stone wanted out of here and quickly. He looked at the two warders, both taller than him, who were standing rock still. They were facing up to him as if he had some fight left in his clenched fists.

'It's usually Xavier who throws the punches. You're a brave man to hit him as hard as you did, sir,' the thickset warder said with a Scottish accent. We know who you are from the visitor records; you won't be allowed in here again, so we suggest you now leave in an orderly way. And if you do that, we'll take no more action against you. But I don't know about your friend Xavier. He's a man who we hear has wide contacts, and I doubt he'll soon forget this little incident.'

'Just get me out of this festering den of thieves, fast,' Stone shouted.

The warders ignored the noise from what they saw as a frail man. He was grabbed by his right arm and led to the door. He did not resist. The warders said nothing more and again Stone suddenly felt the suffocating claustrophobia of the stark, windowless brightly lit corridor. The space was very enclosed – several doors and iron-grid gates had to be unlocked to let him out, and the grip on his arm was not released until he was at the visitor entrance.

Out in the road, Stone suddenly felt good. He stood on the pavement and, for a moment, breathed in the air. There was no more pain he could feel. With blood streaming from his wide nose, Xavier was still confined securely in HMP Belmarsh. And being chased by proceeds of crime investigators for his dirty pile of money.

Stone saw this as a good day's work. But he hesitated. Should he hold back from the attraction of easy money to clear Marine House that had been dangled in front of him by this crook behind bars?

72

The pain from Stone's cancer was now stretching from his right hip into the middle of his back. The diamorphine painkillers were just dulling the growing concentration of the pain that was now coming from his bones, right inside him. And he did not know how this would progress, what was to come. It left him frightened, alone with his solitary feelings.

And there were matters to tidy up.

Even though it was a summer's day, he put a coat on, taking care not to move his bruised shoulder. He took the fast train to London, and it was then just under two hours before he walked into Sol's shop in Hatton Garden. The journey made him tired, but the greeting from Sol was, as ever, warm, and even though it was before midday, the glass of whisky in Sol's private room was nectar.

'I've come to say goodbye, Sol. My doctors are telling me I don't have much time left.'

'Harry, what's going on?'

'Cancer. It's eating away at me.'

'Are you getting the right attention? I know some good doctors; I've sold diamonds to a few.'

'Yeah, I've seen the top people. But today I'm putting my affairs in order before it's too late. And I'm dodging people knocking on my door chasing for money.'

'Harry, I hope you're not giving in to some of the underworld. There's a lot of 'em out there. I see it very often in this diamond business, where some think there's easy, anonymous money to be made. And I don't like to think anyone will ever come knocking on your door to ask where you got these beautiful, rare diamonds.'

'Yeah, let's keep it all close. These are the laboratory certificates you wanted and one last big stone I'll get to you soon. And that'll be it.'

'Don't leave it too long. My Russian contact from St Petersburg is excited at handling another big diamond if it's the same cut and clarity, and I'm meeting him at his house in Regent's Park middle of next week. It'll be worth good money, tens of thousands again.'

'Claire's onto it, and I'll have it with you soon.'

'This has been good business, Harry. And I've got the cash for you, the readies you wanted to settle the balance.'

Stone sipped at his whisky as Sol left the room. He again felt a tinge of nervousness about where he would go after saying goodbye to Sol.

Two minutes later, Sol came back, and he handed a well-worn leather bag to Stone.

'£25,000 all in twenty pounders, Bobby Moores. And be careful how you carry it, my friend.'

They enjoyed another whisky together. Their last. But the parting was quick; lingering with a long farewell was not Stone's way. Just a warm handshake between them was enough as Stone left.

Carrying the leather bag, Stone did not look conspicuous; he did not feel exposed, even coming from a diamond dealer in the heart of London's Hatton Garden. He took a taxi to the Tower of London. He looked at the Tower against a leaden sky. Of course, the Crown Jewels, with the largest diamond ever found and priceless irreplaceable other jewels, were kept there.

But where was that naïve thief Josh with his big diamond?

73

The iconic Tower of London was a place Stone knew well. It held memories that would always be with him. It was with a gang of boys when he was thirteen or fourteen years old that he would ride the Underground trains from this place. They ran bets to see how far they could ride without being stopped by a ticket inspector. Stone was proud that he had won the race many times. And today – a bumpy, noisy ride on an electric train from the Tower of London to Plaistow, a station in London's East End – brought back nostalgic thoughts. For a moment, he saw how quickly his life had passed him by from those days to a finale that would soon be upon him.

From Plaistow station it was only a short walk through familiar streets to Xavier's place in the High Road. He had been there before, two years ago, to deal with the snarling menace of Xavier and his gang of narcotics dealers. It was no more than a squat, and Stone recalled the stench and noise from two aggressive black dogs that Xavier said he kept as pets.

He climbed the twenty-eight steps of an outside concrete stairway to a flat above a charity shop. He banged his fist on the door and then stood back, not knowing what to expect. A middle-aged woman, with short hair dyed a bright pink, gave a wide smile as she opened the door. She looked at Stone for a moment as if she should know him as she did most people who knocked on her door from around this place.

'You know Xavier? Inmate in Belmarsh?' Stone asked.

'What's that to do with me?'

'He told me to call. Bring you something.'

Before Stone had finished, there was the sound of heavy feet in the hallway. The man Stone had seen before with the wispy beard and bloodshot eyes appeared.

'Lynda, leave this to me,' he said, pushing the woman back into the dark hallway. He faced up to Stone, standing squarely, staring at him. 'You brought me something, Harry?'

'Maybe. But you give me something first. Some important information Xavier said you've got for me.'

'Don't know anything about that. Xavier's inside and I look after things 'til he comes out. Won't be long now.'

'Don't try that on,' Stone said and turned, carrying the bag of notes, to walk back down the stairway. He knew how this gang of violent criminals worked.

'Give it to me; give me that bag – I want it.'

A large, wide-bladed knife was flashed in Stone's face. He vaguely saw the woman's pink hair as she yelled at the man.

'Leave him, Ash. Can't you see he's an old man?'

In one quick movement, the bag was snatched from Stone's hand, and he was pushed with force onto the narrow stairway landing. The door closed quickly behind him. Stone felt feeble; he could not resist, and he sat for a moment on the top stone stair to get his breath back. The door opened a fraction and Lynda peered at this aged visitor.

'You alright, darling?' she asked.

Stone put his head in his hands and slowly pulled himself to his feet.

'Do you want a cuppa? Or something else?'

Stone ignored her and started to walk back down the stairs. A flashing knife close to his face, which in a few seconds would have torn his cheek wide open, was too close. Quick, wild thoughts of revenge ran through his head. A lit bottle of petrol through the front door. That would teach them not to play with him.

His rage was growing, but Stone's energy wafted in the air. The last big-money deal, fed by the opium of secret insider information, was now dead. And with £25,000 snatched away, capturing Marine House would now mean turning the screw on the Jackson siblings and their stolen money. But before using that blackmail, he was going to let his lease run down; he wanted to feel the power of being a squatter.

He walked slowly two blocks from the high street until he came to a familiar space. There was a modern two-storey building standing out from the grey Victorian houses around it. It had been built in a spot where a German bomb had demolished eight terraced houses in 1942. The sign said, "Plaistow Children's Hospice". He stood and stared. £25,000 could have been well spent in that place; he would make that up to them.

Stone walked back to the station slowly. He knew he still had over £2 million in the bank; he could buy a village house close by and settle in for his final days. Comfortably, undisturbed. But that was never his plan – it was too easy, and nowhere was as grand as Marine House.

Of course, he had been naïve in trusting anything to do with this venomous gang of narcotic dealers and racketeers, with their own form of sadism. But he gloated as he remembered the blood spurting from Xavier's nose and watching him slump to his knees on the prison floor.

74

It took Stone half an hour on the Underground to get a train back to Brighton. He was feeling tired, fractious and very angry. Sitting alone in the train carriage, he knew he would never make this journey again. He was saying goodbye to the place he had grown up in as a child; the streets were still familiar, comforting even with their unchanged pattern. But his friends had moved away, and his family were no longer alive for him to call on. And with gangsters living in squats, the place had changed.

He closed his eyes and rested his head against the back of the seat, but he did not sleep. However much he wriggled, he could not find any comfort. The train to Brighton was slow, it was rocking on uneven rail, and as it swayed again, he suddenly felt the movement of somebody close to him. The carriage was empty; he stirred to sit upright and looked at the large head of a black man with red, bloodshot eyes.

'Good day, Harry,' the intruder said softly.

'What do you want?'

'I've got a message from Mr Xavier.'

'You tell Xavier to open his ears. Last time, you hoodlums get no more money from me, and if you try on your fist punching again, I'm gonna spill it all. Okay?' Stone's voice was sharp.

'No, you got it wrong – it's good news today. My mate tells me you've called on him with a gift parcel. So, I've got something important in return to give you, something promised right from Mr Xavier himself.'

'That man's a rat, stinking vermin. He's inside where he belongs.

Get out of my way.' Stone moved uneasily in his seat and the pain in his back sharpened.

The intruder leant over Stone and laughed straight into his face.

Stone tried to push him away. He looked up. He had taken enough from these criminals; he tried to stand quickly to land a punch just as he had in HMP Belmarsh. But the train rocked again, and he sprawled back onto the seat.

'Harry, don't do that. I've got a crisp sheet of paper with money written all over it. Another door for you to open to make money, that's enough to repay what you owe. Me and me mates can't wait much longer, you see.'

Again, Stone hesitated. He took the sheet of white paper and, in front of the intruder, noisily screwed it into a tight ball. He held it in his hand.

'You'd better know there's a price on your head worth ten times what I've just given you. Somebody'll be close when you're not awake. It won't be a light tap on your shoulder just outside your big house, it might just be a knife around your throat, or it could be a sharp blade stuck right into your heart. Either way, that won't be a nice feeling to wake up to.'

'Shut it. I've said get out of my way.'

Stone stood and walked to the passage in the middle of the carriage. The intruder looked at him and a hand tugged the back of his jacket. Stone tried to brush his hold off, but he couldn't move.

He flung out his arm into the staring eyes and tugged himself free. With the screwed-up ball of paper in his pocket, he walked quickly along the corridor to the next carriage where people were sitting. He found a seat and stared from the window. The low mood from earlier that morning settled back on him.

Half an hour later, as he walked up the front steps into the sanctuary of Marine House, he felt the ball of paper in his pocket. Was it a rolled-up bundle of notes to pay for the £25,000 snatched from his hand? Stone was revived with adrenalin; this game was not finished, and his judgement had been right all the time.

75

The sun was high in the sky as Claire strolled in Hyde Park for exercise and fresh air after being couped up in her small flat. She sat on a seat under a tree as horses with riders trotted by. It was a colourful scene, and it sharpened her disappointment that today would not be as she would have wanted. Today was the day that Rick had promised he would take Claire to Wimbledon. Front row seats for the ladies' final. A spectacle rounded off with strawberries and cream.

From last year, the colour of the court, the colours in the crowd, even the grunts and the closeness of the players, was still in her memory. Who won did not matter, it was just the hush during play, almost like keeping a secret, until it was let out by the roars of approval as points were won.

But Rick had forgotten. He had said nothing last time he called, and Wimbledon today for Claire, was not to be. Claire's feelings for Rick were growing colder by the day. Perhaps that was mutual.

Claire walked as far as Kensington Palace. The brightness of the day for a short while made her feel good, refreshed, confident and determined to sort out festering, outstanding, unpleasant business. The call to Lady Ruth was short but exactly as Claire had wanted it.

'I can't believe that you want to see me about anything other than Marine House; there's only one week left on the lease; I haven't had the last quarter rent yet so please make sure Mr Stone pays it before he leaves.' Lady Ruth got in first as she answered Claire's call.

'But if I find time to meet you, why don't you want Edith and Josh in this room with me? I have no secrets from them, and they are going to inherit one day.'

There was no high tone which Claire had expected from Lady Ruth.

'What I've got to say is best said to you alone, Lady Ruth. But after that I'm sure you'll want to do what is right for your family,' Claire replied.

'Very well. But I trust you will be quick and concise in what you have to tell me. So, can we say the meeting is only for twenty minutes? And at my house in Mayfair. Later this afternoon.'

Claire agreed.

It was a very hot, sultry day, and Claire would have preferred to have been out of suffocating London, maybe at Arrow Hall site or in Brighton tidying up in Stone's study. Or even, she dared to think, at Wimbledon watching the ladies' final. But for today, Claire felt good just to be able to dress for a business meeting and out of her clothes that she had worn for too long on the dirty site. Inevitably, Claire was feeling tense as she walked into Lady Ruth's bare boardroom. The air was stale, and unlike meeting with Edith, this was no comfortable five-star hotel lounge with coffee.

'Would you like some water?' Lady Ruth asked. Her voice was light, slow and showed cheerfulness, more than the last time they had met.

'Thank you, no.'

'I'm still surprised, Claire, that you are able to work for such a man as Harry Stone. He's uncouth, untutored, brash. You name it, he lacks basic human manners I look for in someone I'm about to do business with.'

'You do realise he's not a well man? He has cancer eating away at him,' Claire said.

'Whatever his health, that still doesn't excuse him. So, for a moment, we put that aside and you tell me what you have come to talk about.'

Claire hesitated. What she was about to say would not change Lady Ruth's perception of Harry Stone. It might even drag it down more. But Claire knew she would only get one chance and she was not going to let it slip away.

'First, Lady Ruth, I have to tell you I'm not here with Mr Stone's approval. I haven't even told him I'm coming to see you. But there's something important I think you should know about Marine House.'

Lady Ruth was watching Claire closely. Almost as if she was interviewing her for an important job and she was going to put Claire on the spot.

'I think we've wrapped Marine House up. We have somebody else we are about to close a deal with. They're people without all the baggage that your man Harry Stone has brought to the property. So, for one last time, there can't be much new, but I'll listen just because it's you, Claire.'

Claire breathed in deeply and she sat upright in her chair.

'Your daughter Edith has had £75,000 from Harry Stone. And it was just as she had asked for, all in £20 notes. I delivered the bag to her just two days ago. And it's not only Edith who's asked for upfront payments; Josh has too. He asked for £100,000. And both promised Mr Stone if they were paid then the deal to buy Marine House would be his. Edith even put this in writing to him.'

Lady Ruth stared at Claire as if she was pained by what she was being told but would fight back.

'I didn't know of it, and it doesn't surprise me. And I did warn you about my daughter Edith. But if they've had upfront money as you call it, that doesn't alter anything. Marine House is a very valuable property, and the family needs to get the best money for it that we can. And we will not be selling to Mr Stone for reasons I have told you.'

'Harry Stone doesn't have much longer to live. He's trying to get his affairs in order, and buying Marine House was a big part of that,' Claire said.

'If he is as unwell as you say, then why on earth does he want to buy a big property like Marine House? Seven bedrooms? And has he still got the time and energy to pull it around to convert into apartments as he says he's going to do? To me that doesn't quite add up.'

'Please, Lady Ruth, I would ask you to consider it. I don't think this is just money any longer for Harry Stone. It is to be a place where he will spend whatever life is left for him.'

'You sound as if you know the man inside that brassy exterior. Are you sure he's got the money? We have never asked for his bank to confirm that. Perhaps we should have done so to stop wasting time on this.'

'Harry Stone has the money. He's done many deals bigger than this,' Claire said, but she was not sure if that was true.

'From what you've told me, it looks like he deals with hard money, bundles of notes. Where he gets them all from, we won't ask. Better we don't know. And the first time I met him, I thought he was that sort of market trader. A lot of shouting, a lot of haggling. But not a lot of substance behind it.'

'Do you know where Josh is?' Claire asked suddenly.

Lady Ruth stared at Claire with a frown as if she was being impertinent.

'No, I don't know. Should I?'

'Harry Stone asked Josh to bring back some diamonds for him from a little island in the Caribbean. And after we met last time in this room, Josh stopped me and gave me the bag of diamonds he had collected. Only, when I gave them to Mr Stone, there was one big, valuable diamond missing.'

'Josh never told me he was running errands for Mr Stone. And to a Caribbean island to collect something unusual, to say the least.'

Lady Ruth again stared at Claire. And Claire felt she suddenly saw disapproval at this visit and what had been said to her.

'I can only say it as it is. Josh is not answering his phone, and I would have preferred to have spoken to him directly about all this,' Claire said.

There was a pause and Claire stood. She had said enough; she was ready to leave. There was a distinct barrier being put up by Lady Ruth when talking about Harry Stone. And Claire was not sure if she had made any dent in that armour. This meeting was now better left.

'Before I go, just something else,' Claire said. 'When I was at Marine House on my own the other day, Edith called. For almost an hour, Edith walked around the house on her own and took away a small painting of London. It might have been by Canaletto and if so, it would have been valuable. She was high-handed in what she did, and I hope you agree she should have asked Mr Stone's permission before wandering around the house. And she should certainly have asked him before taking the painting. After all, his lease has not quite expired yet.'

'I'm still not sure what this is all about. We'll leave today as a confidential meeting between you and I. My children will do what I tell them but please, you or Mr Stone don't talk to them any further.'

'Thank you for seeing me, Lady Ruth. I will tell Mr Stone that you don't think he's a suitable buyer for Marine House and that you are now expecting to close a deal with other people. But one last thing, if I may. Mr Stone has become aware that Josh had a sexual assault case against him. Not wanting to cause any trouble, he has decided therefore that he will not take this incident of his missing diamond to the police,' Claire said.

For a moment, Lady Ruth's stiffness in her face tightened. She sat more upright.

'That's not a threat, I hope,' she said, looking hard at Claire.

'No, please don't take it that way. But I hope you will agree that a missing diamond is a serious matter.'

Two minutes later, Claire left; she was uncertain. Stone would never leave Edith and Josh alone now they had taken enough rope to hang themselves. But today, raking around the grubby bits of the Jackson family to get the can of worms out on view that the siblings had been feeding on, just maybe had stopped the face-off that was looming.

76

Eviction, and all that would mean, was now confronting Harry Stone. Lady Ruth would stand behind her children like a mother hen when trouble came, and that alone would keep Marine House another mile from Stone's grasp. But Claire had no regrets as she drove fast the next day to Brighton.

It was empty, dark in the kitchen as she closed the back door. She called out "Harry" twice. She stood still, but there was no reply. In the Regency lounge, it was eerie in its formality. This was no place for Harry Stone to spend his last days in.

She wandered to Stone's study, a room at the back of the house; it was small, dismal, dark, with no sunlight ever on it. She flicked the light switch, and in that instant, the reality of the whole situation of Harry Stone's deadly illness confronted her. Claire shuddered for an instant at the depressing piles of papers that left little space on the top of his large oak desk and the two chairs. Stone did not have a filing system, important things were kept in his head, and this place echoed his sometimes-chaotic life. He rarely wrote letters, but emails, usually lacking grammar and spelling, were his easy way of communicating. There was a closed laptop and half-empty whisky bottle on a side cabinet.

Claire found a plastic folder with the Panama bank accounts just as she had set up for Stone six years ago in Arrow Hall. Nevis, his mate Sol in Hatton Garden, diamond dealer, were all there, a very neat web weaved by an arch manipulator. But Josh, missing with a large diamond, was a thread leading right back to the Jackson family. Claire would see they paid a big price for it.

She picked out a single sheet of paper – it was a letter from the Plaistow Children's Hospice. She read the thank you for the donation twice and she grinned. She had known Harry Stone to do that before. What was money really to him?

A desk diary rested on the top of a pile of dog-eared papers on the floor, and Claire flicked through it. There was a creased sheet of paper folded into a page of three days ago. It fell onto the desk, Claire flattened it, it was a printout of an email. Claire scanned the two-line message quickly. She reread it before she began to understand it.

'You've had nearly £125,000, and that's all you're getting. I'm being watched; you owe me five grand for what I've done. So this is the end. Keep your man right away from me.'

Claire immediately recognised James's details as the sender, and she recoiled from it. She flipped the paper over and read the second sheet. It was an email back to James.

'My runner who's calling on you for the cash said you were being cocky and teasing him with the last parcel of money. He tells me he gave you a gentle reminder not to do that. Hope he didn't bust you too much.'

This scam of creaming off cash in overpayments to suppliers and odd money sloshing into fake bank accounts now fitted into place. She folded the sheet of A4 and placed it in the diary just where she had found it. The back of her scalp tingled with unbelief and horror where this might lead. James and Harry Stone were in this scam together. Both of them right in front of her eyes. Closing the diary, Claire walked quickly from the dark, untidy study.

But why had he left these emails not even hidden in his diary? And the letter from the children's hospice? Was she meant to see them? Perhaps when he had gone? Claire walked into the brightly lit sitting room and felt the sun warming the place. Stone's diary was like reading ghost letters to her, and even in the warmth of the room, she again shuddered.

She wanted to get away from this soulless, empty place. She should have known better than to get involved with the dubious life of Harry Stone again.

77

There was determination boiling in Claire. Stone's study left her with a growing festering scorn for two people she had once trusted. But Claire could see that Stone's feeble health was closing down – how long did she now have to confront him on this squalid duplicity?

Late afternoon, alone in her flat, Claire's phone buzzed on the kitchen table. Answering, Claire was jolted.

'You haven't been to visit me,' James said. His voice sounded very quiet.

'I have called the hospital a few times. And I've been very busy on something else important.'

'I thought you'd like to know I'm being discharged. I'm getting bored in here anyway. There's lots to do on the site and I need to get back.'

'When?' Claire shot the question.

'Sign off tomorrow, I hope. Scan shows brain all clear. No permanent damage.'

'You've been in intensive care. Broken bones in your arm and leg, they'll take a while to heal, and what about a knife dragged across your back?' Claire replied.

'Just a few weeks walking around on crutches, arm in a sling, usual stuff. But that won't stop me. I expect to be back on site beginning next week when I'll deal with that criminal.'

'I've altered security on the site; we need to talk before you return.'

'Why have you done that?' James's question was sharp; his arrogance was mounting.

'I want everybody off that site and that includes you.'

'Look, it was an accident; I fell off the scaffold – that could happen to anyone.'

'The police will decide that. Knife blades flashing around is nothing to do with an accident.'

'What have you said to the police?'

'Only what I remember. You were scooped up from the wet grass at the bottom of the scaffold, groaning in pain. I don't think you're going to forget that. Do you want more?' Claire did not wait for James to answer. 'I'll call in a day or two,' she added quickly and closed the call.

Claire felt her pulse race. There were volatile confrontations to come. Sipping from a glass of her favourite white wine, Claire was now ready to get Rick's money back, but pricking James's puffed-up ego and facing off Harry Stone for one very last time would be more satisfying than the bank account.

78

'Please answer your phones,' Lady Ruth said to Edith and Josh. 'I do not think it should be necessary for me to leave messages for you to call me.'

The three of them were in Lady Ruth's elegant sitting room at the top floor of her Mayfair house. It was a small space; it was cramped; neither Josh nor Edith would find it easy to avert the gaze of their mother.

'Mother, I don't have long – I've got to be away to the Dalys', and it's a long drive down to Broadway in the Cotswolds. Particularly at this time of day. And you know they don't like people being late,' Edith said. She sat only on the edge of a chair, as if to make her point.

Josh stared at his sister and mother in turn. It was not often that his mother left urgent messages to meet in this small room with high, heavily curtained windows. He was not sure what was to come.

'You'll give me the next half an hour, both of you. And I want your phones switched off; I'm not to be interrupted.'

'This all sounds very formal. And please don't treat us as school children,' Edith said.

'Josh, stop fiddling with your fingers like that, and both of you listen. Why does it take somebody outside the family to see how downright disreputable you both turn out to be? The Jackson name used to shout integrity, but it's being dragged down by the two of you. I suppose you get it from your father. He turned out to be less than trustworthy.'

'Mother, I'm not staying to hear you talk like this. Five minutes and I'm going,' Edith said and looked at her watch.

'You're going nowhere until I'm finished with you both.'

Lady Ruth stood and walked towards the door as if she would block Edith leaving. Josh was silent; he was no match against his sister and his mother.

'I've learned what both of you have been up to. Trying to pinch Marine House away from me. Brick by brick.'

'This is too bad, Mother. I don't have to listen to you and your fairy-tale stories. You used to start bedtime stories with "once upon a time". I suggest you do that again now.'

'Edith, that's enough. I won't have insults from you.'

'Well, you always have had your head in the clouds most of the time.' Edith almost spat the words at her mother.

'£75,000 and all in £20 notes? Upfront payment on the sale of Marine House? How does that sound then? And where is that money now?'

'That man Harry Stone would always try to get in front of the queue to buy Marine House. You've dealt with him; you know full well he's that type of person not short of throwing sweeteners around. But beyond that, I don't know what you're talking about.'

Edith looked at Josh as if she wanted his support.

'I'll ask again, Edith, one last time. Where is that money now? Because I want it in this room before you leave for your drink-fuelled weekend in the Cotswolds.' Lady Ruth's voice was raised to a high pitch, and her face reddened.

Edith let her arms flop over the edge of her chair, and she closed her eyes. She had no answer to her mother's onslaught.

'I've told you all you need to know, and I want to go,' Edith said.

'Don't dare lie to me again. I am prepared to get a lawyer to write you a strong letter. And that is something I never thought I would need to do, even with you, Edith,' Lady Ruth shouted.

She stared hard at Josh, who had looked nowhere except down at the table.

'And what have you done with some valuable diamonds that weren't yours to play with? And where have you been the last couple of days when I've tried to get hold of you?'

Josh stood and, like Edith, he tried to move towards the door. But his mother stood firm, and she looked at Josh in the eye. He tried to push his mother away, but she caught him on his shoulder, and it stopped him still with her unexpected force.

'You both know what I'm talking about; neither of you do yourself any favours with the deplorable way you have dealt with easy cash that that man Harry Stone has let flow through your grasping hands. I expect you both to come and talk to me, with the money that you've grabbed and with diamonds that you're trying to snatch. And I want to hear an apology for what you've done. You've both let the family name down.'

The room was warm, and Lady Ruth left the small, cramped room quickly. She was followed closely by Edith who said not a word to her mother. And Josh slumped back into his chair and put his head in his hands.

79

With a glass of whisky in his hand, at midday, Stone looked along the road from the sitting room balcony of Marine House. He searched for the shadow of Xavier's heavies, but he saw nothing, and he angrily fingered the bruise on his aching neck from the iron bar smashing his shoulder. Leaving the balcony doors wide open, letting in refreshing air, he sat on a chaise longue, now his favourite place to be.

Medication, for a short moment, was easing the pain which was now throbbing across the whole of his back. Carefully, he unfolded the fresh sheet of paper that he had screwed tightly into a ball on the train. With a tinge of excitement at what it might lead him to, he smoothed it on a low table. He held it up to the light, scanned the scribble on the paper quickly, but it meant nothing to him. He threw it back on the table and called Roger.

'How're you feeling, Harry?'

'Okay at the moment, but this illness is not going away.'

'You must know I'll do everything to help you. Are you still buying that big property in Brighton?'

'Yeah, I'm fighting to get it; it'll be my last fling. But there's something that's come up that'll help me on my way. You might be interested too.'

'You shouldn't be fighting anyone the way you are now. What are you up to?'

'I've had another tip, strong one this time, it'll make a lot of cash. What do you know of Circus Inc?' Stone asked. He had a grin on his face, the first time for many weeks.

'What's going on, Harry?'

'I might buy some of Circus Inc's shares on the stock market. That's it. So, what do you know about them?'

'Another one of the leaks? Harry? Don't take that stuff seriously – you might run into a load of trouble. There's been a lot in the news this past week or two; somebody inside Circus Inc has been fiddling. They've walked off with a lot of cash in their pocket; it's a big fraud, money plundered from right in the middle of the business. Which all means Circus Inc is not as valuable as it used to be.'

'You forget too quickly. All the leaked deals I've had have been winners. Just put money up for a few days and you'll double it. So, take it from me, Circus Inc won't be any different.'

'It's your call, but this one does sound way off and for all the wrong reasons.'

'I'm going to have one last push. My lease runs out next week. But I'm never leaving Marine House. Not even to the local hospice that my doctor is trying to arrange for me.' Stone spoke quickly; he knew his position exactly.

'I hope you haven't given Josh the hundred grand he was asking for. He would take it and run, and I doubt you'd ever see it again.'

'Yeh, he's a thief that one, but you don't need to know any more. I'm working on 'em, and I'll tell you when I've bought the property.'

'I thought you might say that.' Roger laughed.

For a few moments, talking about making money, Stone began to feel his usual self. But he wanted to finish the call. He could never tell Roger of just a few days ago, lying senseless on his back doorstep and then walking out of hospital in the middle of the night.

And, as usual with what Roger said, Stone would ignore it if it was not what he wanted to hear. He opened his laptop and unlocked his stockbroker account. He was going to take a big bet. Circus Inc. The name had a ring to it; it was different; and this time, whatever Roger said, he just knew it would be a big win. Satisfied with what he was doing, he sipped his whisky.

Within a few minutes, he placed an order for £50,000 of shares in Circus Inc. He was oblivious to being caught out by any busybody authority in doing these secret, illegal insider deals. Who could link him to fraudsters in prison throwing very secret, plundered information around?

Mesmerised by what he had done Stone, for a while, stared at the screen. When the price of Circus Inc doubled, and he knew it would, he would have cleared another £50,000. Even after losing £25,000 from a flashing blade in the East End, there were still bundles of notes scrambled in his safe, and it left him with just £35,000 to find. And there was a big diamond still out there with Josh that would easily fill that gap. Stone paused his thought. He was nearly there.

He poured another large measure of his favourite malt whisky. Sitting deeply into the chaise longue, he was satisfied. But he did not know that Claire was about to call on him, this time not to talk about the Jackson family.

80

In her car from her apartment, it took Claire just short of half an hour to get to Canary Wharf. She took the lift to the fourth floor of this warehouse that had been converted into apartments, her anger growing. And the tension in her face was building for a short and ugly meeting. Her trust had been betrayed.

James came to the door on crutches and with his left arm hanging loosely in a plaster cast.

'What a pleasant surprise. Come in,' James said.

He leant to kiss Claire, but she stood back.

'We just need to talk for a short while.'

'Don't worry, I'll soon be back on the site, and I'll arrange a driver if I have to. The whole project is getting to a critical point. Everything needs to be rescheduled if we're to finish on time. And I've still to take on roofers and more electricians. Their quotes should be in by the end of the week.'

Despite his difficulty in walking, James sounded in ebullient mood. He led Claire into the small kitchen-dining area and started to press a button on the Italian coffee machine.

'How do you like your coffee?' he asked.

'I don't have time for that,' Claire said.

'I hear that you haven't been to the site for a few days.'

Claire did not move to sit but took a deep breath and walked towards the window that looked out to the river.

'I have some serious things to say to you, so please listen carefully,' she said with her back to him.

'Yeah, I'm really sorry about the accident. Health and Safety will want to know about it. You must let me know when you've checked the site insurance because I'm claiming it all—'

'James, stop.' Claire turned and spoke sharply.

James looked up and stopped shuffling some papers on the table. He sat heavily on a wooden chair.

'There's been a fraud, a conspiracy on the site, and I know you've been part of it. You've been syphoning off cash, probably in collusion with some of the tradespeople. You were put in hospital after a sharp blade slashed across your back, and that wasn't just because you told him you didn't like his work. You can either own up to this now or—'

'What on earth are you talking about? Why would I want to do that?'

'At the beginning I had total confidence in you. And so did Rick. It's a project you should have been proud of.'

'I have nothing to do with the money. You run the bank accounts. And I'm coming back soon to finish it off. So, is this all you've come to talk about?' James asked, his aggression rising.

'Yes, it is. I've looked again at all the invoices you've given to me for payment. I've found duplicates, invoices that don't even add up and even two that are fakes. They're false – I've checked, and the builder just does not exist. And then there are the bank account changes you've been giving me. Mostly they're all fakes as well. And I wonder why all the changed payments are to a bank account just a few steps from your front doorstep here in Canary Wharf.'

'I've only signed off what I know the site should be paying. Nothing more and nothing less. And if I've made a mistake in signing off a copy, then I've told you before we need to correct it and go and get the money back. Let me know who they are, and I'll call the builder myself tomorrow.'

'James, no. You are not taking this seriously. This has been going on almost since the site was opened. It's beyond simple mistakes. This is wilful fraud, planned and very blatant. I don't know how much you've had out of it, but I've added up the total overspend that you've signed off. It's big, over £100,000. I've got all the papers of the whole sordid story safely stored away. They'll go to the police if necessary.'

'Claire, you be careful. If you are accusing me of swindling, that's not something I would take lightly. If you dare say this with anyone else listening, then I'll sue you. I have a professional reputation to keep, and I'm not going to let that slip away from some unfounded, loose accusations.'

James was now hobbling on his crutch; his face was becoming red; and he stood in front of Claire as she moved towards the small hallway.

'I don't want you back on the site. From today, you are no longer employed on rebuilding Arrow Hall. And I've had all the locks, including on the office cabin, changed, so don't try to come and get anything you want to take away to hide the fraud, because you won't be able to.'

Claire spoke quickly. With James trying to deny anything she was saying, her antagonism to him had been rising as she had talked. But James was by now blocking her exit, holding his crutch across the doorway. She tried to push past him to the front door, but he pushed her back.

'Before you go, I want you to admit you've got all this wrong. I want you to show me all the bills you think are wrong so I can—'

'No, James. I've said enough. You know what you've been doing, so let me pass, please. I've got more work to do today.'

James clumsily stood on one foot and grabbed Claire's arm. He put his face close to hers and shouted.

'If that's the case, I'll get my lawyer to send you a letter. And this fancy fraud scheme you've made up'll cost you a lot more money than you're accusing me of thieving. So, what do you want?'

Claire recoiled, but James still had her arm in a tight grip.

'Let me go or I'll get the police.'

She took her phone from her pocket, but James knocked it from her hand and onto the floor. And as James tried to pull Claire back into the small kitchen area, she slapped his face with her free hand. It was enough to send him off balance and he fell heavily to the floor on top of his plaster cast arm. She trod over him, picked up her mobile phone and reached the front door within a few seconds. As she stood on the landing, she looked back at James, and he was scrambling to his feet. She shouted back through the open door.

'You should know that if you try any legal bluff, I've seen proof in writing of what you've been up to. You've been right in the middle of a very nasty scam. And you're going to pay for it.'

James did not answer. He was at the door on his crutches, staring at her. But Claire left him; she was now in a hurry. She walked quickly to the landing that led to the flights of stairs to the ground floor.

A few minutes later, out in the open, she was shaking. She walked across the wide concourse to the river edge where she stood to breathe in heavy doses of fresh air. Clearing this mess was far from settled. There was a big sum of cash that she had let slip through her fingers, and firing James today was the easy part. She still had to tell Rick that there was £120,000 from his bank now missing.

Recovering from his injuries, James was immobile. Holed up in his flat on the east side of London. James was finished. But there was more sharp noise to come. And shouting was all that Harry Stone would be able to do.

81

After driving quickly to Brighton, Claire parked her car and, for ten minutes, sat on a bench facing the sea. It did little to calm her.

Still wary of being caught by the mobsters watching out for Harry Stone, Claire let herself in by the back door of Marine House. As Stone came towards her, Claire hesitated. For the first time with his illness, Claire saw Stone in shirt sleeves, and she was stopped in the doorway. His face was gaunt and ashen, his arms thin and his hands almost skeletal. His shirt hung loosely at his waist, and she could see a blue and black bruise on his temple that stretched down his neck to his right shoulder.

'Come in,' Stone said with a grin on his face at seeing her.

He walked slowly through the kitchen to the sitting room. Claire followed. She wanted to ask about that bruise, but now was not the time. Almost with his eyes closed, Stone fell into a deep sofa with a heavy sigh.

'Good to see you again. I didn't expect you to come so quickly. There's lots for you to do, Claire.'

'I've only got ten minutes,' Claire said, her mouth dry as she stood facing Stone. 'And I've got something serious to sort out with you.'

'You've come to help me, Claire. That's all I want to know. I want you to sort out all my papers and then I want you to look after my medical care. There's a nurse coming in, and I want you to meet her. And I haven't heard anything from the Lady Ruth Jackson crowd. And have you found where that inveterate thief Josh has got to? I need that diamond; it's getting urgent.'

Claire stood the other side of the spacious room and faced Stone. He looked vacant. It was as if she was not there. This was a picture of a sad and broken man. But Claire was sure that he could still erupt with anger at what she was going to say.

'Do you want a drink?' Stone raised his voice as if that is what he wanted.

'No. Not today. I don't have time for that.'

Stone pointed to the whisky decanter on a sideboard.

'Pour me a big one will you, Claire?'

Claire hesitated. This is not what she had come for, and the longer she was here, the more difficult it would be. She walked to the sideboard and poured a full measure into his glass. She had done that many times at Arrow Hall, but she would never do it for him again. As Claire placed the cut glass tumbler on a side table, he looked away from her as if he had felt the sharpness in her voice.

'Is everything all right with you?' Stone asked.

'There's a problem on the Arrow Hall building site,' Claire said.

'I'll come and see it again before I'm finished. We'll make a date before you go,' Stone said.

He fidgeted on the deep sofa, but he still did not turn to face Claire.

'I don't want to see you at Arrow Hall again. Ever,' Claire said. 'You will soon understand why it's best you keep right away.'

'So, what else have you come to tell me?' Stone asked.

Claire walked a few paces until she was facing Stone on the sofa. She looked at him as he sipped his whisky, and there was not even a thin smile on his drawn face. But she saw a slight tremor in his arm.

'I've uncovered some double dealing on the Arrow Hall site. A lot of money's been raked off into somebody's pocket. It's cost Rick £120,000 so far.'

Claire searched Stone's face for a reaction. But there was none. He just sat quite still, sipping his whisky, and then he slipped lower into the sofa. There were many seconds of silence before he spoke.

'I hope you can sort it out,' Stone croaked.

He was still not facing Claire. He was in pain, severe discomfort by the frown on his face.

Claire momentarily felt she should quickly leave, and she turned towards the door. But Claire stopped. There would never be another time to clear up his cheating. She put her bag on the floor and sat facing and close to Stone. He looked up and with a flicker in his eyes.

'You've been getting a feed of cash out of the Arrow Hall site. I don't know why you've done it, but unless you pay it back, Rick will take action to recover it in the courts if necessary before it's all finished.'

'How do you know all this, Claire? And don't try to take revenge on me from times long gone by.'

'I found a note in your study when I was tidying your papers. It was tucked in your diary. You're in collusion with James the surveyor who Rick hired to run the site. Between the two of you, there's over £100,000 skimmed off. Fake invoices, duplicate invoices, altered bank accounts, they're all there.'

Stone pulled himself upright on the deep sofa.

'I had hoped you would keep on sorting my papers. I know what you've seen. Claire, just leave it; I'm too tired even to talk about it.'

'I've kept the sheet of paper which tells all that you've done. And we're going to deal with this now. It's a fraud; it's a nasty little scam. Do you want to be remembered by the big lump of cash that has been creamed off? A last deal that was downright thieving?'

'I sold the wreck of Arrow Hall too easily, too quickly. Rick grabbed it before I could think about it properly. I was not feeling good at the time. I was hustled into the deal when I was low. He can't grouse now if I try to get some back. He'd do the same.'

Stone, just for a few short minutes, was lively, just as Claire used to know him. He looked at his whisky before he took a long sip.

'You've got to repay it.'

'Come on, Claire, I've not had much. Rick's wealthy; he won't miss it.'

'You knew what you were doing. You probably set up the scam and drew James into it.'

'I did it because I wanted the money back that Rick underpaid on Arrow Hall. So, it now leaves us square,' Stone said.

Stone spoke slowly in a controlled and determined voice.

'No, only when you've repaid it to the last penny does it leave you square.'

'Don't try to bully me, Claire. I'm not well enough for that. I haven't got the cash, so I couldn't repay even if I wanted to. And I sold Arrow Hall—'

'You leave me with no option then. I'll have to call the police,' Claire cut in. 'I desperately had hoped I could settle with you and your accomplice James without bringing in the heavy arm of the law. The fraud squad will come and ask a lot of questions. They won't give up on some shallow answers.'

'How much?' Stone snapped.

'£120,000. That's the exact figure; I've traced it all.'

'That'll dent my hopes of raising the missing cash for Marine House. The lease ends next week, and then I'll be a squatter waiting to be evicted.'

Stone's voice had gained strength and an edge that reminded Claire of days with Stone at Arrow Hall. But if this was begging for sympathy, it would not work.

'Marine House, that's finished – I've had that straight from Lady Ruth. Even if they would sell to you, I'd still take back this money you've cheated Rick for.'

'But that sticky-fingered lot have still got my money, £75,000 and a valuable diamond, maybe worth near a hundred grand. They're not going to get away with this blatant stuff, treating me as if I'm an idiot. Go and tell 'em I'm never leaving here.'

'It's time you saw the other side of the coin, now you know what it's like to be cheated,' Claire said.

Claire placed a sheet of paper with Rick's bank details on a low table.

'The details for repayment to Rick are there. Make it by this time tomorrow and that will be the end of it.'

But Stone stood. He hobbled slowly to the whisky decanter and refilled his glass.

'I'll repay Rick half and the other half, £60,000, I'll pay to the Plaistow Children's Hospice.'

He looked at Claire, almost pleading in his sunken eyes. And Claire smiled, unsure how far to press Stone on this. She nodded.

Stone opened his laptop and for a minute fumbled with the keys until he found his bank account. Claire then watched closely, silently, as he keyed in the payment of £60,000 to Rick's account and £60,000 to the children's hospice. It was a slow and painful process for him.

'And don't leave it beyond a few more days before you come to see me in Marine House again, Claire. It's a big house, too big just for me. I'd like you to be there when the cancer finally does its job.'

Claire did not want these few minutes to be the way that summed up all she had known about this man. His days were now numbered, and what she had now made him do would last in her memory. Certainly forever. Claire's emotions wavered between unease at his abject state and the trust that had been severed.

She quickly left the room. And once at the back door, tears were running freely down her cheeks. For Claire, this was the end of knowing Harry Stone. She would not now ever be able to face up to returning to Marine House to see him again.

And she was trembling.

82

It was early evening when Rick left the Peninsula hotel in Hong Kong. Sitting in the back of the hotel's green Rolls taking him to the airport, he wished he had planned for a longer visit on this stopover. The chauffeur drove for a last look at the waterfront – it was humid warm; the place was buzzing with boats and never-extinguished twinkling lights from the high-rise buildings.

As a wind-down from New Zealand, just yesterday evening, he had taken a leisurely ride around the harbour on a junk boat with bright red sails, soaking in the sights and sounds of the harbour and skyline.

And earlier this morning he had shopped in the Peninsula Arcade. Buying a present for Claire, five bottles of assorted Chanel eau de parfum, was the least he should give her. It was as much the elegant design of the bottles that he thought she would like as the intense lasting aromas of the spray. But with Claire, he had more to do. He had been absent for Wimbledon ladies' final day, and he also had an important admission to make to her.

As he settled into his seat for the twelve– and half-hour flight to London, he shuffled through the papers for the New Zealand wine estate he had been trying to buy. He carefully read, for the third time in the last two days, a letter demanding a twenty-five per cent increase in the price they were willing to accept. The agent had told him three times there had been a lot of interest in the estate and that would be reflected in the final price.

The stewardess in the cabin brought him an aperitif, a glass of wine from the very estate he was trying to buy. It tasted good, and it increased his frustration of his failure to secure the winery that would have been an interesting sideline. No more than something to brag about at parties when the wine was on the menu.

But today, the whole reality was different. He had invested a big six-figure sum of his own money which would now be lost if this did not proceed. An investor had withdrawn from the deal, leaving Rick on his own. He was going to spend his time in London looking up a list of contacts, people who could be interested in providing some money to fill that gap. Otherwise, the whole project was likely to collapse.

As the aircraft left the runway on its long flight to London, Rick enjoyed another glass of the Marlborough estate wine. He folded his papers back into a neat bundle, and it was then that Arrow Hall came clearly into his thoughts. Whatever he had promised to Claire, that was a promise he could no longer afford at this time. The wine estate or Arrow Hall. That was the crossroads he was now facing. The short, snappy calls in the past few weeks with Claire he knew had shown his impatience with New Zealand. And the more he thought about it, he was certain that $750 of perfume would not clear those memories.

Inevitably, the overnight flight to Heathrow left him with little sleep, and by the time a chauffeured limousine dropped him at his Mayfair apartment, he felt far from refreshed. It was early morning, and as Rick walked through his front door, he expected to find Claire there. But his wide penthouse apartment was quiet, empty. There was no colourful display of flowers enlivening the lounge; there was none of Claire's clutter in the bathrooms; and when he opened the wardrobe, her clothes had gone. As he collected the pile of post from the box on the landing, he could see that Claire had not been there for a few days.

Rick showered, changed from the crumpled clothes he had travelled in, and after running through all the post that had accumulated, it was late morning before he called Claire.

'Long journey and I've just got home. Thought I'd find you in the apartment. Where are you?' Rick asked.

'I'm in Brighton. I've been looking up somebody, so I stayed over.'

'Claire, could we meet at Arrow Hall?'

'Have you decided what you want to do with it, finish it, sell it or just leave it?'

'First, I'd like to walk around the site with you as soon as possible. You can then tell me what we've spent, and I hope you've been able to work out what's still needed to finish it all off. And I have to leave again at the end of the week, so I don't have much time.'

'You really should have called or texted to let me know you were coming home. I haven't heard from you for almost ten days.'

'My fault,' Rick said tersely.

'I'm staying over in Brighton for another day. I'll call as soon as I've finished here.'

'Yes, there's a lot to catch up on. I'm sorry I was so unthinking in sending in my surveyor without talking to you first,' Rick said.

'Do you remember James? I've sacked him. He wasn't much good.'

'Claire, please. Of course I do, and I'm ready to listen.'

There was a pause and Rick knew this was going wrong. Yeah, he had put James on the site, but he had not yet listened to Claire about what she was accusing him of doing. And he had not asked her any more about the accident to James.

The short call ended; Rick was again surprised at the coolness in Claire's response. He would have been surprised too, to know that Claire was not in Brighton when she took his call, but she was alone in her own new flat.

Rick started unpacking his papers from buying the wine estate and he could feel the tension within himself. It was a blunt reminder that they had not spent much time together in the last few months even just to talk. Chasing his own vanity project, he had let the demands of travelling and buying a wine estate overtake him. And he had not been here for Wimbledon ladies' final day, Claire's favourite outing of the year.

He busied himself at his desk, but he was not concentrating. Rick wanted Claire to stay; he wanted to sit down and talk to her. But Arrow Hall was difficult. The rebuild was now no more than a cold lump of money which he had to get back. Quickly.

Unsure of Claire's feelings towards him, he walked moodily around the large apartment. Whatever he now said to her, it would be letting Claire down on Arrow Hall. That, he was certain, was what would finally cause her to walk away.

83

Stone was not expecting good news from anywhere. He had not eaten during the day – there was still not much in the fridge – but he was not hungry. His mood was downbeat; Claire had turned against him.

And when his phone rang, it awakened him from his dark thoughts.

'I got this one wrong.' It was Roger, who sounded almost excited. 'Circus Inc. The price has doubled. This one caught everybody out.'

'Surprised to hear that you agree I was right. That makes a change, Roger. I went in big on this because I knew it was going to happen.'

'Don't get too excited yet. You'd better not tell me where you got your illicit information from, but it's been picked up that there has been some heavy buying just before the news that somebody was buying Circus Inc became public. A lot of alarm bells shouting out loud. Somebody in a pinstriped suit will be expecting that there's a bit of a fraud going on. So be careful with what you've got.'

'Roger, you sound like a schoolmaster scolding a pupil for looking over the shoulder of the person next door in an exam. It happens all the time. Have you never done it?'

'I don't have to answer that. But okay, you make money big time, so have you now cleared the lot to buy Marine House?'

'Just, little bit to go yet.'

Those words echoed in Stone's head as he finished the call and looked again at the sheet of paper he had pressed into a tight ball on a train from London. He opened his laptop and peered eagerly into his stockbroker account. He liked what he saw. Circus Inc was another big win.

Stone had already poured two measures of whisky that afternoon, but he now poured another one. He sat still and the pain he had been having during the whole of that day dissipated. The back of the sofa was a soft spot as Stone rolled his head onto it and his eyes just shut. Stone wanted to sleep. Manipulating money for Marine House was like playing a game of poker, and this time he had not held all the right cards to keep it.

Stone was awakened from his reverie to take a call from Sol in Hatton Garden.

'Harry, my friend, have you got that last big carat diamond?'

'I'm still waiting for it. A couple of days, okay?'

'My Russian client is now in London. He's here 'til middle of next week, doing his shopping. He's eager to handle the last big diamond. Get it to me before then, and if it as sharply cut and well polished as the others you've brought me, it'll be £85,000. How does that sound?'

'I like it.'

'Harry, I know you're not too well, but are you alright? I'll come and collect it from you if you prefer.

'My lady, Claire, is dealing with it for me. I'll tell her it's getting urgent. But we'll get it to you in good time.'

Delivering the last diamond was becoming urgent. Eighty-five grand was big money; Stone was not going to let it slip away, like a high tide going out.

84

Manipulating people was a life skill that Stone had learned over many years of practice. Anyone would bend and be coerced if enough damage was threatened to them. It always gave him satisfaction that he was in control. But today Stone tried to stop his anger simmering as he called Claire.

'Where's that Edith woman you gave £75,000 to? I want to see the receipt she signed to make sure it isn't an outright lie they'd sell Marine House to me.'

Stone's voice was raised, but it sounded hoarse, as if it had no force behind it.

'I've got it safe; I'm working on it,' Claire said, trying to be evasive.

'There's enough out there now to pull that family down. I never trusted Josh; I knew he was an outright liar and a thief who'd walk off with a diamond. But he's played right into my hand. It's time to spill their thieving and sexual promiscuity secrets right onto the street, until they cry for me to stop. Or sell me Marine House at a knock-down price.'

'Be careful how you deal with this. You don't want to get into a legal fight; you've got your own secrets to hide. Like how you're going to pay for it. And they'll want to know where your funds have come from to make sure they're not being paid in laundered money. And diamonds from a tax haven in the Caribbean will not sound good,' Claire said.

'You're being negative. I don't want to hear that – the end of my lease is close, and I don't have much time left.'

'I know it's difficult for you, but be patient for a couple more days.'

'Yeah, you've said that before. But where are we now?'

'Calm yourself. Raising your voice to me is not going to help you,' Claire said.

'Get me Josh. Get me that diamond. I'm going to frighten him so he runs to his mother.'

Stone's voice trailed off; he had not meant to shout at Claire. She was right about his money – it was tainted, laundered to a far-off island in the Caribbean. And trading diamonds, no, that would not sound good either.

As he hauled himself from the deep sofa, he eased his back slowly as he stood. At the front door and then the rear door, he tested the heavy bolts that held them securely. He was never going to move away from Marine House, and if Lady Ruth thought she could take it with her aloofness and contempt, it wouldn't work. He would let the Jackson family stew for a few more days. And this was a place to squat and relish the rage from that tribe that would be fired at him.

85

Anxious that everything as she had known it was fast running away from her, this morning Claire drove at speed. Just before mid-afternoon, as Claire weaved down the small lane, her nostalgia for Arrow Hall returned. It was the old iron gates that had made the entrance to the first Arrow Hall that set it off. They were always there, wide open, shrouded in a green canopy of moss and with a large bush growing through one side. This part of Arrow Hall had never changed, and it was Claire's hope that she would never see those gates moved from their open welcome. But as she entered the site, Claire quickly reminded herself that she had to move on from all that.

There was only one contractor's vehicle parked on the grass; the cabin door was closed; and Claire held the new keys tightly in her hand. She walked to the half-finished building, through the front door to what would be the entrance hall and then straight into the morning room which had been Stone's study. But this time it was different; Harry Stone would never again sit at his desk in this spacious room, often his voice raised on the phone.

Inside, building work had not yet reached the first floor, so it was not possible to see through the rooms that had once been her flat in the west wing of Arrow Hall. Someday, this place would be free from the clutter and noise of building work, but Claire stood and gazed for a minute, saddened that she would never be here to finish what she had started so eagerly just a few weeks ago.

She walked quickly to the cabin. Inside, James's laptop, papers and drawings were still on the table, gathering inevitable dust. It even felt mouldy and damp in this cramped place, but it was ready for a fresh start just as she had left it. As she watched from the cabin, waiting for Rick, tension returned, tightening the frown lines on her face. A few minutes later, Rick, dressed casually in a fresh, deep-blue, short-sleeved shirt, came into the cabin. He looked as sophisticated as she had always known him. The difference between seeing James and Rick in this small space was stark. Rick kissed her on her cheek as she tried to avoid looking at his eyes.

'Claire, it's good to see you again. I feel I've been away a long time.'

'Yes, Rick. You've been away five and a half weeks, and in that time, I've barely had three calls or even texts from you. And each time you did call you were too busy to listen. So, what's going on?'

'I don't want to talk about New Zealand now.'

'Have you thought about Arrow Hall at all while you were away?'

'Only when we've spoken, which hasn't been easy, I know. But, Claire, first, before anything else, I need to say sorry about being so sharp the other day. I was very travel weary, and I should not have spoken like that. Please forgive me,' Rick said.

There was a pause and Claire looked down to the floor.

'I need to see Arrow Hall finished. Urgently. So where are we on the rebuild? How much have you spent so far?' Rick shot the question quickly at Claire.

'Over £300,000, but looking at the original tenders for the work still to be done, it's going to take double. And maybe more to get the gardens landscaped and the old moat reseeded to make it look green again. I've printed a detailed list of exactly what has been spent, and I've tidied the papers – they're all in here. The surveyor you send to replace James will soon follow the trail of where we are.'

'The site looks derelict, abandoned. So where are all the contractors?'

'It's James, you appointed him to run the site. He's too arrogant. He lost control and none of the builders would work with him.

Some just walked off; he was lucky not to have a brick thrown at his face, and when it got serious, he had a knife flashed over his back. I sacked James two days ago. And when you've got time to listen, I'll tell you what he was up to.'

'Claire, please, I've always got time to listen,' Rick said.

'Did you ever check James out before you let him onto the site?'

'I had no reason to.'

'I wonder how much he's creamed off working for you on other sites. Nothing sophisticated, just fake bills from a carpenter that doesn't even exist. Invoices that don't add up, invoices signed off for payment twice. Shady bank accounts to receive all this money. Why you gave him £15,000 in cash I can't imagine. I was never able to get from him where even one penny had gone.'

'You are scathing, so let's have it. Who else was in on this?'

'Probably a contractor or two on the site, probably the one who knifed James, and then there was Harry Stone, you remember him?'

'How could I forget. That man must have seen you coming.'

'He says he should have held out for a bigger price when he sold the site to you. This little trick was his way of making up for it.'

'What's the total that went missing? How much are we talking about?'

'Just a penny or two short of £120,000.'

'Wasn't it missed before it got to that enormous sum?'

'Rick, I didn't miss anything. I found what was going on; I've confronted James and Harry Stone. And Harry has repaid you £60,000 and sent £60,000 to Plaistow Children's Hospice, a charity he supports. It's finished. And so is James.'

'I think we should go to the police with this,' Rick said.

'Harry Stone is dying. He only has a short time to live. Prostate cancer. Going to the police is not going to do much good. And, Rick, the clear-out of Arrow Hall is complete, ready for you to do what you want with the place.'

'I'm not having Harry Stone tell me which charity he wants to send my money to, so go and tell him I want the £60,000 back.'

'Rick, I've told you he's dying. Please let's move on,' Claire shouted.

'I come home to find this place spinning out of control. And I only bought the derelict building because I thought you loved Arrow Hall.'

'You bury yourself in New Zealand on a vanity project; we don't talk for several weeks; and then all you do is criticise when what I needed was for you to listen. Rick, that's not good enough.'

'I can't let it go on like this, you know that, Claire.'

Rick quickly shuffled some of the papers on the desk as if he wanted to hide something.

'I know this is not what we set out to do here. But I'm needing to sell Arrow Hall. I've got to raise some money quickly. And quite a big sum.'

Claire knew those words were coming. They had never really been hidden. Her tenseness again tightened the frown lines on her forehead.

'In the past few weeks, I've cleared up an undercover fraud, seen fights on the site with large knives slicing at James and all I get now is that you're going to sell the place.'

Claire's anger at this whole debacle was growing. She turned away.

'Please, Claire, I had something planned if only you would stay and listen to me.'

'No. It's final. If you're going to sell, then I'm finished with it. All I can say now is goodbye. I never wanted it to finish this way. I've rented my own apartment, and I've cleared everything out from your place – I've moved out. I won't be back. And thank you for the good times. There have been many, Rick, and…' Claire struggled to finish.

The keys to the cabin and the large metal industrial gates jangled as she put them on the table. She turned and walked quickly from the small, enclosed space. There was nothing more she wanted to hear from Rick that would make the break easier. And Claire did not wait to listen.

86

Standing on the top step to Marine House, Stone leant down to inspect the repair which the carpenter had just finished to the front door. It had not even been painted yet and, grudgingly, he handed over £300 in notes for what he saw as an expensive piece of wood for two panels and for boarding up the broken window in the sitting room until it could be reglazed.

He closed the front door without looking along the road for the thug who had loitered menacingly around Marine House. Even handing over Xavier's demand, with a knife flashing in his face, would never leave this place secure from the heroin addicts who would do anything for a payday.

He walked down the wide hallway and into the sitting room where he poured a whisky. Today his pain was never far away; it was showing in the lines of his thin face. The hurt in his back was very intrusive; Nurse Carol had called earlier that morning with his medication, but it was slow to work and there was little he could do to get comfortable.

The boarded broken window stared at him as, with the large glass of his favourite malt in his hand, he stood on the small balcony and gazed across the road to the sea. Unusually for Stone, introspection caught him for a moment. This illness, or any illness come to that, he did not understand.

His intake of whisky had grown over the years; of course, it was now far beyond his doctor's guided limits. But that was nothing new, and he had always been fit and busy. So why was this insidious disease inexorably spreading around his body, making him lose control of his life? Even the buzz of making money from insider dealing was waning. His brooding left him angry with himself.

The bell to the front door of Marine House suddenly chimed into the hallway. Stone heard it clearly; he looked up from his glass of Glenfiddich and swore. Nurse Carol came into the sitting room.

'Do you want me to get it?' she asked.

'No, ignore it – I'm in no mood to speak to anyone. There have been some hoodlums around this place, and I'm beginning to feel very tired.'

Nurse Carol looked at Stone – she knew what he was saying; she had picked up the pieces lying on the back doorstep. She watched as Stone took a long sip of his whisky and sat back and closed his eyes. But the caller persisted with a long ring of the bell, as if they knew he was there.

His instinctive irritability increased; he pulled himself from the chair and started walking slowly to the hallway. But Nurse Carol stood in front of him.

'Please go and rest and I'll answer it,' she said.

'If it's those hoodlums, tell them to clear off before I call the police.'

Stone walked slowly back to his chair and his whisky. A minute later, Nurse Carol came back into the sitting room.

'I think you'd better come to have a look and listen before I open the door. It's somebody who says it's vitally important and they urgently need to see you. But be careful, there are a lot of cold callers with scams around this part of town. You've seen one on your back doorstep, so this could just be a hoax.'

Stone waved Nurse Carol away and ambled slowly down the hallway.

The video connection showed a clear picture and, as he took it in, he stood back. The person standing at the front door of Marine House was positively someone he did not want to talk to. Ever again.

He recoiled for a moment and stood still.

87

What had this woman come for? She had no right to be interrupting his tiredness, with his glass of satisfying whisky. She was here for only one reason – she had come to chastise him. Just a week away at the lease end, she was here to make sure he was tipped out of Marine House. And today she was here to poke around like her daughter with the big ego had done. And probably looking for any damage that she could charge him with before she sent in the bailiffs. Stone knew how these things worked. But what was worse, she would do it with a commanding voice, just like a headmistress reading a school report that had not been good.

Early next week, he would have all the locks to all outside doors rechecked. That would then be the end of antagonistic members of the Jackson family interrupting the peace of his next few days. It heightened his antagonism.

'What're you doing here?' Stone snapped.

'I want to talk with you, Mr Stone, so please let me in.'

He flicked the intercom video off and, turning his back on her, walked away down the wide hallway. He reached the sitting room door when the bell chimed again, even louder, longer, he thought in his irritated state. Painfully, he walked back to the front door.

'Clear off.' His voice echoed with a satisfying bellow down the wide hallway.

'Mr Stone, you really must listen to me. And please remember just one thing – I own Marine House. Not my wayward children, Edith and Josh, but me.'

Stone looked at Lady Ruth on the video. Out of sheer frustration, he impulsively pressed the button to open the front door of Marine House. Why not enjoy, at last, giving her, right to her face, what he thought of the thieving Jackson family? And even taunt her with sexual assault charges against Josh. Or he could go straight to his study, top up his whisky glass and shut himself in.

Lady Ruth came into the hallway quickly; she stared at Stone as he stood, whisky glass in hand, ready to walk back to his seat in the sitting room. From Stone's contorted face, the ashen pallor on his forehead and hollow cheeks, she saw he was unwell.

'Thank you for letting me in. I didn't want to use my own key to this front door; I don't want to be intrusive, but I have something important to say. I want to say it to your face, and I want to say it now.'

Stone did not turn to confront her. But he heard her calm voice as she spoke to him.

'It would be easier if we could sit down,' she said.

'What're you here for? Just to inspect your house where you think I might have left a few dirty marks on the carpet? Is that it?'

'Please, Mr Stone. When Claire called, she told me you're not well. I want to make this easy for you. And I promise you it won't take long.'

Lady Ruth walked past Stone into the elegant Regency sitting room. This was a place where, in the last few years, Stone had often spent time alone drinking an energising glass of his favourite malt whisky. He did not want the memory spoiled. He resented her intrusion, heightened now as Lady Ruth stood in the middle of the room as if she was in control. Stone had seen enough; he wanted her out.

'What do you want? Tell me why you've come here and then get out.' Stone's tone was aggressive.

'Would you please pour me a large G&T. I usually take a double with lemon and ice.'

Stone blinked and stared at Lady Ruth for a moment. Without thinking, he turned and shuffled to the seventeenth-century cocktail cabinet that stood in a corner of the room. He laboriously mixed the drink, with lemon and ice, topped up his whisky and gave Lady Ruth her glass. He did not look at her; he was again feeling tired, agitated, and he slumped onto a deep sofa. This was all a bad nightmare as Lady Ruth followed, sat facing Stone as close as she could and tasted her cocktail.

'I heard something the other day that I don't like. And when that happens, I do something about it,' she said.

Stone closed his eyes and slumped deeper into his seat. He had heard all this before. The gossip of a police raid on Marine House just a year ago. She had had her spies out watching the place; a rough-looking tramp had been seen lurking around the front door.

Stone sipped his whisky, turned away and tried to ignore her. But Lady Ruth watched him closely and leant further forwards in her chair. He felt her presence.

'I'm going to call you Harry. I understand from my son that is what you like best.'

Stone sat more upright and nodded, his eyes still firmly closed.

'And please call me Ruth while we're sitting here together. I know from our previous meeting you don't like titles, so for today we'll be informal.'

Lady Ruth sipped her drink and put the glass on a low table with a noise as if she wanted to awaken Stone.

'We had many parties in this fine room. I hope you like it. I see you haven't changed it much.'

Stone opened his eyes and stared at the woman who was intruding where she had no right to be. He sat upright on the sofa, looked at her glass and then took a long sip from his whisky. What was happening, what was she talking about? Stone was not sure.

'Harry, I've found that you have paid £75,000 all in notes to my daughter, Edith. It's a strange thing for you to have done, and why all in notes, I wonder. It's dangerous and not the right way to deal with that amount of money. Don't you know about bank transfers?'

Lady Ruth looked intently at Stone. But her face was straight. Bundles of notes like this was not something she had seen before, and she didn't approve of it now.

'I wanted to buy this place. It's what your daughter asked for to get me the deal. I have it in writing from her.' There was a single sheet of paper on the table and Stone handed it to Lady Ruth.

'I have dealt with Edith. She understands my displeasure at her asking for such a sum in notes in a bag to be collected in the cocktail bar of a hotel. Edith now knows where she stands. And then there's Josh. I understand you gave him a diamond, not a big one but a diamond none the less. I believe that was to be given to Edith. But I'm afraid Josh has gone and pawned the thing and got a few hundred pounds for it.'

Lady Ruth finished, but she had not looked at the paper Stone had passed to her. For a moment, she stared intently at Stone.

'I don't want to hear all that,' Stone shouted almost as if, suddenly, he had woken up. 'Get out and go back to London; you're all as slippery as each other. I'll get my lawyer to write to you about the money you've taken.'

'Let me speak just for a few minutes longer. I find it very distasteful what my children have done. They're trying to get money out of me, by the back door, if you please. And until I give it to them, it's money which is not rightfully theirs.'

Stone sipped his whisky noisily.

'Your son Josh is a thief. He's walked off with a very valuable diamond I was asking him to collect for me. I don't know what he's done with it, probably tried to sell it on by now just like the last one,' Stone said, trying to raise his voice.

Lady Ruth fumbled in her pocket and took out a handkerchief. She unfolded it and a glistening diamond shone even in the dull light of the sitting room. Without speaking, she leant forward and passed it to Harry Stone.

'I hope, Harry, now I have retrieved this precious stone, that you won't feel the need to press charges against my son. It will not be the first time that I have had to intervene to keep that young man out of prison.'

Stone took the jewel placed it on the low table by his chair and ran his hand through his hair. He was agitated; he wanted this woman to leave. She had said enough; he knew the rest.

'All I have really is my house in Mayfair, Marine House, some investments, a house near Cambridge, not much more. I'm going to offer Marine House to you, Harry.'

'The Jackson family has got a lot to hide.'

Lady Ruth paused. She was enjoying her cocktail and she took a long sip from it.

'Yes, I hear you've dug up a nasty episode surrounding Josh. It was all very shady, and I don't like to talk about it. So please listen to me carefully, Harry. I'm going to repay you what you've given to my children. That is money they should never have had. So, the price of Marine House to you comes down by – let's round it for all the mistakes my children have made – £200,000. And, Harry, to make it easy, and I'm sure you can do that sum quickly, we will fix the price together at just £2.3 million. I do hope you find that a fair way to resolve this.'

Stone's natural instinct quickly surfaced when anyone was talking money to him.

'No, that price is too much. Take another £100,000 off and you might have a deal,' Stone replied.

'We'll split the difference to £2.25 million. I want to be sure that your money is legal and that this is not money laundering, but my lawyer will deal with that. Then there's one important condition about all this. You undertake not to talk to anyone about how my children have behaved in taking money from you. And I include the unfounded accusation of sexual assault against Josh.'

'I never want to know or hear any more sordid detail about your children. I've seen enough.'

'Very well. I'll leave you with a copy of the contract for sale. Why don't you put in the figure £2.25 million and sign it – it'll bind us both into the deal. Then this is settled, finished. Our lawyers will clear the rest of it, and it'll be as quick as that.'

Lady Ruth placed a large envelope on the low table between them.

Stone raised his glass towards Lady Ruth. It was not his way to say thank you, but this acknowledgement of a deal was as far as he could go. And Lady Ruth raised her glass too. Harry Stone was a sick man, she could see that, but she had paid the price to keep the family name intact. She finished her gin and tonic quickly and walked to the door.

'Harry, thank you for letting me in, and I hope you will still have plenty of time to enjoy this lovely house. But before I go, something else. You kept me standing on the doorstep for a while, and I noticed that you have had to make a big repair to the front door. And it looks like you have a broken window here. I won't ask why you have that damage, but I do hope you will look after the house when it is yours.'

Stone merely raised his hand and listened as, a few seconds later, the front door closed. He did not know what this woman was trying to do; he was not sure he trusted her. He went to refill his whisky glass. For some time, Claire had told him that Marine House would never be his, and in his antagonistic frame of mind, he had even been looking forward to a long period of squatting beyond lease end. Stone paced the room. He stared across the road to the sea; the sun was now low in the sky and its brightness was almost golden in colour.

He opened the large white envelope Lady Ruth had left, took a thin document out and, after skimming it quickly, threw it onto the table. But he could not leave it; he picked it up again and read it closely. Lady Ruth's strong, bold, looping signature took up a big space at the bottom. For once in his life, Harry Stone was stunned into silence.

He had made enough to clear a price of £2.25 million with a bit to spare. After sitting still for almost ten minutes, he went to his study, sat at his desk and made a quick call to his lawyer.

But then, more importantly for him, he pushed papers aside to make space, and he wrote a short letter.

88

This morning, a taxi took Claire to South Audley Street in Mayfair. She had an appointment in a glitzy but comfortable beauty salon, a place once owned by her close friend Jennie. Claire was going to take time out; Arrow Hall was a scar she was going to blank off for a few hours. A back massage, her hair cut and styled and her nails manicured was pampering to restore her belief that she was doing the right thing.

There were several brightly lit mirrors around each room where Claire unavoidably saw herself, and each time it did nothing to lighten her mood as what she saw was the frown lines on her forehead deepening. It was not helped as she checked out of the salon. As Claire took the receipt from using her credit card for a very costly few hours, she was sharply reminded once again that, moving away from Rick, she would have to settle all accounts when they came. Spending the money this morning did not give her the timely boost she had expected.

Late afternoon, Claire walked back to her flat and spent time putting her clothes from Rick's apartment in a small wardrobe. She had turned her phone off since early that morning, but she now saw four missed calls. They were all from Rick. He had texted too. He had something to say to her. Could they meet and talk again just for a short time?

That did not help to lift a level of growing sadness surrounding her. And another hour passed before Claire replied to Rick. She made it a quick message.

Yes. We'll meet just to say goodbye properly. From the good times I want to keep memories. But anything to do with Arrow Hall, we'll keep out of it. Why don't u find my new flat in Knightsbridge. Tomorrow in the afternoon.

As she finished the text, Claire knew that seeing Rick again would be difficult. Sitting on her own in the small, confined space of her flat, it felt gloomy; there was no elegance to it, nothing that she could ever make into a comfortable space. How long would she be able to stay here until her money ran out? And what a contrast it was against the light and spacious buildings where she had always lived.

And what would Rick think of it? That no longer mattered, and Claire blotted it out. What could she say to Rick tomorrow afternoon? Why had she let herself be drawn into a corner, with a small bank balance and little chance of finding work?

89

Claire spent half an hour in a florist shop a road away from her front door. There was a lingering scent of fresh flowers, and she bought an arrangement of red roses and carnations set off with white breath flowers. In her flat, Claire placed them carefully on the table in her kitchen dining area. It brightened up a dull room. It was a tiny step to making this small space feel like home.

Rick laughed as, half an hour later, he gave Claire a large spread of similar flowers and saw her own display. He leant to give her a light kiss on her cheek.

'Of course, I should have known you would have flower arrangements. The bright colours in my apartment were always placed there by you.'

'There's not much to show you round here, but it'll be good when I've finished shopping to put some more colour in the space,' Claire said.

They sat at the small kitchen table. Rick gave Claire a box wrapped in silver paper with a red bow tied over it. He took Claire's hand across the table and gently squeezed it.

'I've brought you a little present from my stopover in Hong Kong. Don't open it now but delve into it when I've left.'

Claire looked at Rick, unsure what to say. She did not really want a goodbye present.

'Thank you for agreeing to meet so soon, Claire,' Rick said. 'I wanted you to know that before I left New Zealand, I had bought tickets for you to come back there with me. They're first class all the way. Would you come?'

'Rick, I think that's going to be impossible.'

This was not what Claire had expected. And Rick saw Claire's hesitation and the deep frown lines on her forehead.

'You and I have never enjoyed a real holiday together. You would like New Zealand, laid-back, beautiful countryside. We could spend some time there and you could help me unravel the knot that is tying up the vineyard deal.'

'Rick, I don't think you understand how I've felt these past few months. You've not been here to talk to; even going out to dinner is a distant memory. So, what's been going wrong?'

'I have no excuses. Getting too busy can't be good when it interferes with personal life. I've been under pressure to satisfy some outside investors, and I'll never let that happen again. I stopped over in Hong Kong on the way to London just to step back from it all for a few hours and yes, I owe you a big apology. And, Claire, I do have an admission to make to you.'

Rick hesitated. Claire looked back at Rick and quickly looked away.

'In New Zealand, I did meet somebody three or four times. It was quite by chance, somebody I had known before in London – she happened to be in the same hotel in Auckland. It held me up by two days from returning home, but there's nothing there now, so please forgive me.'

Claire had already seen too much pain in Harry Stone's face in the last few days and she wanted this to stop; she wanted to move forward, away from confrontations. Claire stood to put Rick's flowers in some water in the kitchen sink. She would arrange them later. She turned to face Rick.

'When are you going back?'

'Wednesday, middle of next week with a stopover in Singapore.'

Rick again took Claire's hand as if it would help what he was now going to say.

'We agreed not to talk about Arrow Hall, but I think you should know I've got a buyer, a developer I've known for a long time. He will take the building from where it is now, and I know he will be sympathetic to how it should look when its's all finished. Will you help him with the finishing details when the time comes? Only you really know how it was before the devastating fire.'

'You are asking for the impossible, Rick. I've walked away from the site with some bitter memories, so I'm not going back.'

'Please think about it. I feel guilty already; I don't want to stir up your feelings, but the offer will be there for you.'

'This isn't turning out how we had planned it a few months back. Remember, it was to be our country home, so my answer will still be no. I want to leave it for now.'

'I will have to go back next week but, Claire, will you please follow me when you have a chance to come? They're first-class tickets, so they can be changed. Let's not make this a final farewell, Claire. I want to repay you for the hurt I've caused you; I want you to come and enjoy the laid-back lifestyle for a couple of months. And then, when we come back, you can decide how closely we want to live together. Be independent, but let's not say goodbye.'

Claire stared at Rick. Yes, this was amicable, and it was how she wanted the parting to be. And an hour later, as Rick prepared to leave, Claire did not know how to hold back an emotion that was telling her this might be the last time she saw Rick.

Alone in her quiet apartment, she opened Rick's present. She dabbed the perfume from each of the elegant bottles on her hands and the scent stayed with her as she tidied and arranged Rick's flowers. The frown slowly relaxed from her face.

But going to New Zealand? The offer was unexpected; it was too soon after shutting out Arrow Hall. At that moment, Claire had no reason to think she was ever going to travel there.

90

It was 2.00 in the morning when Claire took the call. She was alone in her new flat and, in the middle of the night, it was absolutely silent. As Claire quickly woke, she felt that it was very cold.

'Is that Claire? Claire Watts?'

'Yes.'

'I'm sorry to call you at this hour, but I am the homecare nurse looking after Mr Harry Stone in Brighton. He said you were the first person I must call, whatever the time. I'm sad to tell you Harry Stone passed away just an hour ago. I was here; the doctor had called and made him free of pain; and he was peaceful at the end. He'd had a terrible gash to his shoulder that maybe hastened his end, we shall never know. But we did the best for him that we could.'

Claire by now was sitting at the end of her bed, and she was very wide awake.

'I could see the disease had eaten away at him. When I last saw him, Harry was not in charge of where he was and what he was doing, and he didn't like that. I'm sure the end has come as a relief,' Claire said.

'Please go back to your sleep. I will tidy up here, and I too can then go home for a few hours' rest. But Harry Stone left a letter. It is addressed to you. He left it in a white envelope on the top of his study desk. He told me you have a key to the house, but would you prefer that I post it to you?'

'I don't remember the last time Harry ever wrote a letter. It was not his way. Thank you, but I think leave it just where it is. I'll come down as soon as I can.'

Carol had a very calming voice, but this was a time, even though expected, that Claire found difficult to think about. With her head in her hands, Claire sat still for many minutes. She then fumbled in her purse and found a small diamond. Holding it up to the kitchen light for a moment, it glittered for her. She had known Harry Stone for at least twenty years. Living in her own flat in Arrow Hall, working for him, she had seen and been part of the ups and downs of his spontaneous and fast-moving business deals. And watching him, Claire had always been quite sure that he was as much interested in the excitement of the chase as the money that might flow afterwards.

But, of course, there was much more to Harry Stone than a small diamond could ever tell.

Harry Stone was Arrow Hall, an Elizabethan manor house deep in the countryside. The two were closely woven together and, for Claire, that could never change. The indelible image of Harry Stone, sitting at his desk in the morning room, surrounded by untidy papers and a glass of whisky in his hand, flashed before her. But in her night-time tiredness, Claire desperately tried to brush that image away as, even now, it stirred tarnished memories for her.

Claire's eyes felt heavy and watery. The call, coming in the darkness of the night, somehow made the news worse. It heightened her sense of finality to something she had known and been part of. Alone in the kitchen of her meagrely furnished flat, Claire took a sip from a mug of tea. Harry Stone, someone Claire had once shunned for his shady dealing, had died cruelly and quickly. A tear of emotion crept from her eye. After going back to bed and turning the light off, inevitably, her thoughts were running, and Claire had difficulty in keeping her eyes closed for the rest of the night.

What was really keeping her awake was Harry Stone writing her a letter. That was as unlikely as being hit by a thunderbolt of lightning. Curiosity was driving Claire to read it and quickly.

91

In the early morning, as she left her bed, the gloom in her small flat surrounded her, just as it had since the day she had moved in. Claire wanted to get away; this was not a place where she could ever feel comfortable. But Claire took her time – she showered; she nibbled some toast and ate a yoghurt. She did not feel hungry, and with a last cup of strong coffee, she sat at the kitchen table.

The flowers that Rick had brought stood out right in front of her. She had arranged them in a large glass vase; she leant over to enjoy the scent but, inevitably, that jogged her thought to New Zealand. The reality she faced hit her, and she breathed out heavily. She would not see Harry Stone again, and she had moved away from living with Rick. They had both gone from her life. And the scam that had encircled Arrow Hall was still leaving a nasty taste. Rick had a buyer for Arrow Hall; she would no longer ever have her own space there which she could call home.

Rick dealing with it so quickly, taking it away from her, made everything very final. This really was the time to start again.

The ringtone on her phone suddenly interrupted her.

'Could I please speak to Claire Watts?' the caller asked.

Claire momentarily looked at her phone; she did not know the voice, and she hesitated.

'Yes, speaking. I'm Claire Watts.'

'George Mates. I am the solicitor appointed by Harry Stone to administer his estate. First, may I share with you commiserations on the death of Harry. The nursing agency rang me half an hour ago to give me the sad news. And Harry had instructed me to call you personally as soon as I could after hearing of his passing. Is now a good moment to talk, Claire, just for a few minutes?'

'Yes, of course,' Claire replied.

'The reason for calling you today is Harry Stone's funeral. He wanted me to specifically ask if you could be there. We are expecting to arrange it for two weeks today. Plaistow crematorium, 10.00 in the morning.'

Claire again hesitated. This was too sudden.

'I would attend anyway, so why would he request that?'

'I understand how you feel. But it was a very specific request because he believes, other than you, there may be nobody else at his funeral. I assume you are aware he did not leave any family, and of course, his business did not make him many friends.'

'Two weeks from today. I'll put it in my diary. And I'll be there.'

'I shall not be able to meet you at his funeral, but I shall be winding up his estate in due course. Harry has suggested I call you again if there is anything outstanding as you will probably be able to help and know the answer.'

Delving back into Stone's ragged study again would be very tedious and not what she ever wanted to do. There was nothing more to uncover; she no longer had the time to give to his messy papers, piled high one on top of the other around the small room. So far, he had given her a small diamond – that was not a real salary for the time she had spent shadowing the Jackson family. Claire closed the call.

Would she be the only person at Harry Stone's funeral? That would leave it as a cold, unreal ceremony, a most awful send-off for anyone, let alone for a man whom, though she had not always trusted, she had worked with closely for many years.

92

In the new day, Claire drove quickly to Brighton. But it was still two hours before she arrived at the garage to Marine House. The back façade of the building was, as always, hidden in shade. Would the racketeers searching for Harry Stone and his money now drift away? He was now beyond their grasping hands, but just the thought that these thugs could still be loitering, searching for the ghost of Harry Stone, bothered her. Claire fumbled with her key to unlock the back door.

Marine House felt forbidding in its silence. And the antagonism of this place, Harry Stone's final home, immediately touched Claire as if it was hanging in the still air. This was a house that some members of the Jackson family had demanded ransom money for.

In the kitchen, she quickly switched the lights on, but it did not relieve the tension she felt just being in this now silent, grand building. She walked straight to Stone's study. The room gave her the shivers. It was untouched since she had last been here, with no attempt by Stone to cover over what she had found in the scam.

The piles of untidy paper scattered across the desk and the floor, as if they had been thrown randomly by Harry Stone, were like a barren area, a hostile place for doing any work. But the oasis was in the centre of Stone's desk. A new large white envelope with her name, Claire, written on it in large capitals stood in the middle. It was Stone's handwriting, and she felt the envelope staring at her as a mirage, something not real, as if he was there in the room with her. With the long silver paperknife, that had always rested on his desk, even in Arrow Hall, Claire carefully slit open the envelope addressed to her.

Her hands shook slightly as she unfolded a sheet of plain white paper. There was a short paragraph, written in a spidery scrawl that was Harry Stone's handwriting.

Claire,

Sorry I'm not here to see you open this.

You've worked not only for me but with me; many times you've slowed me down. I owe you for that. I say sorry for my messy attempt to squeeze more out of Arrow Hall. It was never going to work while you were in charge there.

I had a visit from Lady Ruth. She squared with me what her children had taken; she didn't want me to talk about Josh's sexual assault accusations; and we did a deal to buy Marine House. I've signed the paper to start that running. You told them what a mess that family had made – it got Marine House for me; I always knew you would. So, you're in my will. I've now left this big house to you. And I know Her Ladyship will be satisfied with you as the new owner.

Harry

Claire sat on Stone's chair facing the desk. Before folding the letter back into the white envelope, she read it again twice. A short, brief note saying it how it was without emotion. It was typical Harry Stone. It was the person she had known better than probably anyone else. And the short note left her stunned. Claire had wanted today to be just another way of closing off this chapter of her life. But this place was to become hers. That left the final pages too wide open.

It was ghostly quiet as Claire walked back to the kitchen, and she made a strong black espresso coffee. Holding her hands round the hot cup, she tried to warm herself before she wandered around the large rooms of the house. The elegant sitting room had been tidied where Nurse Carol had been round. Opening the French doors let the air flow through, but Claire continued to feel the detached formality in the place. The room was grand, with high ceilings and a large chandelier in the middle which she had hardly noticed before. But there were no touches of untidiness, with scattered papers, that said Harry Stone had lived there. Or ever been in that room for that matter.

Claire walked into the wide entrance hall to gather up the letters delivered that morning. Three junk mail envelopes she left where they had fallen, but a crisp white envelope addressed to Mr Harry Stone caught her eye. She pulled out a letter from the same children's hospice in East London.

Thank you, Mr Stone for your further gift of £60,000. Your continuing generous support will enable us to complete the new garden play area and to refurbish two of the bedroom suites.

Claire put the letter back into the envelope quickly and shook her head. Harry Stone's gifts to the hospice in the past few weeks Claire knew was part of the measure of the man. Some surprising generosity made the picture of him complete.

Alone, her own thoughts now racing with excitement, Claire settled into a comfortable chair in the elegant room and reread the letter to her for almost the tenth time. Marine House? This large, empty building with seven bedrooms? A formal, grade-II-listed, prestigious Regency house on the seafront built for a bygone age? Claire had twisted the arm of Lady Ruth for Stone, but this place could surely never be hers.

For an hour, Claire wandered again around all the spacious rooms, but she got no feel of the place. It was a large, impersonal building, cold and silent, and its time as a grand family home was surely coming to an end. Locking the back door of Marine House, Claire walked to the front façade where the midday sun, in a cloudless blue sky, was shining with a dazzling brilliance. She strolled across the road to the beach and sat on a bench facing the sea.

How would the funeral go? A quick half hour in an empty crematorium? No fuss. No observing by anyone but her how Harry Stone's life had been lived? Yes, she would deal with that, even with all its gloomy sadness surrounding it.

Along the side of the beach, from a kiosk she bought an ice cream and, like a schoolkid, walking slowly along, it tasted good even as it messily melted in the heat of the day.

93

Claire walked for ten minutes before turning back to Marine House. Looking across the road, again Claire suddenly saw the contrast with Arrow Hall. The bold presence of Marine House was an imposing building that tried to show off, as it dominated with its wide façade. But Arrow Hall, hidden in the countryside, surrounded by its own grass and trees, with a moat that had once been full of water, had a long, interesting history.

And Rick, soon to sell Arrow Hall in its half-built state, would leave Claire no longer part of that.

Her phone pinged. She did not want to talk to anyone at that moment. Feeling breathless with tension and shielding her eyes from the glaring sun, Claire answered. It was Rick.

'I looked at my bank account and it was wrong of me in asking you to get another £60,000 from Harry Stone. I'll send the money he did pay me back onto the children's hospice. We'll call it square.'

'No, I don't want you to do that. I'm paying that sum to the hospice myself. It will be in memory of Harry Stone. It's the only way I can find some finality to this torrid time.'

Claire caught her breath. It's funny how fate would ensure that the name of Harry Stone would live on in the children's hospice. She looked across to the imposing building that was Marine House, and she managed a half smile.

'Have you decided any more about a holiday in New Zealand?' Rick interrupted.

'No. This is not the time to think about that. I'm in Brighton. Harry Stone died yesterday.'

'Claire, are you alright? You sound tense.'

'Yes, I've just had a very sleepless night.'

'I'm sorry to hear that news. But does that mean you will come to New Zealand with me?'

Claire hesitated.

'No. I'm going to Harry Stone's funeral. Two weeks' time.'

'I can have your ticket changed. You can follow on when you're ready.'

'I've had some very unexpected news. Harry remembered me in his will. He's left me Marine House, his seven-bedroom mansion right on Brighton seafront. But I don't think I would ever want to live there.'

Again, Claire hesitated. With Stone's legacy, Claire felt the frisson of suddenly, unexpectedly, being able to start her new life. But going to New Zealand? That was chasing after Rick, and that she was not now going to do.

'Claire, are you there still?'

Claire heard Rick talk. She stopped. Yes. What did it matter where she was, or where she went? Claire was going to take the last chance given to her, a present from Harry Stone, to buy Arrow Hall.

This book is printed on paper from sustainable sources managed under the Forest Stewardship Council (FSC) scheme.

It has been printed in the UK to reduce transportation miles and their impact upon the environment.

For every new title that Matador publishes, we plant a tree to offset CO_2, partnering with the More Trees scheme.

For more about how Matador offsets its environmental impact, see www.troubador.co.uk/about/